Break Bone Fever

A Finnerty and Liccione Mystery

Mary Rae, M.D.
&
Wanda Venters, M.D.

Advance Praise for *Break Bone Fever*

"Rae and Venters have combined to create an exciting page turner in this murder medical mystery. *Break Bone Fever* is entertaining and thrilling."

—Jay Rabinowitz, M.D., Clinical Professor of Pediatrics, University of Colorado

"What a timely murder mystery! The authors of *Break Bone Fever* draw the reader into the equally intriguing worlds of scientific research, viral infection, Galveston history, conspiracy, and murder."

—Marsha K. Kohn, J.D.

"Murder, money issues, and a deadly medical epidemic merge to create the stage in *Break Bone Fever* for a taut, fast-paced mystery."

—Charles DuPuy, P.A., Retired, and Author of the E.Z. Kelly Mystery Series

"*Break Bone Fever* has many layers of intrigue—I was hooked before the end of the first page! This murder mystery is relevant to current events on so many levels and interwoven nicely. Having gone to school in Galveston, the authors capture the unique essence of the city known only to those who have lived there."

—Natalie Dryden, M.D.

"Expertly crafted with intriguing characters, *Break Bone Fever* is a page turner."

—William Maikovich, Esq.

Break Bone Fever

A Finnerty and Liccione Mystery

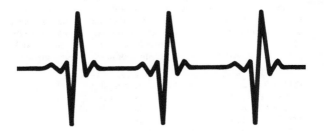

Mary Rae, M.D.
&
Wanda Venters, M.D.

Written Dreams Publishing

Green Bay, WI

Publisher/Executive Editor: Brittiany Koren
Cover Art Designer: Ed Vincent, ENC Graphics
Interior Layout Designer: Katy Brunette
Ebook Layout Designer: Maria Connor
Category: Eco-Medical Thriller/Mystery
Description: Two friends in the health care field work together to solve their friend's murder.

Hardcover ISBN: 978-1-951375-47-8
Paperback ISBN: 978-1-951375-48-5
Ebook ISBN: 978-1-951375-49-2
LOC Data: Applied for.

First Edition published by Written Dreams Publishing in July, 2021.

Green Bay, WI 54311

To our mothers,
Catherine M. Rae and Anne L. Venters

This book was inspired by the quiet majesty of Galveston Island and an underlying fear that its fragile beauty will not survive global warming. It is also a tribute to all the government workers who are tirelessly doing their jobs to try to protect our people and our world.

Prologue

September 26, 2018

Galveston, Texas

Working quickly, he pulled the wire cutter from his backpack. He snipped off the dead man's fingers and put them into a sack. The oversized duffle bag was barely big enough for the task. He dragged the mutilated body to his car, past the empty beach houses, and heaved it into his trunk.

It was a short drive to the East Beach parking lot. A pavilion on stilts loomed in the dawn's mist. When it was high summer season, the pavilion offered snacks and restrooms. It was now closed until March. The Dumpster behind the building would be rarely emptied. It took all his remaining strength to heave the bag over the edge of the blue metal container.

Finished, he walked to the jetty that protruded into the bay, fished out the small sack from his pocket, and casually tossed the fingers into the roiling waves.

Chapter One

September 26, 2018

Galveston, Texas

As the automatic double doors of the Emergency Department whooshed open, the refrigerated hospital air collided with the terrarium-like atmosphere of an autumn Galveston evening. Louise Finnerty braced herself for a twelve-hour, overnight shift. She wished she had reached Marnie earlier. *I hate the way she screens my calls.* It had been a challenge to provide support without invading Marnie's grieving process. Walking briskly, transitioning into work mode, she cleared her head of home/life tasks.

"Dr. Finnerty, we need you right now!" a voice yelled.

This was not the first time Louise had heard a call for help upon entering the ER. Already in her scrubs, she threw her lunch bag on the cluttered counter the physicians used and rushed into Room 1.

"The patient is a seventeen-year-old male, first name Diego, with fever, altered mental status, hypotensive," said Bob Janssen, the evening charge nurse.

"I've got a line!" called another nurse at the bedside.

"Great," Louise countered. "One liter normal saline wide open. Let's get another line and run in another liter. Get a norepinephrine drip ready to go. Can someone get a Foley catheter in him? We need to watch his urine output."

Louise looked up and saw one of the techs had already drawn several tubes of blood with different colored tops—a rainbow of tubes. "Get me CBC, CMP, lactate, blood type and screen stat so we can get some idea where we are right now. Save the extra tubes until we know what else we need."

"Doc, his rectal temp is 103," said Bob.

"Add on two blood cultures and give him a gram of cefepime. We'll follow the sepsis protocol," Louise said to the tech as she watched the monitor above and behind Diego's head. His blood pressure was creeping up but was still low at 80/50. Heart rate 150.

"Good," Louise murmured.

Then she looked over at the Foley bag hanging off the bottom of the gurney at Diego's feet. A few milliliters of cola-colored urine had collected.

"Not good. Hemorrhage, kidney failure, liver failure, or all three," she muttered under her breath.

Glancing around the room for the first time, Louise saw a diminutive woman in the corner. Allowing family members into the critical care suites had improved communication and history taking, and most definitely, cleaned up the staff's language. When the first round of orders had been repeated back and completed, the staff looked at Louise with the unspoken question, what do we do now?

She answered aloud, "Now we wait."

In the next five minutes, Diego's vital signs crept into the range of minimally sustaining life. She turned her attention to the silent woman huddled in the corner. "I'm Dr. Finnerty. Are you Diego's mother?"

A nod confirmed the relationship.

"Would you be more comfortable speaking in Spanish? I could get an interpreter." Louise's Spanish was functional, but an official interpreter ensured nothing was lost in translation.

After the woman shook her head no, Louise continued, "He's doing better. We're going to take good care of him. His blood pressure was dangerously low.

We can fix that, but we need to find out why he's so sick so we can give him the treatment he needs."

She took a seat on one of the stools in the corner next to the woman and leaned in to hear Diego's mother.

Mrs. Jimenez spoke slowly and carefully. "English is best. We don't want no trouble. He woke up with a fever. Then, his pain was too much. Next, he couldn't talk."

"Hey, Doc, look at this," called Bob.

Diego's clothes had been removed. His arms were covered with angry red nodules that were easily identified as bug bites in various stages of healing.

His mother had gained enough strength to come to the bedside with Louise. "Yes. Too many mosquitoes behind the restaurant where he works. He has to take the trash out there."

At the sound of his mother's voice, Diego began to stir. His blood pressure continued to improve, and he showed signs of waking up. He opened his eyes and started to move on the bed. His movements quickly progressed to writhing.

Louise carefully inspected Diego's vital signs and obvious discomfort. "Let's give him two milligrams of morphine and repeat in five minutes if his blood pressure holds."

"He said his bones hurt bad, then he passed out and I called 9-1-1," his mother said.

After another set of vital signs confirmed improvement, Louise gave Mrs. Jimenez a quick smile. She explained that he needed to be moved to the ICU to continue his treatment. She assured her that she would be just outside Diego's room making arrangements to admit him to the ICU.

"We need to find out what made Diego so sick," she repeated, as much to herself as to Mrs. Jimenez.

Louise called the ICU intensivist and placed a stat consultation with Infectious Disease. Ten minutes later, a team of residents swooped into the room.

Sensing Mrs. Jimenez's fright at this invasion,

Louise returned to the woman's side, speaking calmly and slowly to her. "These new doctors are going to take good care of Diego. You will have to repeat your story many times, but everyone is trying to do what's best for him. If you get confused, just ask for an interpreter. I will get a social worker to help you navigate the system."

Mrs. Jimenez nodded her thanks.

Louise organized a space for herself on the messy counter that physicians used for computer charting, eating, and napping with their heads resting on their arms. Then, Louise walked to the breakroom to place her lunch in the refrigerator. She used the walk down the hallway to collect her thoughts.

Next, she logged on to her laptop to see what other patients were in the department. The non-acute patients waiting for care had no idea of what was occurring on the critical side or the toll it could take on the doctors. And why would they? It's just how it is in the ER.

Louise was taken aback when people asked her if she went into Emergency Medicine because she was an adrenaline junkie. Nothing could be further from the truth.

Passing the ambulance entrance, she caught sight of Brian, one of the EMTs who regularly transported patients to the ER. He was in a large closet wiping down and stacking wooden backboards used to transport accident victims. It almost looked as if he were setting out surfboards for rental in a beachside shack. A strong whiff of disinfectant hit Louise's nose.

"Hey, Doc, how's the kid doing?" Brian asked. "He was my last call. Had one just like him yesterday—still in ICU."

"He's holding on. He'll make it to the ICU," she said.

As Louise answered, Ned came around the corner with a cafeteria tray heaped with a cheeseburger dripping with an egg and stuffed with bacon, and a side of fries. A recipe for a Texas heart attack conveniently available right there in the hospital.

Dr. Ned Forrest, one of her newer colleagues, had been on the day shift. He liked to fortify himself before his commute home to a suburb on the southside of Houston. Louise followed him into the breakroom.

"What the fuck was going on with that son of a bitch with no blood pressure?" Ned asked. No sanitized talk in the breakroom. Rarely did Ned complete a sentence without an expletive or three. It was not uncommon for him to refer to patients as young as two as sons of bitches.

He didn't wait for Louise to answer and with a fork in one hand, burger in the other, said, "We had one just like him the night before. Still in ICU. Still alive. Infectious Disease on the case. Possible dengue fever." He continued stuffing his face and talking at the same time.

Louise sighed. "Tough way to start a shift. Glad he made it up to the ICU."

"Take a look at the son of a bitch in room 8 if you want to have a laugh," Ned replied.

Needing a laugh, she set off to resume her shift.

Louise had little time to ponder Diego's case. Patients were waiting. Patients were always waiting in the ER.

Louise's first patient on the non-critical side of the department was the guy in Room 8, whom Ned had mentioned. He had checked in just after noon with a chief complaint of "my pants are too tight."

Louise patiently, but efficiently, asked him the questions needed to rule out a brewing intra-abdominal catastrophe. Finally asking the question that she knew she should always ask, she said, "Is there something you're concerned about? Have you checked your symptoms online?"

"Yes, ma'am, liver failure like my daddy. He blowed up like a toad at the end and couldn't even button his britches."

Louise was grateful for the tests the staff had automatically completed. After a few more questions, an exam, and a review of the labs that included normal liver functions, she reassured her patient that the cause of his waistline expansion was not from liver failure.

"I guess I've just been puttin' on then," he said.

So, after eight hours in the ER and twelve minutes with Louise, the patient left with a new lease on life.

Hurrying to the next waiting patient, Louise reflected on the inadequacy of medical resources for patients like Room 8 whose liver was fine but who was on his way to diabetes, hypertension, and heart disease.

The night progressed with the march of humanity that enters ERs across the country. Ambulances and EMTs arrived and departed with regularity. The staff numbers picked up during peak times in a feeble attempt to meet the needs of the rising daily census. Police officers were present to follow up on accidents and altercations.

Her last patient of the shift was a garrulous senior citizen with a laceration on his palm from a cat food can. As Louise repaired his wound, he took the opportunity to recount some youthful hijinks. Louise finished her procedure as he wound up his story.

"So, I snuck out with some buddies for a midnight swim down past the seawall. Next thing I remember was diving under water when bullets were whizzing over our heads. Turns out we swam right into the crosshairs of some bootleggers."

"Only in Galveston, right?" Louise replied, well aware of the colorful history of her city. She placed a dressing on the line of sutures. "Okay, sir, you're good to go. That cat owes you one."

As the sun came up, Louise felt the exhaustion that came from shift work. She finished her notes, hoping Didier, her husband, was managing the home front okay.

Wouldn't it be nice to just kiss the kids as they went off to school and then collapse in bed?

To make sure she had not left any details unattended, she glanced at the view on her computer where all the

ER patients were listed. Dread filled her heart as she recognized a name.

Gennifer Drake, 49, Critical Care Room 6, DOA.

No. It can't be. Not Gennifer. No way was her friend the person listed as dead-on-arrival in Room 6.

Louise rushed to the room and almost collapsed when she recognized the body.

"The EMTs tried their best. We did, too. It was too late. She…" Dr. Jane Torson said, her voice trailing off. As she started to decompress by telling Louise about the resuscitation, she saw Louise's distress.

"Oh my god, did you know her?" asked Jane.

Louise nodded and she sank into a chair. "Yes, she was a very good friend but please, go ahead and tell me what happened."

She knew Jane needed to unload the events of the failed resuscitation. As in all ERs, the doctors in Louise's group knew that it never gets easier when a patient dies. Barely able to understand what Jane was saying, Louise listened, knowing that's all she was meant to do.

"She was found on East Beach by some early morning beachcombers. Their dog was checking out what looked like a pile of towels. But as they got closer, they could tell it was a body. A woman. She was already blue. They tried to see if she was breathing. The woman started CPR while her husband dialed 9-1-1."

Jane went on and Louise followed the story, able to fill in the blanks herself. EMTs arrived and took over. They intubated and started bagging her. They placed her on a "thumper" to administer chest compressions. The heart monitor showed no activity. Unable to start an IV, they squirted epinephrine into the tube in her throat as a last-ditch effort to reawaken her heart.

The beach was a five-minute run from the hospital. Her core temperature was 92 degrees when she arrived in the ER. They gradually warmed her to avoid sending her heart into a chaotic and deadly rhythm. But, even after her body reached a normal temperature, and after a prolonged resuscitation attempt, there was still no heartbeat.

"We just pronounced her dead," Jane concluded, whispering at this point. "Are you going to be okay?"

Louise nodded silently.

Jane finished her tale and went to complete paperwork after giving Louise a hug. Louise looked up to see Officer José Torres hovering nearby. She had known him since joining the ER group fifteen years ago. He was tall, nice-looking and wore his hair slicked back, helmet style. No matter what the weather, José was in uniform shorts that he wore at least an inch shorter than regulation. He had an infinite supply of spearmint gum and offered a piece to everyone. When José saw Louise's shattered expression, he understood.

"You know her," he said, and automatically offered her a piece of gum, which she took and folded up into a tiny square.

They sat together as the medical assistants prepared Gen's body for the trip to the morgue where the medical examiner would do a forensic exam. Louise watched as the nurse opened the kit which was used to prepare the body for transport. Years ago, she had been surprised to learn that it included a filmy sack with a zipper referred to as a shroud. It had seemed like a sad supply to have on hand.

"We've been friends since medical school," Louise said. "We kept in touch. I just saw her last month. She works in the lab. I mean, the Gulf National Lab. She does—did—research there." Louise looked at José. "Did you take the call? Were you on the beach when they tried to resuscitate her?"

"Yeah. A couple walking their dog found her on the beach and called 9-1-1. I was pretty sure she wasn't going to make it. But the guys did everything they could. They're pretty broke up, too," he said, unable to meet Louise's tearful gaze.

He fiddled with his radio, then he handed her a

tissue. His phone rang. "I gotta take this call. I'm sorry, Doc." Abruptly, he left.

People came in and out of the room. It took a minute for Louise to notice the presence of Detective Iliana Sudhan who was married to Bob, the evening charge nurse. The detective was a compact middle-aged woman. Her quick movements suggested agility and strength. Her clothes were business casual, neatly tucked and pressed, which looked somewhat formal on The Island. Her smooth light brown skin made guessing her age difficult.

Louise had always respected Iliana's calm, business-like demeanor. With her warm brown eyes, the detective imparted empathy to the victims of crime who frequented the ER. Louise had taken a fish hook out of the detective's son and treated her mother for angina. Iliana had helped Louise when a lonely loser of a patient had stalked her. The detective had paid him a visit to explain that his expressions of love were appreciated neither by the lady doctor nor the Gulf County Police Department. Over the years, their professional interactions led to friendship.

The detective gave Louise a moment to compose herself before speaking. "Hi, Louise. So sorry for your loss. I remember meeting Dr. Drake at some of your get-togethers. I know she was a good friend of yours. If you can stand it, I would like to ask you some preliminary questions."

Louise nodded. Iliana had a job to do.

"We found her phone in her pants pocket. It had her license and a credit card in the case. So, we were able to make a preliminary identification. I hate to put you on the spot right now, but can you confirm that this *is* the body of Gennifer Drake?"

Louise nodded. "No question. She's even wearing the earrings I gave her for her last birthday. Opals were her birthstone."

"Do you know if Dr. Drake had family here?"

Louise shook her head. "No. She grew up in Iowa,

and after med school she stayed here to work in the lab. Gulf National Lab. I don't think her family ever understood her decisions. They didn't communicate much from what I could tell."

"Significant other?"

Hunched over now from physical and emotional exhaustion, Louise whispered, "She's been seeing Garrett Mancinelli, the owner of Garrett's Seawall Trattoria, for a while."

"Was she depressed?"

"God, not that I knew of. She worked a lot. But she was in the process of adopting another cat. People don't do that if they plan to commit suicide."

Iliana took in Louise's distress. She paused before continuing softly. "We don't know if it was suicide, an accident, or foul play. At this point, we have a person found dead on the beach. I'll let you know what we find out from the medical examiner. Here, give me a hug. You going to be okay? Should I call Didier?"

"No, I'm okay. He's with the kids and I've got my car here. I'm off as soon as I write my last note."

With Iliana's departure, Louise was all alone in Room 6 with Gen's lifeless body. She walked over to Gen and lovingly took her hand. Gen still wore her favorite blush polish. Not wanting to leave her, Louise stood for a long time by her bedside, tears streaming down her face. "Oh, Gen…"

Soon, a transporter arrived to take Gen to the morgue, and Louise had to relinquish her hold on Gen's hand. Reluctantly, she said good-bye.

***

When Louise left the ER at 8:15 a.m., it was already hot. She tossed her three part "office" —white coat, briefcase, and lunch box—onto the passenger seat. As an emergency physician, her actual office consisted of a hook on the wall in the physician's lounge that she shared with nine partners.

She exited the parking garage and headed to the western side of Galveston Island. Generally, she didn't mind her fifteen-minute drive at the end of her shift. It gave her a chance to decompress before re-entry to family life. Today it was especially needed.

Looking out over the Gulf of Mexico to her left and then the marshes traversed by fingers of Galveston Bay to her right, she wished the calmness of nature would soothe her raw nerves today. She had called Didier to tell him about the tragedy and that she would be late. He had given the children a kiss from her and taken them to school.

Louise wandered through the empty house, thankful that she didn't have to work for another twenty-four hours. She dropped her things on the bedroom floor, stripped off her scrubs, and headed for the shower.

Clean, if not refreshed, she pulled on one of Didier's tee shirts and collapsed onto the unmade bed. Exhaustion took over and she fell into a deep sleep.

Louise awoke two hours later, startled by the realization that the nightmare of Gen's death was no dream. After a half hour of tossing and turning, she gave up on escaping reality.

She dressed, went to the kitchen and made a pot of strong coffee. Taking her coffee out to her veranda, she ignored the hungry egrets as they paced slowly through the grassy shallows. One question kept returning to her.

How will I tell Marnie about Gen?

Chapter Two

Four Days earlier—September 23, 2018

Galveston, Texas

Running his fingers through his close-cropped Afro, Bert Springer was glad to reach the Third Coast Hotel. The walk along the seawall in the bright September sun had been hot. Though travel from Oklahoma wasn't hard, he was in the busy fall semester at O.U. where he taught a full course load in microbiology. This survey assignment with the U.S. Biosafety Association had been rather last minute. Apparently, he was filling in for another surveyor who had a medical emergency. As he waited for his room key, the concierge, a small, neat blonde, emerged from behind her desk in the lobby and cornered him.

"We are so excited to have you and your partner staying here. We hope that we can make your stay very pleasant. We're always eager to support our Gulf National Laboratory," the concierge gushed.

"It's a lovely hotel," Bert said as they waited for the slow-moving elevator.

"Oh, it's just gorgeous and so historic. It was built ten years after the Great Storm of 1900 wiped out The Island. Of course, multiple storms followed, but the hotel is still standing. Every window leaked during Hurricane Harvey." The concierge sounded strangely proud.

Bert hoped for clear skies.

Once inside his room, he tossed his carry-on onto the bed and looked around. Without any functional desk or work area, it seemed totally inadequate for a business trip.

Sitting in an armchair juggling his papers with his laptop, he reviewed the agenda for the next day's work. He and his partner, Ernie Pedersen, were there to make a site survey of Gulf National Lab's Insectary Services Division—a daunting assignment. The Gulf National Laboratory was one of a handful of Biosafety Level 4 labs—or as insiders say, BSL4—in the U.S. It was even more unusual in that it housed levels 2 and 3 in the same facility. Despite the lack of national standards for operating these facilities, the Gulf National Laboratory was eager for a stamp of approval to show they were on the up and up. As chairman of the survey, Bert had researched the pre-survey documents. *This is going to be a big job.*

The lab's website stated: The Gulf National Laboratory is a high containment research facility that is fighting global infectious diseases. The lab's researchers work on the world's most threatening contagious diseases, including Ebola, dengue, plague, and Zika.

Bert's job was to make sure that this one division, Insectary, which was dedicated to arthropod borne disease, was doing its job safely. The U.S. Biosafety Association would grant certification for two years if all was in order. This coveted certification indicated to the Centers for Disease Control that the lab operations met accepted safety and quality standards. To avoid sanctions and suspension of operations, the lab was meticulous in keeping all of its certifications up-to-date.

Being fully aware of the public scrutiny aimed at these facilities, Bert took his responsibility seriously. A recent syndicated article scared the pants off readers with examples of lab-created outbreaks, theft of pathogens such as anthrax, and deaths of researchers. Many scientists believed that the H1N1 flu re-emergence was actually an accidental release from a lab source. The Gulf National Laboratory had been quick to point out that there was no hint that any of these incidents had occurred at its facility.

While Bert had remained in the academic arena, his partner for the survey, Ernie, had accepted a job at a biomedical company for better pay. Both men were certified biosafety professionals. They did the surveys to enhance their résumés as well as for the supplemental income.

The U.S. Biosafety Association was careful to rotate surveyors so that no pair became too complacent, and to keep down the complaints when one guy didn't pull his weight. That was Ernie's reputation. He was a nice enough guy, but he didn't prepare for the surveys, which made it hard to cover all the bases. More irksome was his generally distracted manner. He was often on his phone in one hallway or another. At least their names provided some comic relief when they introduced themselves.

Bert headed downstairs to meet Ernie for dinner and go over the game plan for the next day. He found Ernie in the bar staring at his cell phone with an empty glass at his elbow.

"Bertram!" he called out a little too loudly for the pre-dinner crowd. "So, we meet again. This one's gonna be a bear. I started looking at protocols on the plane."

"Hey there, Ernie. You bet it's a toughie. A job like this used to take four days but with cutbacks, we get two."

"I hear you," Ernie agreed. "I sure as hell wouldn't be here if it weren't for the compensation. Last time I saw you was in Phoenix."

Bert laughed. "Never did figure out where that rat came from. At least it was the last presentation, and we got the incident logged."

"And it didn't run up my leg." Ernie chuckled.

"Yeah, that lady doctor got the shock of her life."

"Poor rat," said Ernie.

Bert remembered the incident well. The lab was put on an every-six-month follow-up inspection for two years.

"Let's hit the terrace and see if we can scare up a few more drinks," Ernie said. "You ever been here before? It sure is toasty outside, but it's damn cold in the A/C."

Bert agreed. "It's a constant battle between comfort and misery in this climate."

The hotel didn't have a patio bar. They settled for a sunny spot on the couches in an enclosed veranda. It offered a great view of the Gulf of Mexico through the floor-to-ceiling windows.

Bert had been to Galveston once before. He knew that the lab and medical school were nestled into a corner of the island between beaches, cruise ships, and cheap tourist dives. It's what his mom would've called a Redneck Riviera. The sand was brown and the water browner. The hotel brochure described the sand as honey-colored and explained to the reader that the water in the Gulf was clean, just full of churned up silt. It claimed that the tar that got on your feet when walking on the beach was from a natural deposit offshore, not from unnatural industrial sources.

Looking out the windows, Bert could see that the beachgoers appeared to love it. The shoreline was full of families, dogs, pickup trucks, and fishermen. On the horizon, oil tankers were visible, waiting their turn to head up the ship channel to Houston, the Petro Metro. Once settled and in better light, Bert saw that Ernie looked a little rough around the edges, more so than he remembered. He had heard that Ernie had gotten divorced and remarried, to an Allison if he recalled correctly. He wondered if the new marriage was working out.

As the sun set over the Gulf, the line of tankers appeared like a string of party lights in the distance.

The men found their way to the pastel toned dining room where the crowd was sparse.

"Slow night?" Ernie asked the waitress after placing his order.

"That's how it is during the week. Unless it's Mardi Gras or a Harley convention. Then it's a whole other scene," she said with a smile.

Their conversation was kept to generalities—weather, health, and sports.

In their own way, the two surveyors were content with the quiet setting. Bert wanted to continue prepping for the survey. He thought Ernie looked as if he was wrestling with his own problems.

After dinner, Bert headed to his room to work. He alternated between the armchair and the bed, never getting comfortable. He decamped for the bed and continued his reading and note taking until his neck and back complained too loudly. Nonetheless, he had finished reviewing the scope of the survey. He was glad they had only been assigned the Insectary Services Division.

He got ready for bed and drifted off, still mulling over topics such as maintenance, containment, and safe disposal of infected arthropods. Knowing what diseases these bugs could carry would only bring nightmares.

***

In his room, Ernie reviewed his dinner with his partner. Bert looked trim and fit. *Was he ex-military?* Feeling unkempt in comparison, Ernie wondered if Bert had noticed. His divorce settlement from his first marriage included paying for his daughter's college tuition. This arrangement had added an additional pressure to Ernie's financial woes. Of course, her mother had encouraged their daughter, Gigi, to go to a private school in the Midwest with a hefty price tag instead of the state school fifty miles from home. He could hear his ex-wife carrying on about it, "*USA Today* says it's a top ten for students wanting to run for political office."

Like Gigi was ever going to run for any office higher than social chairman of the Kappa house.

Tuition would have been manageable if he hadn't lost so much of his savings in the stock market—not to mention his gambling habit. Ernie had tried to recoup some losses with an insider trading tip, but instead lost a bundle. He had long been aware that there were U.S. Biosafety Association surveyors making some money on the side through anonymous sources willing to pay for favorable reports or reports that omitted unfavorable details.

He had no problem following a lead and reaching a certain Susan in St. Louis. She had done such extracurricular work. Within a week, he had his first call.

His first few "assignments" were easy to pull off. It was mid-August when he received a call from Galveston where he was scheduled to perform a survey. The caller didn't give too many details over the phone, but he indicated the price he was willing to pay for the right results—and that's what got Ernie's attention.

After twenty minutes in his room, Ernie quietly headed down to the elevator and out the back door of the hotel. With his cell phone in hand, he walked through quiet streets, following a GPS route to the assigned location.

It was warm, with what felt like 110% humidity still in the air. The light breeze carried the salty aroma of the Gulf. The streets behind the hotel were lettered and half lettered, such as N Avenue and N ½ Avenue. These ran at right angles to the numbered streets. It seemed odd to him to see such an organized grid layout in an unzoned, quasi-urban setting. Bars and tattoo parlors were nestled in between well-preserved southern mansions and elevated shanties. The latter had entryways at least a story up, approached by rickety steps. Even with the dim streetlights, he could see the houses were brightly painted. While others might find this mish-mash charming, he did not. He preferred his gated community back home with its strict overlay of architectural regulations and its harmonious appearance.

Arriving at the designated spot, he hesitated before entering the Fisherman's Folly Bar and Grill. This place was seedy, even for Galveston. But considering his escalating financial ruin, there was no turning back. Though he was out of shape, he thought he could hold his own if need be. Plus, he had the foresight to carry a Glock 26, just in case. He assumed everyone in Texas was packing.

He took a seat at the bar and then looked at his watch...9:40. He was expecting a call at 9:45. With a beer in hand, he took a few minutes to soak up the atmosphere. There was no indication that the Folly had a working grill, despite its name. His khaki pants and pastel pink golf shirt were definitely out of place. The dress code was shorts, wife beaters for the guys, tank tops for the ladies, and flip flops for both sexes.

In one corner, there was a table of five White guys huddled over an iPad. They were watching something that had made them hi-five each other every few minutes.

His phone vibrated at the appointed time. After greetings and confirmation of identities, Ernie said, "Nice place you picked out."

His contact responded, "I wanted you to have a real Island experience. Besides, I need you to know about this place in case we need you back here for some networking."

Planning on his role ending with the conclusion of the survey, Ernie decided not to ask about further networking. The two dispensed with niceties and got to work on the details.

The guy on the other end of the line explained to Ernie that a scientist in the Insectary Division was deep into research of dengue fever. She had discovered a mutation of the virus which threatened to cause an epidemic in the U.S. The researcher's premise was that the ever-increasing numbers of Aedes aegypti mosquitoes were delivering a dengue virus that would kill people. Lots of people. Mosquito populations were getting bigger, heading further north and often remaining active all year round. All as a result of the rising temperatures.

The scientist was pushing to get this in front of the CDC, the press, and anyone else who would listen. She wanted funding for a dengue vaccine that was effective and safe. She also wanted to show the imminent danger to human health from global warming right here in the U.S.A.

"Okay," said Ernie. "Where do I come in?"

"Dr. Drake is going to present her research to you when you ask to review a current project. She knows you're going to be looking at process and safety rather than the validity of her conclusions, but as I said, she wants to get this in front of everyone. We want you to keep it out of your report, and for that, my people are ready to pay you big money."

"Okay," he repeated. "Shouldn't be a problem." Ernie realized he would need to pull one over on Bert, but that could be managed. He had deep-sixed problem data before by padding other parts of his reports and no one was the wiser. "Anything else?"

"Perhaps there will be more later." The voice paused before continuing. "Let's see how the meeting goes. It's essential that her research doesn't see the light of day. Whatever it takes."

Ernie was a bit surprised about the concepts of "more" and "whatever it takes," but tried not to worry about it.

Starting to sweat, he wondered if a wet spot was appearing on his back. Fiddling with academic reports was one thing. *I mean, who did that really hurt?* Since his benefactors were often drug companies, he assumed his interventions would either help or hurt the development of new drugs. *Don't we have enough drugs already?*

This little subterfuge would bring about an infusion of funds which would go a long way to solving his problems and allow him a fresh start financially. *Eye on the prize.*

Chapter Three

September 24, 2018

Galveston, Texas

The next morning, Ernie slid into his seat in the dining room across the table from Bert. Facing the window, his eyes widened as he took note that the Gulf water actually looked blue. Pelicans were hovering above the water, appearing almost motionless in flight. They were looking for breakfast, too.

Bert opened the conversation. "You noticed? The water looks inviting today. Our waitress said this happens now and then after a storm at sea sweeps out the silt. People hear about it and the hotel fills up for a while."

Bert looked rested and ready for their day at the lab. Ernie wished he felt the same. He had slept poorly. He gave a weak smile of appreciation for the nature fact. What he really needed was a strong cup of coffee.

"So, are you still good with the game plan?" Bert was referring to the division of labor they had worked out the night before. Neither had been to a Biosafety Level 4 for over a year and knew it would be a long day.

"You bet. I think it makes sense for me to review the Human Resource credential checks and records since I'm going to review the research project they're using as an example," Ernie said.

Bert agreed. "I like doing the site inspection and learning what's new in the field. I'll allow an hour to observe a mock donning and doffing of the "space suit" the researchers wear in level 4. I'm also curious as to how the air filtration hooks up to the Insectary Division. It seems from the floor plans that the filtration equipment takes up an entire floor. Mr. Williams, Chief of the Insectary Division, said he would pick us up at 8:30."

Ernie had been glad to turn over the chairman duties of the survey to Bert. For the little extra pay, the role was not worth the extra work of pre-survey arrangements, such as contacting their hosts and working out logistics. Then, there were the post survey tasks, including compiling both surveyors' notes and checklists into one report and signing off on the final version. Bert had told Ernie that he wanted the credit for his next performance review at O.U.

It was already warm as the men waited outside for their ride. Ernie saw Roy Williams pull up in his Honda Civic. The man got out to shake hands with the surveyors who would be snooping around his department for the next day and a half. Williams had an elegant demeanor, set off by his fine facial features, steel gray eyes and a nicely tanned bald head. *Some guys could pull off the bald look.*

Williams didn't show his impatience with the prospect of a survey. "How was your trip? Where do you gentlemen come from?"

It was clear he'd been through this kind of inspection before and knew it was best to create a bond and favorable first impression with his inquisitors.

"It was a pretty easy hop to Houston from Oklahoma City," Bert said.

"I flew down from Minneapolis," replied Ernie.

During the short drive to the University of Texas Medical Branch campus, home to Gulf National Laboratory, Williams launched into his prepared thumbnail history of U.T.M.B. Ernie felt like a captive audience. The medical school was founded in 1891 as the first medical school west of the Mississippi. Galveston was chosen as the most suitable location because it was a busy port city with a high number and variety of illnesses. The recurring epidemics of yellow fever continued to decimate the Island's population into the 20th century, killing up to twenty-five percent of those infected. The high mortality rate persisted until the medical community finally learned that the disease was caused by mosquitos. The death rate plunged when mosquito control measures were instituted.

"Wouldn't The Island's medical forefathers have found it ironic that we're breeding the little bastards right here? Having levels 2, 3 and 4BSL in one place facilitates work that requires samples and experiments conducted at all three levels of security—as long as researchers are not overly protective of their data," Williams explained.

"What is one of your success stories?" Ernie asked.

"Currently, two of our researchers have been instrumental in developing an effective vaccine for Ebola."

As they entered the lab, Ernie noticed that it looked like an old security checkpoint at an airport. Fewer bells and whistles than the body scanners now used. Still, it was staffed by state police who took the surveyors' driver's licenses and made them security badges. Bert and Ernie had sent in their credentials for verification previously. After going through the metal detector, Williams approached and stared at a black rectangle on the wall to scan his retinas.

"They say this doesn't work on dead eyes—in case you're wondering."

Ernie realized he had never even considered the possibility before but wondered if he should.

Williams whisked them through two more doors that required his employee badge to operate. The surveyors were cleared for entry as long as they were accompanied by a designated host.

Ernie knew that this BSL 4 lab was built like a fortress. Even though the façade of the lab had windows, the inner building was a sealed prism.

"The lab is built to withstand a class 5 storm," Williams said. "We were one month from opening in 2008 when Hurricane Ike hit. It turned out that flooding and a storm surge, not high winds, caused the most damage. The Island was wiped out, but the new lab was undisturbed. Hurricane Harvey in 2017 packed a punch that was a lot worse for Houston than it was down here. The lab stayed dry and solid."

"These windows must be better sealed than those at the Third Coast Hotel," Bert joked.

They took an elevator to the third floor, home of the Insectary Division. Ernie would've never known he was in one of the world's safest inner sanctums just by looking at it. Offices and conference rooms lined the hallway, many with magnificent views of the Gulf of Mexico. He saw a sign indicating that the labs and insectariums were further down the hall.

Williams ushered them into Conference Room C and promptly excused himself to attend a conference call. This would be their home for the next two days. Here they would meet the senior staff for their introduction to the department. The room was furnished with an oblong table that had seen better days. All but four of the black leather chairs had been pulled back to the wall, allowing for laptop chargers to snake onto the table. Piles of documents were neatly arranged at the far end. Ernie's heart sank as he saw the mountains of paperwork.

A stocky middle-aged woman dressed in a pantsuit stood when the surveyors entered. She had a steady gaze. Her short brown hair was tucked behind her ears. "Hello Dr. Springer, Dr. Pedersen, I'm Kathy Walsh."

"Pleasure to meet you in person, Ms. Walsh. Thanks for setting us up here," said Bert. He had informed Ernie that Kathy Walsh was the go-to person in the department.

"Let me introduce Maria Moreno and Julia Mills," Kathy said, looking at her colleagues. Maria appeared to be well past retirement age. "Maria will answer any questions you may have regarding our departmental budget and research expenses."

"Good morning. Happy to help. This isn't my first rodeo with your outfit, so I'm sure I can find what you need," said Maria.

Kathy continued with a nod to the remaining woman. "Julia oversees our IT. She can set you up with your temporary access and help you search our policies and procedure manuals online."

Julia looked pale and much younger than her coworkers. Ernie thought she looked anxious. She gave the surveyors a nod and a brief smile but appeared as if she wanted to bolt from the conference room.

"Many thanks, ladies. It looks as if you have us all set up," said Ernie. It was evident to him that Williams had surrounded himself with very capable work wives.

After the surveyors signed confidentiality agreements regarding the full gamut of the division's activities, they were off and running.

Ernie requested coffee as he got started on his policy reviews. He noted Bert's undisguised excitement about his day of inspection. Bert even had a nerdy belt with a flashlight and gizmos on it to check for leaks and loose connections to and from the air filtration system. Ernie heard him asking hopefully if he could take a look at those double-lined pipes that were used to carry water in and out of the facility.

"Don't forget to visit the little boy's room before going to Level 4, even if you don't need to," Ernie teased him.

They both knew there were no toilets in level 4. The staff inside had to hold it or remove and disconnect from the air supplied to their suits if nature called. The process in and out of level 4 was time consuming.

The morning passed quickly. At noon, Ernie was pleasantly surprised when Kathy came into the conference room with sandwiches and a plate of cookies. Bert had returned by then and both men were working on the checklists that the U.S. Biosafety Association required to confer certification. They told her it was going well.

"Once you've done a few surveys, you can almost sense a pass or a fail the minute you walk in. You can smell it," Bert said to Ernie after Kathy had left the room.

It wasn't till 4:00 that Ernie prepared to meet Dr. Drake for his last—and most important—meeting of the day. He had read her proposal and reviewed the research methodology and statistical analysis. With his background in microbiology and his years in and out of research labs, Ernie remained sharp and incisive when it came to study review. Despite the downward spiral of his personal life, he retained a bit of self-esteem regarding his professional capabilities. He vowed to apply himself more once this was all behind him. Maybe he would put in for a promotion to team leader at the lab back home.

The study was sound, and the conclusions would be hard to dispute. He could see why completion and publication would give the climate change deniers some serious heartburn. He couldn't say they didn't deserve it with their undisguised toadying up to the oil and gas lobby. The evidence for global warming was accepted scientific dogma. But under the current administration, even the Environmental Protection Agency leadership appeared dubious.

Is this who the voice on the phone was referring to when he mentioned "his people?" I mean, how could someone work at, let alone run the EPA and not believe in climate change? Yet here Ernie was getting ready to derail a solid attempt to shine light on EPA's cynical denials.

As Dr. Gennifer Drake walked into Conference Room C, Ernie looked up. She was a striking woman, almost 6 feet tall, with a graceful and powerful walk.

Her mid-length brown hair was neatly styled. She was dressed in a conservative but feminine manner, brown slacks and a tailored white blouse. Her white lab coat was neatly pressed.

"Hi Dr. Drake. Interesting research you have going," Ernie said as he stood up to greet her. "Sounds really scary," he added with a weak smile. He could see Dr. Drake was not impressed by his first comment.

"I would say that my report isn't "scary" but terrifying and time sensitive. I think it's crucial that we get this report out as soon as possible. I've had trouble getting people upstairs to see the urgency in this public health emergency," Dr. Drake replied.

"I agree, I agree—if the methodology bears out. But that's not really my job here today. I'm here to make sure the research in the Insectary Division is carried out in a fashion that is safe for employees of the lab and the community-at-large. Our association wants us to look at the metrics you use to make sure your research conclusions meet the standards of certified institutions."

Ernie then asked her several questions based on his review of the project. She was able to answer them all and he had no choice but to appear satisfied. It was all there. He indicated that the interview was over by shuffling his papers together and standing up.

Dr. Drake shook his hand and thanked him for his comments.

Chapter Four

September 25, 2018

Galveston, Texas

Back in Conference Room C on day two of the inspection, the surveyors ticked off the remaining areas to inspect. Ernie was dreading his second meeting with Dr. Drake.

"Jeez, I wish I'd toured the insectariums yesterday," said Bert. "It's BSL3, so no space suit, but listen to all the items…"

Ernie nodded without looking up as he continued his policy reviews.

"Hazard lights, alarms, check to see if the zappers are functional, check the logbooks. Did you know the researchers have to count out the mosquitos they use in every experiment and then account for them, dead or alive, when they finish?" Bert continued.

"No margin for error," said Ernie. "Those little buggers are escape artists. Do the researchers have to autoclave their clothes when they leave?"

"Yup. Looks like a busy morning," Bert said as he left the room to start his inspection.

Ernie made the rounds to interview a sampling of staff members about safety procedures. His quiz always made his victims nervous, but he could usually put them at ease and get what he needed for his report.

He didn't like to make it a punitive experience.

On this survey, he was the one who was a bundle of nerves. He had to pull off one more deception to defang Dr. Drake's research. He needed Bert elsewhere when he met with the doctor. He knew it wouldn't be pretty.

As luck had it, Bert returned to the conference room to make some notes just as Dr. Drake arrived for the scheduled meeting.

Ernie grabbed his laptop and some handwritten notes that he had made the night before.

"Shall we head to your office, Dr. Drake, so Bert can concentrate on his work?"

After a second's hesitation, Dr. Drake agreed.

"Hey, don't mind me. I wouldn't mind hearing a bit about the study while I'm doing this busy work," Bert said.

"Nope, I'm overruling the chair here. Our report's due in forty-eight hours and you'd better get cracking!" Ernie responded with false bravado.

Turning to Dr. Drake, Ernie said, "Lead the way." As he followed her through a series of corridors to her office, he used the brief interlude to calm his jangled nerves.

Ernie took in Dr. Drake's office. *For someone with an M.D/Ph.D, it's pretty spartan.* The desk was crowded with IT equipment and colored folders, all neatly arranged. *This is where I'm going to lower the boom on Dr. Drake.* As he proceeded to lay out his instructions on how she must change the purpose, methods, analysis, and conclusions of her study, he saw her disbelief.

"You want me to do *what*?" she stared at Ernie incredulously. "That's the whole damn project! Where is this coming from? Why would I do such a thing?"

Regaining her composure, she leveled her gaze at him and said, "No. I refuse. I don't know how this even has anything to do with you. You're here to give us a merit badge before the CDC comes for the real thing. You asked intelligent questions about the study yesterday. What the hell has changed?"

Ernie was looking at his shoes. He mumbled something about discovering shortcuts and safety risks to the staff after reviewing her material the night before.

She had taken no shortcuts; there were no safety risks.

Rising to her full height, she looked down at Ernie, who was avoiding her gaze. "I'm going to get this in front of Dr. Thatcher upstairs. I'll tell him exactly what you asked me to do. Mark my words, I am not going to let this ride. Certification or no certification, I'm *not* compromising my professional integrity."

She walked around Ernie to the door, grabbed the knob and thrust it open so hard it hit the wall. "I think we're done here."

With that, Ernie shuffled out of her office without another word.

***

Hearing the commotion between Ernie and Dr. Drake, Billy Stanton, her assistant, came to see what was going on. Dr. Drake looked so furious, Billy thought he could almost see steam coming out of her ears.

"Everything okay?" he asked.

"Who does that sniveling creep think he is? Our research and methods are sound. There are no safety risks," she said, still staring at the open door. "Williams will be his usual dickish self and stay out of the fray. It's time to move our game up a notch."

She remembered that Billy had come to her office to review the protocol for the next day's data collection. "Sorry Billy, let's sit down and take a look."

Thirty minutes later, her cell phone rang, and she put it on speaker so that she could keep working on her computer. "Hello," she said.

"Dr. Drake," said a synthesized voice on the other end

of the line. "I do not think you have fully understood the importance of not pursuing the publication of your research. There are some *very important* people who do not want this research made public. We know all about your past, and how little information you wish anyone to know about your life *before* Galveston. You should gracefully accept Dr. Pedersen's suggestions. You have much to lose." Click.

Billy saw the shocked look on Dr. Drake's face.

"Who was that? Are you okay?" he asked.

Dr. Drake turned aside to compose herself. After shuffling a few papers on her desk and logging off her computer, she looked up at him. "Actually Billy, I feel great, freed actually. The survey is over. And something else that I was worried about for a long time just got resolved. I'm calling it a day and plan to celebrate. We all need to take a step back and enjoy life. Congratulations again on your new baby. Treasure every minute with him."

Giving him a big smile and a thumb's up, she left the room before Billy could respond.

Billy stood at the office window looking out to the seawall. He wasn't sure what to do next.

Having clawed his way into the middle class, Billy was horrified at the thought of unemployment. Because his parents were drug addicts, his grandparents had stepped up to take care of him and their other grandkids. Despite their own health problems of multiple sclerosis and diabetes, they had done their best to stretch their disability checks. The small amount of foster care payments had barely been enough to keep a roof over their heads and food on the table. He and his younger sister had gotten scholarships and worked through college to pay for their living expenses. His brother had succumbed to the family disease of addiction. That had broken his grandparents' hearts.

Billy was determined to do better, even if it meant bending the rules a little. His wife's teaching job had anchored them with health care and a steady paycheck. The unexpected second baby, so soon after their first, threatened their economic security. Because of undiagnosed pre-eclampsia, his wife had almost died, and her recovery had been slow. As was more common after a complicated birth, she was suffering from postpartum depression. Her return to teaching anytime soon looked doubtful.

This postdoc position with Dr. Drake wasn't giving him the exposure he needed. Without telling her, he had contacted Dr. Drake's superiors to see what he needed to do. Another path forward might be to talk to Dr. Pedersen. He seemed to be making a successful career in the private sector.

***

Ernie tried to collect himself for the final meeting of the survey. He headed back to Meeting Room C, wondering if anyone had overheard his dressing down by Dr. Drake. He was taken aback when Billy Stanton came up behind him.

"Dr. Pedersen, do you have a minute?"

Ernie was in no mood for a conversation with Billy. He frowned and shrugged. "Not right now," he said as he picked up his pace. He heard voices from further behind them. "I've got to get to the last meeting."

In an attempt to appear unruffled, Ernie turned to Billy and added, "Maybe later."

The summation conference was a parenthetical meeting with the same staff leaders that the surveyors had met the previous morning. Kudos were handed out to the sections with no deficiencies. Constructive criticisms were made where appropriate.

As chair, Bert explained that Ernie and he were the eyes and ears of the U.S. Biosafety Association. They would get their report in by the end of the week and let the lab know if the division would be granted two more years of certification.

Ernie added that he didn't think they had anything to worry about. A collective sigh of relief could be heard at this point.

Scanning the room while the good news was imparted, Ernie noted that Williams sat quietly in the front row with only the faintest of smiles. Billy Stanton was present. But no Dr. Drake. Billy looked flushed and kept fiddling with his watch. Ernie wondered if it was a smart watch which was giving Billy more information than he could process during the meeting. He noted Julia, the antsy IT specialist beat a hasty retreat from the room. Thinking back on his confrontation with Dr. Drake, he wondered if he had made a terrible mistake. He was more than ready to say good-bye to Gulf National Lab.

Hailing a ride, the surveyors left directly from the lab for Hobby Airport south of Houston. Ernie and Bert were quiet as they rode across the causeway that connected Galveston Island to the mainland. Looking west, the bay was aqua blue. Sailboats were catching breezes. Fishermen and pelicans completed the picturesque scene.

But looking to the east, Ernie saw a dystopia. A railroad trestle framed a seemingly endless landscape of refineries and chemical storage tanks. Ominous flames shot who-knows-what into the atmosphere. The contrast was a good metaphor for Ernie's mental state. He was cheered by the prospect of putting his financial woes behind him, just as he was disgusted to find himself embroiled with such lowlifes.

Once through security at the airport, the men sipped beers at The Bayou Bend Cafe and enjoyed large servings of gumbo on their expense account. They exchanged small talk. Ernie was tired of survey chat. As Bert got ready to go to his gate, Ernie wished him a safe and pleasant flight. He said that he would manage the bill and promised to send Bert the completed sections of the report by the 48-hour deadline. Ernie's flight to Minneapolis wasn't scheduled to leave for another hour.

The flight left on schedule—without Ernie. He made his way back down I45 to Galveston. He had received another phone call. Dr. Drake had not backed off. She was actively exploring other avenues to expedite the release of her findings. Ernie's contact said that plan B was needed.

Once he was back in Galveston, Ernie checked into a no tell motel near the seawall and close to the Fisherman's Folly. Trying to minimize his electronic footprint for the next 24 hours, he paid cash for the car rental and the motel. He called his wife to explain that the survey had gone over schedule. When she didn't answer, he left a message. *Hope she's not suspicious when she hears me lamenting missing an evening at home.*

He decided to finish up what he could from the survey. He completed the electronic checklists he was responsible for and shot them off to Bert.

With time on his hands before being due back at Fisherman's Folly, Ernie changed into his running clothes and braved the heat for a quick run. That usually cleared his head, although he doubted it would that afternoon.

The seawall extended in both directions from where he stood at 29th Street. It was an actual wall with a sidewalk on top. Perfect for walkers and runners, Ernie mused. He had picked up a glossy tourist magazine in the motel which described the history of the seawall. Seventeen feet high, concave toward the water, it allowed for engineers to raise the altitude of the town by pumping sand harvested from the bay behind the wall into a platform upon which to rebuild the neighborhoods of Galveston after the devastating hurricane. With successive additions, the seawall now stretched about 10 miles long. The concave face deflected the power of raging storm surf upward instead of allowing it to go straight at The Island's buildings.

In an effort to pass more time, Ernie read on.

The storms kept coming. Ernie was amazed at how stubbornly the citizens of Galveston reasserted themselves and rebuilt on a disaster-plagued sandbar. Similarly, he had read how folks in Houston had rebuilt their homes in the same floodplain four times, counting the recent devastation caused by Hurricane Harvey.

His run provided the needed distraction. The other visitors enjoying a late afternoon on the seawall gave him a lot to look at. Galveston attracted an eclectic crowd. He made his way back to his motel room as the sun was getting low and the shadows of the remaining beach umbrellas were getting longer.

After showering, he changed into the clothes he had been instructed to wear to his meeting—jeans and a tee shirt. It was best that nobody remembered a country club client appearing twice in one week.

He found his way, again on foot, to Fisherman's Folly. As instructed, he took the last seat on the left side of the bar. The mirror in front of him reflected a table of guys huddled in the corner. All were about thirty to forty years old and wearing tee shirts, black or white, with the letter Q emblazoned on it. Oh Lordy, thought Ernie as he squirmed on the bar stool. *Is this a gay thing I've walked in on?*

Not that he cared about anyone's choice of partner, he just didn't want to be propositioned. His evening was destined to be bad enough without that complication. Yes, he had also read how Galveston had been a safe haven for libertines and practitioners of alternative lifestyles. He flinched when one of the Q guys took a seat next to him.

"I'm Travis."

The hit man was gay? Ernie wondered. Not that it mattered, he reminded himself again.

The man noticed Ernie's gaze drop to his tee shirt and proudly explained.

"QAnon, man," Travis said. "Have you seen us on TV? We're coming out of the shadows since the president showed us that he's on our side."

Ernie was vaguely aware of Q-Anon. He knew its membership consisted of a bunch of conspiracy-obsessed nut jobs who inflamed each other online. When he'd stumbled upon an article about the organization, he'd learned that the members believed an intertwined narrative—including that all the presidents since Reagan had been servants of the "Deep State." Their theories bounced all over the place, from belief in politicians who were involved in child trafficking, to the existence of a cabal of Jewish financiers, and yes, to that hoax that scientists were peddling about climate change.

Somehow, they'd concluded that it was President Donald J. Drum who would finally bring this all to light and a new day would dawn. Q referred to a shadowy figure in the Department of Energy with a high level of security clearance. Q-Anon was the community of people who tried to decode his or her messages. They found significance in the number seventeen, as Q was the 17th letter of the alphabet.

When Drum mentioned, in his fiery rallies, that he'd only been to the swamp that was Washington, D.C. seventeen times and that the Mueller investigation was being run by seventeen angry democrats, the Q-Anon faithful went wild. They could be seen at presidential rallies in their Q shirts waving their Q posters.

As Ernie faced Travis at the bar, his anxiety increased with Travis's obvious infatuation with his group. To Ernie, they sounded like raving maniacs. *Better to get this over with.*

Getting down to business, Travis said, "I've been told to take out some lady scientist and that you're the guy to give me the specifics."

Ernie tried to disguise his horror at Travis's blunt declaration. He hadn't bargained for this, but Ernie couldn't walk away now. He was already in too deep with these people, whoever they were. Not only would he forfeit his payment, but he was sure they had the wherewithal to ruin his career. His job was to provide details, given by his source, to Travis about the target and arrange payment.

As they talked, Ernie learned more about the man. It turned out Travis worked on an offshore oil drilling rig, a job that required twenty-one days at sea and then twenty-one days off. The timing worked out quite nicely.

"My next *tower* starts in two days," he said.

"Tower?"

"That's how we pronounce *tour*. Don't ask me why. I can do the job and then disappear."

They covered the bases in fifteen minutes. It felt like an eternity to Ernie.

Travis slid off the stool and regrouped with his Q people.

Ernie knew his own payoff was contingent on keeping this operation under wraps. That, and destroying Drake's plans for releasing her results. He wondered for the umpteenth time what on earth he had gotten himself into. He was sickened by the idea of murder. In the end, he rationalized, he wasn't the one committing the deed. If he didn't agree to play his part, surely they would find someone else. And Jesus, he needed the money. He was in deep, and the people on the other end of his calls would not let him forget it.

Ernie tried to calm himself with a double scotch. It didn't help. He abandoned the bar and made his way back to the motel for another restless night.

Chapter Five

September 26, 2018

Galveston, Texas

The next evening, Travis sat in his car outside the 24-hour HEB grocery store. Ernie had provided him with the details regarding Gennifer Drake's car, license number, make and model, her home address, and hours of work. It was easy to follow her to and from work, and on her afterhours errands. He was glad she was a night owl and had popped out at 10:30 p.m. to do some shopping. The lot was almost empty. In the stiff breeze, the sabal palms lining the asphalt were casting crazy, dancing shadows.

Although he wasn't much for self-reflection, the spooky atmosphere caused him to wonder how he was here, about to commit a crime. A really *big* crime.

His job with Rotterdam Energy after his discharge from the navy had been a lucky break. He had enlisted after high school simply because he didn't have any other options.

He was an only child, born after his mother had a series of miscarriages. She always blamed her inability to maintain a pregnancy on the water where they lived in Texas City, just up the road from The Island. It was home to many of the biggest refineries and petrochemical companies in the world. Outrage over spills and contamination bubbled up every few years, although no direct link to miscarriages or other illnesses had ever met the definition of causation.

Despite the efforts she had put into becoming a mother, his mom turned out to be a distant parent. Travis figured she was worn out from raising him, working a minimum wage job at a convenience store, and plodding through an unhappy marriage. All he remembered about his father, a worker at the Mobex plant, was that he was angry all the time. Travis assumed his father harbored resentment towards him. A kid was a financial burden in their strapped circumstances.

Since his dad took off as soon as Travis started high school, Travis knew he would have to take care of himself and help his mom. When a U.S. Navy recruiter visited his school on his eighteenth birthday, he took that as a sign that he should enlist. He liked looking for signs and secret meanings behind ordinary events.

He certainly didn't "See the world!" during his enlistment. But he did learn some skills, including welding. When he finished his enlistment in 2010, he had no problem signing on with Rotterdam Energy for his first offshore job on an oil rig. The money was good. As a single guy, he was able to make ends meet and help out his mother. He still had enough left over to spend on some toys, including the sweet little twenty-four-foot bay boat he had moored in a marina out on the Bolivar peninsula. He also had plenty of discretionary time on his hands during his twenty-one days off between tours. Galveston had plenty of temptations for a young man with time and money. He liked to drink but found out he liked the high he got on oxycodone even more.

He had collected his share of on-the-job injuries, typical of those performing the grueling work on the rigs. At first, he and his coworkers had no problem getting prescription drugs. When the worthless occupational medicine docs quit handing out narcotic prescriptions like candy, the workers turned to the underworld, never far from the surface on The Island.

It wasn't until he discovered Q that he finally found something that fully captured his interest. Q was all about making things right for people like Travis and his mom. With his inclination to overanalyze coincidences, he fell into their web of conspiracy theories. Plus, he had inherited his father's sense of resentment. He got stoked up with the rush he got from hating the "animals and criminals" that the president railed against. It was easy for him to hate the groups that Q targeted. Especially the "eco-terrorists" with their climate change hysteria and environmental regulations that were handcuffing the industry providing him a paycheck and benefits.

He saw the job at hand as a means to make a difference by shutting up a whiny bitch. He was sure someone high up in the organization, someone pulling the strings, would become aware of his commitment. They must have selected him for the job. Even though he had expended no effort in obtaining a promotion while enlisted in the navy, Travis wanted to climb up the shadowy ladder of the Q organization and make a difference.

That guy he met at The Folly didn't have a clue. No way could Travis stuff a body in a duffel bag and bring it aboard the rig, then manage to toss it off the side a hundred miles at sea. When his tour started, he would be transported by a chopper to the rig. The weight limit was super strict. Plus, he and his coworkers worked 24/7 on alternating twelve-hour shifts. There was never a quiet dark moment to toss a body off the side of the rig. His plan was to dispose of the body out in the Gulf, the day before his tour was to start.

So, yeah, it all makes sense for me to be waiting in a supermarket parking lot late at night. I will make a difference.

With that realization, Travis sat up straighter and took a few deep breaths.

Suddenly the target appeared, heading to her car with a bag in each hand. As Dr. Drake groped for her car keys, Travis approached her from behind with his syringe of fentanyl. He tripped her as she hunched over the trunk, and covering her mouth with a gloved hand, he jammed the syringe into her thigh through the thin material of her pants.

Dragging her out of sight, he then lay on top of her, pinning her right arm under her and securing her other arm with his left hand. Using both his legs and steel toed boots, he immobilized her. Her scream was muffled by the thick work gloves he used on the rig.

The woman struggled enough that he had to bear down to keep her still. She was a few inches taller than him and a lot harder to subdue than he predicted. He lay on top of her until he felt her muscles relax and her breathing slow.

He heaved her into the backseat of his car and put her on top of a drop cloth, wrapping it around her. At the last minute, he remembered to collect her grocery bags and purse. He shoved them in the backseat beside her.

Travis took another look around the lot. The shadows were still swirling every which way, wilder now than before. No one was in sight. He felt himself tense up when he saw the bright green eyes of a possum emerging from behind the Dumpster. It locked its gaze on him for a few seconds before moving on with its off-kilter gait. One possum, no people in sight. *Keep cool.* He made himself slow his pace and casually got into the driver's seat. He wanted to hightail it out of there but managed to keep his speed at 5 miles per hour. His passenger was completely motionless, and he wondered if she was already dead. Travis had given her a big hit. Unless she was a junkie, it should've done the deed. He hoped the brisk breeze blowing through the parking lot wasn't the leading edge of a storm. His work was far from done.

Pulling up on Harborside Drive next to the marina

where his boat was moored, Travis finally relaxed. It was dead quiet. Except for the wind. He could see whitecaps between the bay side of Galveston and Pelican Island.

He parked within ten yards of his boat. He looked at the woman's form on the backseat. She was covered by the drop cloth which he had fastened with plastic chip clips. He didn't see any sign of life, nor did he get any resistance when he used every muscle to pull her out onto the sidewalk. *This is what they mean by dead weight.*

He dragged her down to the edge of the dock and jumped into his boat, the Suzy-Q, named for his mother Sue and his newfound second family. A brackish stench rose from the mooring. He pulled the woman from the dock and onto the boat deck. The added weight made him lose his balance for a second as the craft rocked back and forth. *You'd think in three years in the navy I'd have grown some sea legs.*

He untied the boat, started the engine, and edged out of the marina. He looked around and was relieved to note he was still alone. Well, except for his passenger. He picked up speed as he left the boatyard.

As soon as he passed the sleeping ferries, Travis turned right, heading into the Gulf of Mexico. The wind hit him hard in the face and the rain stung his bare arms. He wanted to get out far enough to dump the woman overboard without risking her washing up on the beach. Because flotsam from the oil tankers and the influx of Sargassum seaweed were huge turn offs for beach goers, the city constantly cleaned the beaches. He definitely didn't want his package to turn up there.

He was only five minutes out onto the gulf when three-foot swells caused the boat to rock and roll. The rain was coming down harder. It was still hurricane season. *Did I miss a warning?* He needed to get out to deeper water.

"Oh, fuck!" he shouted when he realized the shape

under the wrapping had started to move. He edged over to where she was freeing herself from the loosely clipped drop cloth.

He lunged at her just as a wave broke over the side of the boat. He fell, hitting his head on the starboard rail.

When he opened his eyes, Travis couldn't believe what he saw. She was standing up, wobbly, but up. She was staring at the shore, where the lights could be made out through the rain.

She looked at him with glassy eyes before throwing herself at him. Despite the accelerating fury of the storm, everything seemed to happen in slow motion. She was kneeling on his chest, choking him as rain pelted his face. He tried to get some air. Another wave struck the boat. Now rain, salt water, and air rushed into his lungs. He took a breath. Then another. "Fuck me, fuck me, fuck me!" Travis half screamed, half cried.

He couldn't see anything as he made his way over to the portside of the boat. She was gone. He tried to tack back to see if he could see her in the water. His flashlight was useless against the roiling seas.

He tacked again. No luck. The wind had picked up even more. He feared he'd capsize the boat if he waited any longer. He had to get to shore to save his ass.

But still, how could she have come back to life like that? He realized that the purity of the fentanyl he bought on the street was questionable. *Why hadn't that asshole told him how big she was?* He would have given her a larger dose. He just wanted this night to be over. Wiping sea spray from his eyes, he positioned himself at the wheel and headed back to shore.

After he had managed to moor his boat at the marina, Travis tried to collect himself. Things hadn't gone as planned. He was supposed to call when the deed was done. It was hard to bring his phone to life and punch in the number. His hands were shaking from cold and fear.

***

The shock of the water awakened Gen, but she was still drugged and disoriented. *Am I dreaming?* She tried to make sense of it all. She remembered seeing the shoreline. Without any idea how far it was, her instinct for survival started her arms paddling and legs kicking. She was so confused. *Why am I out in the sea at night?*

After a few strokes, Gen was hit in the face by a breaking wave. She gasped as she inhaled a mouthful of salt water. Her arms and legs felt like heavy weights. She tried to take another breath but got a mouthful of water instead. She thought of Garrett.

Then it all went dark.

***

Waiting for Travis to call him, Ernie needed to fill his time. He rationalized that he might as well try to make a bit of money. He had no trouble finding Aces High Casino, an old tub dressed up to look like a Mississippi riverboat and moored in dank water off Port Industrial Road. He'd just play the slots and gave himself a one-hour limit while he drank a virgin margarita, his lucky beverage.

When he started to win, he thought he might as well stay another hour and take his good luck to the poker table.

He kept winning. He was $1,000 up.

One more hour and another margarita, and he was still up $500. For once, he had enough sense and self-control to get out while he was ahead. At least, he could cover his costs in cash before leaving this god-forsaken sandbar.

When his cell phone went off, Ernie picked up on the first ring. "Yeah."

"It's done," Travis managed to croak out. "But I'm not so sure…"

"Not so sure of what?" Ernie shot back.

Travis stammered out the words. "My chopper flight to the rig was delayed by weather so I took the body out in my boat. There was a squall. I lost control of the boat and she went over the side," he sputtered. "The waves were huge. I saw her go under. But it was too close to shore. If there's an onshore wind tonight, her body could turn up somewhere between Stewart Beach and Beachtown. Anyway, I'm outta here tomorrow morning."

"You worthless redneck dickwad!" Ernie yelled. He heard a dead signal, then tried to call Travis back. His call went straight to voicemail.

Ernie consulted the map on his phone. Stewart Beach to Beachtown was a one mile stretch on the eastern tip of The Island. Trying to look natural, he hustled to his rental car.

When he arrived at the empty parking lot at Stewart Beach, he realized he had run along this stretch the day before. Earlier in the day, while the sand hadn't been exactly white and the water had been far from blue, the beach had been inviting. The fine, light brown sand had been firm and easy to run on. The dunes had glowed with yellow wildflowers.

The surf was up, at least for Galveston. He could hear the water rushing up to the sand with small continuous waves. They stirred up the pebbly shelf which created a low-pitched rustling he could hear before he could see the water. Dense fog engulfed the beach.

He tried the flashlight on his phone, but it only made the visibility worse. He walked down to where the water just met his feet. Then, he turned and started walking east. *How did I ever get involved with such fucking inept lowlifes? Travis and his loony friends?* He answered his own question. He needed the money to get out from under his losses in the stock market and from gambling. He had accepted the deal as soon as it was offered. He had told Allison his financial concerns were all related to paying Gigi's tuition for the next four years. But it was worse than that. Much worse. He tried to think about how big the payoff was going to be. He could put all this behind him.

He passed the high-rise condominium, recognizable only from the red lights on its twenty-third-floor roof. He had no idea how far he'd walked. He could see about ten yards ahead as the fog started to lift in spots. Thinking he saw something, he went closer to the water's edge. Before he could make it out, his feet slipped out from under him.

Breaking his fall with his hand, it landed in a gooey substance. The pain was almost immediate.

"Jesus Christ!" he shouted without caution. "Jesus H. Christ!" Even a land-loving Minnesotan could identify a jellyfish.

Ernie ripped his tee shirt off, then dunked it into the water and tried to scrub the jellyfish off. His hand was swelling, and the burning was intense. He wrapped the shirt around his hand like a huge mitten and continued his trek. He was walking and rewrapping his hand when he almost fell again.

"Ayyy!" he screamed. The pitch was so high that Ernie was surprised by his own voice. He thought he was having another run-in with sea life. He steadied himself to keep from falling on top of a sodden mass tangled in seaweed. It was about his size and heaving. Activating his flashlight with his good hand, he lurched back.

He managed to turn the body over and was confronted by a ghostly pale Dr. Drake. Her gaze fixed on him.

Can she see me? He couldn't bear the sight of those piercing dark eyes. She was pleading with those eyes.

He couldn't handle it. He used his shirt-gloved hand to conceal them. The big mitt covered her nose, mouth, and her eyes. He pressed down harder.

When he could no longer sense her attempt to breathe, he slumped onto his back beside her.

It took him awhile to realize the moisture on his face was from his own tears. This entire situation had devolved into an uncontrolled shit storm. He was broke, a washed-up loser committing fraud that would benefit some assholes on the wrong side of history, and now a murderer to boot.

He pulled himself up onto his elbows. The fog was starting to lift and there was a glow on the eastern horizon. He had to figure out what to do next.

That's when he became aware of a dog barking and a couple coming his way.

His next move was pure reflex. He got up and ran toward the sandhills. The dune grass slashed against his skin.

Ernie lay flat, hoping the gentle terrain formed by the dunes and grass would be sufficient cover as the sun began to rise. His hand still throbbed from the jellyfish sting. He could barely make out a warning on a sign at the edge of the dunes telling people to stay away from the dunes as they were nesting areas for sea turtles.

For a brief minute, he remembered when Gigi was seven and they were on the beach in Mexico. She squealed with delight as she "helped" baby sea turtles get to the water by picking them up and running them to the water's edge.

Then, the self-recriminations resumed. He'd never considered suicide before. *Wouldn't it be better if I just died, here and now? Allison and Gigi would at least get something from his underfunded life insurance. Does it still pay if I kill myself? If I'm found guilty of murder?*

He took out his phone and dialed the only person he thought could help him. "I need help…" Ernie said.

"Where the hell are you?"

Ernie was able to describe the beach homes he could make out behind the dunes. He must have made it to

Beachtown. He could see a dimly lit street further on, in front of the homes.

"Yeah. I know those houses. Stay where you are until I call you. I'll be on the road in front of the sand dunes and will let you know when the coast is clear for you to run to the car."

Ernie lay in the sand. *How long will this take?* He closed his eyes and surrendered to exhaustion.

Suddenly a sound brought him instantly awake. He looked up in time to see a sledgehammer coming at his head. He didn't even have a chance to yell.

Chapter Six

September 27, 2018

Galveston, Texas

Louise looked at her watch. She had avoided calling Marnie but there was no putting it off any longer. Today was going to be busy and she had to tell her friend. Hopefully, Marnie would pick up the phone. It was an hour earlier in Colorado. *Maybe just give her another hour to wake up.*

***

Aurora, Colorado

Marnie Liccione looked at the maple tree outside her window, now golden in the autumn sun. Ever since she and Adam planted it together two years into their marriage, she had watched it grow. In springtime, its little red buds were the first sign that winter was ending. After living here for twenty years, the shade from the tree extended so far that Marnie had to change what she planted. To live in a place long enough to see its microclimate evolve still shocked her. But everything shocked her now. Ever since Adam left five months ago for a men's rafting trip and never came home.

She stood and stared at the tree, its yellow foliage the color of hope. Marnie felt she was drifting in a place between this life and the next, paralyzed by her grief. She had taken a leave of absence from her pediatric practice as she struggled through the minimal activities of life.

She felt Jack and Harlee dancing around her feet. She'd lingered in her pajamas to fool the dogs that it was not time for their walk. They knew it was past time. Leaving the window, she changed her clothes and headed out.

The crisp autumn air revived her. They set off for the reservoir. She smiled at her neighbors and kept walking. The thought of another well-meaning question about how she was doing exhausted her. Her eyes followed a flock of geese as they headed south and west. Looking at the majestic mountains that gave the Front Range its name, she listened to their honking call that winter was coming.

When they returned from their four-mile walk, the dogs went into the sunny living room for their daytime nap. Marnie was both envious of and grateful for them. She would probably never get out of bed without their enthusiasm for life pushing her forward.

As she joined them, she thought about what she might actually *try* to get done today, but her thoughts were interrupted by her cell phone.

She looked at the caller ID. Louise. Louise had been great about calling and trying to keep Marnie functional. She had stayed for a week after the funeral—leaving her two children with their busy schedules in the care of her husband and their ever-helpful grandmother. Resisting pressure from her friend to return with her to Galveston, Marnie convinced Louise that she needed some time alone in the space she had shared with Adam.

Failing to muster the energy today to talk, even to

her closest friend, Marnie let the call go to voicemail. Louise called again. That was unusual. Reluctantly, Marnie picked up.

"Marnie, something terrible has happened," Louise said. "Gen is dead."

***

Galveston, Texas

With the sunrise, Travis wondered if the events of the previous evening had been a bad dream. As the details returned, he knew the nightmare was real. He stood looking out his living room window. The view of the Gulf usually brought him peace. This morning, the blue sky with the fluffy white clouds reaching down to the water didn't help. His mom had always talked about living someplace with a view of the water, and he guessed it had rubbed off on him. This condominium had been his first big purchase from his earnings on the oil rig.

He wasn't sure if it was the view or the fact his mother was more financially secure with his help, but she seemed to enjoy spending time with him now. She made frequent visits to the condo, often staying to cook a meal for the two of them. With the payoff from this nightmare gig, he would have more money to help her. He hoped she would finally be able to quit her job. But to make sure it all worked out, he had to get off The Island and out of sight. That was part of the deal.

He finished packing his bag and then called his mother to say good-bye.

Hearing his voice crack, she asked, "What's wrong?"

Clearing his throat, he replied, "Nothing, Mom. Just had a late night out with the guys before flying out. I'll see you in three weeks."

"You be careful out there, son. You know I worry until I see you back on solid ground."

"Don't worry, Ma. I always make it home in one piece. I'm tough."

At thirty years of age, he was still what he, and the women he dated, considered a good specimen. His chest was broad and his arms well-muscled. He had to watch that beer gut, though. Even after his years in the navy, he kept his sandy hair cropped short. He thought it looked good atop his five feet, nine inches.

People, especially girls, said he had sad eyes. Travis tried to remember to smile more so people wouldn't ask him if he was having a bad day.

He felt something on his neck. Closer inspection revealed a scratch on the left side, and he saw another on his left arm. He recalled his victim putting up a fight but didn't know she'd left any marks. With everything that happened out in that squall, he wasn't surprised he hadn't noticed.

He still couldn't believe he made it back to the marina in one piece. The marks weren't concerning in themselves as they were hard to see superimposed on his tats, but it added to an uneasiness he couldn't shake. He was sweating and thought he would jump out of his skin. Maybe it was the energy drink he just downed, or perhaps, the result of hitting the oxy and meth a little harder than usual this last stretch on shore.

Knowing he had to stop before going offshore, his last dose had been the day before. There was always the chance of a drug screen if someone on his team screwed up and had an accident. The safety officer hauled them all in to pee in a cup when that happened.

Since he didn't think there was much chance of that in the first thirty-six hours, he decided to risk a little hit.

By the time he got to the heliport, Travis felt almost normal. There were sixteen of them heading out that morning. He joined the others in the stuffy waiting area.

He glanced around to see if he recognized anyone. He said "hey" to a few of the guys he had worked with before. With the tours being as long as they were, a lot of the crew lived out of state and would fly in and out for their work. It could be hit or miss when he might overlap with the same guys.

It still amazed him how diverse the crew was. He wasn't thinking of diversity in terms of race, but the fact that they weren't all young, husky, male bruisers like himself. Some of the women on the rig worked in support areas, such as cleaning and food service, but some of them worked right on deck along with the guys. And there was Jeff, the skinny chemist. A stiff breeze would blow him right off the deck. There was a chemist on duty 24/7 checking the purity of the oil they pumped out of the seabed. Technicians spent their entire twelve-hour shifts looking at computer screens, monitoring everything from the ballast of the rig, to the amount of oil being sucked out of the ocean floor. Some of the safety staff were in their sixties.

Travis preferred getting to the rig, which was located a hundred miles offshore, by helicopter instead of by boat. The helicopter could land on the pad above the rig. Getting lifted onto the rig from a boat by an open-air basket gave Travis the creeps. A crane was used to swing it over the open water onto the deck.

Everyone waiting with Travis had been through helicopter safety training, including a mock crash landing and the ditching-at-sea exercise. Man, woman, skinny, fat, old or young, they all had to suit up in survival gear for the ride.

As they waited an extra thirty minutes to let a squall pass by the rig, Travis glanced at the Bolivar Ferry. As a child, he had loved taking the ferry over to the Bolivar peninsula. It was one of his few happy memories. His dad probably liked the ferry because it was free. Together, they would scan the bay for the dolphins that famously followed the boat.

"Ready for another tour?" the guy next to Travis asked.

Travis nodded. "More than ready."

Then, they were cleared for takeoff. Each of them filed into the chopper and buckled up. Travis did a quick survey to see if he recognized anyone he didn't want to bunk with. He was on the day shift this tour and he hoped his roommate would be on nights.

Damn, is that Maples? He'd had a run-in with him a few tours back over using the washing machines. Things escalated, and Maples called Travis a redneck asshole and threatened to kick his ass if he disrespected him again. Travis kept clear of him for the rest of the tour.

The platform came into view as the chopper started its jerky descent. The Titan, a newer platform, rose an impressive forty stories above the water. No wonder this rig, like most others, was baptized with a name of a mythological giant. It had been constructed to withstand hurricanes and the impact of an ocean liner and was secured by a support structure that stretched 3,100 feet down to the seabed. Drilling and storage facilities were connected by catwalks that looked perilously insubstantial from above.

Travis remembered being freaked out by all the metal mesh walkways and stairs on his first tour. He could look right down, over 100 feet, to the water. Waves broke against the rig's supports and sent currents swirling in all directions. At first, the view made him dizzy. More than most Americans, he came face to face with the reality of oil rig safety after the BP Deepwater Horizon explosion in 2010. For millions, the ongoing crisis was environmental. For Travis, it was the death and injury of twenty-eight guys that got to him. A federal moratorium on construction of new platforms went into effect.

When construction resumed, with ever increasing safety regulations, the price tag to complete a rig rose as well. As long as the price of oil stayed up though, offshore drilling could still turn a tidy profit and new rigs continued to sprout from the seabed.

After the chopper landed on the pad, the new arrivals gave high fives to the sixteen crew members who had just finished their tour and were swapping places in the helicopter. They were clearly relieved to be heading home for twenty-one days off.

Travis's group was greeted by Tibo, short for Thierry Thibodaux, the sixty-five-year-old rig vet from Louisiana. He'd been working offshore for over forty years, doing just about every job that needed doing on a rig. He had the battle scars to prove it. As a roughneck, manually screwing the drill segments together, Tibo was lucky to have held on to all ten fingers. Now the sections were fit together by an automated pipe handler managed by a guy in the drill shack. Travis had even seen a woman working the controls.

Tibo was now a "camp boss," overseeing the housekeeping and cooking staff. Today his job was to settle the new crew in and attend to their creature comforts. The first order of business was handing out room assignments.

Travis tried not to look too relieved when he learned his roommate's name. It wasn't Maples. But it was another guy on days. He hoped he didn't snore.

They headed off to drop their gear in their rooms. The rooms had been cleaned and the beds made up by the housekeeping staff that morning in anticipation of their arrival. The company brochure described the rooms as "similar to college dorms." Each room had a set of bunk beds, a desk attached to the wall and a couple of lockers, all within about eight by eight square feet. The ceiling was also eight feet high, and the room was windowless. Travis couldn't imagine what college would have such shitty accommodations. To him, it was what he thought a prison cell would look like. *Don't go there.*

The first item on the agenda was a safety meeting. On the way there, Tibo escorted the group through the employee lounge fitted out with recliners, desktop computers and TVs, then on to the gym, furnished with some worn out equipment. Next, came the mess hall—a contrast to the utilitarian appearance of the rest of the living quarters. There were no windows, but the ceilings were higher, tables set with attractive place mats, and a magnificent, all you can eat buffet. *Were those flowers real?*

The kitchen was headed by an actual chef to oversee the preparation of four meals a day for 130 souls. Food on the rig was unlimited and high quality to keep the captive troops satisfied. Without much to look forward to on any given day during their twelve-hour shifts, mealtimes were a welcome distraction. The company played this aspect of rig life up, even as waistlines and BMIs were on the rise within the workforce.

And so, it started, just like all his other tours. Safety meetings twice a day, work assignments, meals, a few hours of internet with access to adult entertainment, sleep, lather, rinse, repeat. The familiarity of the routine and the distance from the mainland helped Travis's restless mind settle down.

Chapter Seven

September 27-28, 2018

Aurora, Colorado

After the conversation with Louise, Marnie had sat stunned in the kitchen chair. The world was off kilter. *First Adam, now Gen.* Adam had drowned in a rafting accident on the Colorado River. His body had been barely recognizable. Marnie shuddered at the memory. Gen's death made less sense. An accident didn't explain why she was in the sea that night when she was expected to eat dinner with Garrett.

Would someone murder her? What was she up to?

For five months, Marnie had been unable to consider her future. Now she knew what she wanted to do, at least in the short term. She would follow the geese's example and go south. It made sense to spend the fall and holidays in Galveston. Her daughter, Ellie Jean, who was studying abroad in Amsterdam for the year, could join her in Galveston for the holidays.

Ellie Jeans had tried to take a year off as well, but Marnie could not see them both drifting around the house. She encouraged Ellie Jean to keep her plans. Without Adam, Marnie couldn't face the traditions they had made together as a family. She smiled thinking about the times they had skied in the mountains on Christmas Eve, taken long walks at home on

Christmas Day, and then played golf on Boxing Day. These thoughts made her dissolve into tears.

Picking herself back up, Marnie turned her thoughts to planning her trip. She called her trusty house-sitter who said she'd love to stay for three to four months and take good care of Mateo, Marnie's Seal Point Siamese. Texting Louise to say she was coming for an extended stay, Marnie went online to rent her own place.

For once, money was not a large factor in her decisions. Adam's life insurance had been incredibly generous. Perhaps the only "lucky" aspect of his death was that it occurred before their planned reduction in their term life insurance. Now that task, initially slated to happen after the bustle of summer activities, was off the to-do list for all the wrong reasons.

Keep focused. Keep moving.

She went through the house, prioritizing what needed to be done. Then, she emptied the refrigerator and packed for a mild Galveston winter. It had been years since she'd not dealt with a cold winter—eighteen years to be exact.

Staying on task, Marnie loaded the car with her immediate needs. The dogs were thrilled to see their traveling beds get packed. After labeling boxes that she wanted sent in a couple of weeks to Galveston, she took a sleeping pill and fell into her bed.

She awoke the next day somewhat rested—a rare feeling since the accident.

"I guess a plan helps the brain," she said to Harlee and Jack.

She navigated the stairs carefully to avoid tripping over their bodies buzzing with uncontained excitement. After a walk and breakfast, Marnie finished downloading the audiobooks she would need to survive a three-day, thousand-mile road trip.

"Ready to go?" she asked the dogs.

Their excitement was answer enough to get them all into the car.

As she headed down I-25, she thought about the countless times she and her parents had trekked south—before their untimely deaths. They had loved traveling to all parts of Colorado and the southwest. Mesa Verde and Durango. The Great Sand Dunes National Park. Santa Fe and Bandelier National Monument. After just such a lovely road trip, she had headed back to college in 1994. Everything had been falling into place. She had gotten through her sophomore year at Yale, her parents' alma mater.

Then, the first major tragedy in her life had struck. Her parents' deaths shook her to her core. She had managed to finish college early and returned to Colorado. Settling her affairs, she had looked for a new start. It must have been fate that led her to Galveston in 1995. She was looking for a warm spot that was within driving distance. Florida was too far. California was too California. Texas was unknown. No memories there. Galveston seemed doable. Two years later, she was enrolled in medical school and met Adam. Her new life had begun.

Now twenty-three years later, she was driving the same route. She was as awestruck by the grandeur of the mountains which framed the Front Range as she had been in her youth. She could see the imposing peaks of Mount Evans and Longs Peak. Her eyes traveled south to Pikes Peak, which stood proudly alone with its snowy top. She often thought about the pioneers who, after climbing the relentless slope from the Mississippi River to the mile-high plains, paused on their journey west to make homes along the South Platte River in Denver. Those peaks could discourage even the most determined. She was leaving the Front Range again. Another chapter in her life had closed.

Being an active participant in the care of her aging grandparents and raising her young daughter, Marnie was a member of the sandwich generation. Those years seemed to be a constant treadmill of work and caregiving. With Ellie Jean off to college, the last several years were blessedly simple.

And then another tragic accident—a one in a million event. Marnie couldn't decide how to approach this new reality.

Was she guilty of some crime in a past life?

In her own career, she'd had to help grieving parents adjust to the illness and death of their children. And death seemed a fickle master, taking some and sparing others. Still, the unexpected loss of someone left the survivors unmoored. And Marnie was completely untethered.

Perhaps that was why Gen's death held such a grip on her. Her death had to have an explanation. She and Louise would figure it out.

Marnie left I-25 at Raton, taking US 87 to Amarillo. As the sunlight and her attention were fading, she had the strangest feeling that the road was moving. Suddenly, she bolted upright, realizing she was in the middle of a tarantula migration. The road was covered with them.

The sound of her tires crunching the spiders made her skin crawl. She had heard about this migration but never expected to see it, much less drive through it. Marnie shuddered. *This seems like a bad omen.*

She made her way towards her first destination. A pet friendly hotel in Amarillo provided the perfect stop after the first day of driving.

After a long walk the next morning, the puppies and Marnie settled in for another long drive. Like yesterday, it was memories, not one of the many audiobooks that she had downloaded, that kept Marnie awake.

Marnie thought back to when she met Gen. Gennifer Drake was the tallest woman in their medical school class. At five feet, eleven inches, she beat out five-ten Marnie. With a quiet way about her, Gen studied a room carefully before settling in. Gen was a slow-to-warm-up personality type, guarded in her approach to strangers. It was much later in their friendship when Marnie learned the real reason for Gen's reticence.

Throughout the stress of medical school, Gen was

a rock. Initially, both she and Marnie were unsure of joining the University of Texas Medical Branch sorority, the only med school sorority in the country. But ultimately, they needed a family. Marnie could always trust her friend to look at the big picture. It was at the sorority that Gen and Marnie met Louise. The trio became fast friends.

When Marnie had turned up unexpectedly pregnant in her third year at U.T.M.B. and was unsure of what to do, Gen had helped her figure out the important things.

Did she want this baby? Yes.

Did she want to finish medical school? Yes.

Did she love Adam? Yes.

Then, the details of life had fallen into place.

Gen was that way for all of their classmates. She had spent a few years after college working in a microbiology department. Consequently, she was almost five years older than the average student. It was her lab work which had made her want to go to medical school. She was grounded when it came to the big things in life, but she had a wicked sense of humor. When someone was being a pompous ass, Gen would look over, a twinkle in her eye with eyebrows raised, and cause everyone to burst out laughing. The world could be going to hell in a handbasket, and she would lament the narrowness and avarice of the people in charge. Then, she would tell a joke or get excited about the latest NBA game.

Loving Ellie Jean as if she was her niece, Gen had been a reliable babysitter. Louise's mother, Nancy, had been the main back-up for their nanny, but even she couldn't fill all the gaps that two residents' call schedules created at home.

Caught in the memories, Marnie almost stopped the car in the middle of the road. The last few days had been so crazy she hadn't called Ellie Jean. The news of Gen's death would be devastating for her. "Forgetting" to call was probably not being honest. She couldn't face breaking the news to her daughter. *First thing tomorrow.*

After residency, Marnie, Adam and Ellie Jean had moved to Colorado where they had more family support. Adam's parents and Marnie's grandparents were eager to have them closer and help with childcare. Gen had stayed at U.T.M.B. to finish her M.D/Ph.D. program. Louise had stayed close by in Houston to complete an emergency medical residency, returning to The Island to join a group of emergency physicians.

The three classmates had seen each other over the years—girls' weekends here and there. There had also been family get-togethers—frequently on the ski slopes in Colorado and more recently during the summers enjoying the mountains' activities.

Marnie had been thrilled when Gen had first brought along Garrett. She deserved a good man. Gen had been glowing. That was two years ago. Who could predict the tragedies of this summer?

***

September 28, 2018

Galveston, Texas

Louise pulled into her driveway, which consisted of crunchy shell remnants and Galveston's honey-colored sand and parked under the house. Despite looking insubstantial—many permanent residents of The Island had come to the conclusion, often after several previous homes had been destroyed by storm surges—that homes built on stilts were the safest bet. The front garden consisted of an assortment of native grasses, lantana, and oleanders which banked the stilts. It was a struggle to find plants that would survive a climate that included both a four-month heatwave, known as summer, and frigid winter days with storms, that might consist of a wintry mix of freezing rain and snow flurries. At least this architectural style provided a shady, open-air carport.

Louise eavesdropped on the family banter from the porch before opening the door and calling out, "I'm home!" After the last forty-eight hours, family life and daily routines were essential in helping Louise regain her footing. Cora and Noah bounded out of the kitchen to welcome her with hugs, and then ran back to their places at the table.

Cries of "I'm winning!" and "My turn!" punctuated an ongoing game of Go Fish with their dad. Looking up from his cards, Didier greeted her with a smile and squeezed her hand as she stood next to him, peeking at his cards.

"I think you're in trouble," she said.

Cora continued on a roll, collecting packs of four. She was five and had just started to join the family in card and board games without fear of humiliation. Thankfully, Noah, at seven, was so secure in his card sharp mastery that he didn't fuss when his little sister trounced his dad and him.

"Mommy, can we have a second dessert?" Cora and Noah asked simultaneously.

They knew she was a pushover after work. Ice cream sandwiches were produced, as the children wandered into the family room and were granted thirty minutes of TV before bedtime.

This was the best strategy to snatch a few minutes with Didier.

"How was today?" Didier asked as he poured two glasses of wine.

Louise spooned lukewarm macaroni and cheese from a saucepan on the stove. The rosé wine made a perfect accompaniment.

"Better. Today was better." She paused for a bite and a sip, then looked up at Didier. "I just can't wrap my head around it."

Didier patted her hand, encouraging her to continue.

"At first, I couldn't stop wondering what I had missed. Was she depressed? I don't think so. It doesn't fit with what I know was going on in her life. So, if not suicide, her death must be either an accident or foul play. But who would want to hurt Gen? Is it wrong for me to feel better that Gen was murdered and didn't commit suicide? Man, Didier, this is twisted. I keep thinking about the last time we were together. She was so involved in her work. And seemed so happy with Garrett. Remember?"

"Of course. They seemed like a great couple."

Realizing that she was ruminating yet again, Louise asked, "And how was your day? Did you have a good group?"

"Yup. Three couples from Oklahoma for a full day's tour. We spotted some Black Skimmers, and they got some good photos. I think the thing that impressed them the most was the alligator we saw across the bayou. I thought it was a garbage bag, but by using a scope that one person in my group had, I could see I was wrong. I bet they're still laughing about it."

"Hah! Some Born-on-the-Island naturalist I married! BOI, indeed!" Louise knew how proud Didier was to be able to trace his LaSalle family roots back to the earliest European settlers.

"You have no idea!" Didier protested, laughing.

Bending down to give Louise a kiss, Didier continued. "I'm going to take the kids up for baths and bed. You take yourself and your wine out to the veranda and watch the sunset."

"Thanks, hon. I will."

Louise walked out to the veranda, letting the sounds of the birds calm her. She sat down in one of the chairs and tried to keep her mind off of Gen. She started thinking about how she ended up on this island. Where did her story fit in with its busy past?

The Island, always referred to with a capital I by its residents, was really no more than a sandbar thirty miles long by three miles at its widest part. It was a great disappointment to the first Spanish explorers who arrived in 1528. Nearly 500 years later, The Island had withstood the assaults of hurricanes, welcomed waves of immigrants, been home to bootleggers, gangsters, and legitimate businessmen. Since its port economy had been eclipsed by Houston in the last fifty years, it had become a popular beach town with an intriguing history. Today, as a Gulf town flush with artists and free spirits, there was an uneasy truce between those ascribing to the "Everybody's welcome here" sentiment and a lingering social caste system of the BOIs. She wondered which camp she fit in.

Didier came out and joined her on the creaky porch swing.

Louise looked at him, grateful for both his presence and his silence. It still amazed her that they had found each other.

It was at the Feather Fest 1999 that she met Didier LaSalle. He had been volunteering at the annual island gathering of birders, timed to take place shortly after the arrival of the sand cranes. Under the urging of her medical student classmates, Gen and a very pregnant Marnie, Louise had reluctantly agreed to attend the Saturday 7:00 a.m. breakfast program. It took a lot of urging because Louise was on a punishing med school rotation in general surgery and had exactly one Saturday off the entire month.

After a surprisingly good meal of breakfast tacos and strong coffee, and an informative presentation of the crazy 10,000-mile migration of the cranes, Louise's outlook improved. The women hopped into their assigned van to be shuttled to the first sighting stop. Didier was leading her group. The majority of the group had binoculars. Some had their own telescopes. Louise was unprepared. This worked out fine for Didier because he was able to help Louise spot the birds with his equipment. He had to sidle up beside her to point her in the right direction.

They still joked about the corniness of the situation

which had allowed two strangers to brush shoulders within five minutes of meeting. Didier later confessed he'd made sure he was driving the van with the girl with the long blonde braid.

Now, he was the one to break the silence. "Oh yeah, I meant to tell you that Marnie called. She's on her way and will be here for the memorial. She asked if she could stay with us for a few days, and I said of course she could. I told her you'd call."

"Sure. When did she say she was arriving?"

"Tomorrow or the next day. You know your friend can be hard to pin down."

Louise was glad she was off for a few days and hoped she had at least one whole day to prepare for Marnie's arrival. The guest room/study was a disaster. Between tackling that chore and the kids' busy schedules, she hoped she would get a few minutes of quiet to grieve.

Then she remembered she needed to study up on dengue fever. Was it really only forty-eight hours ago that she had cared for that poor boy? Was anyone following up on Ned's observation that they had admitted several similar cases? But, yes, tomorrow.

Finishing her wine, she and Didier went inside.

After a restless night, Louise awoke to the sounds of songbirds singing. She looked at Didier sleeping soundly. Perhaps she should have gotten her degree in environmental science and become a birder. Four years at the University of Houston had prepared him for a life of studying and painting birds. Good thing for both of them that he tapped into his more mercantile DNA and established a small company to provide visiting birders with excursions, lodging, and educational sessions. His store, Feathers, sold binoculars, cameras, books, birding attire, and avian art. His business was thriving. What had previously been a hobby for aging oddballs was now mainstream. Their life on Galveston Island, long recognized by bird nerds as a mecca, was a perfect place to meld her medical practice and his business.

As she quietly got out of bed and went to the shower, she thought of her busy day ahead. She looked longingly at her partner's unruffled sleep. Her career choice had taken her on a rockier path. Despite the stress and strain of medicine, she never questioned her decision to become a physician. She made a mental note to read up on dengue and figure out why her ER was seeing a surge in cases.

Chapter Eight

September 29, 2018

Galveston, Texas

Louise took a few minutes to regroup after the melee of a typical morning at home. She had prepared breakfast for the kids, then moved on to their lunches. Next came a quick examination of the backpacks to see if all was in order for Cora's kindergarten "homework" and the actual homework Noah had in second grade.

"What's this permission slip for?" she asked Noah.

"I need it today," he said. "Sign it. Sign it now!"

"Okay, okay! Let me see it." Looking over the form, Louise could see it was a planned field trip to tour the *U.S.S. Seawolf*, a submarine that was mistakenly sunk by the U.S. Navy during World War II. Of course it was on a day she worked, and she'd miss another excursion. As she signed the form, she felt badly about being a working mother for the millionth time, yet relieved to have an out.

As the clock ticked down, the kids hurried to the car with Didier. He would drop them off on his way to the store and office, where he'd spend his day catching up on business. He had told her earlier that morning that he planned to meet with his staff to discuss inventory and their first official snowbirds fall tour. Snowbird season had been a financial success for the last five years, and Didier wanted to keep it that way.

Taking her coffee to the porch, Louise sat in a comfortable chair looking east. She surveyed the property, again lamenting her struggling garden. She had resorted to hearty survivors after her early years of trying to reproduce her mother's garden from the family's Fort Worth homestead. The beach climate was punishing towards her favorites—roses and black-eyed Susans. She realized she had repeated her mother's error. Mom had attempted to grow peonies, cosmos, and hostas when she moved from New England to Texas.

Louise walked back to the kitchen for the last half cup of coffee. A framed picture that was askew among the jumble of LaSalle and Finnerty photographs on the wall caught her attention. It was of Louise and her brother, Blake, dressed up for some occasion. Maybe Blake's high school graduation? Graduations had been a big deal in their family.

As the children of educators, it was fortunate that academics came naturally to Louise and Blake. Their parents, Claude and Nancy, weren't nearly as directive as the helicopter parents of today. Louise and Blake were raised at the tail end of the glorious years of under-parenting. However, their parents' hopes and expectations were clear to both children. Having majored in journalism at Northwestern, Blake took a job as a stringer for Reuters and bounced from trouble spot to trouble spot—from his parents' perspective—reporting on tragedies and calamities.

Louise majored in geology at Boston University and to everyone's surprise, including her own, applied to medical school after starting her masters in geology at University of Texas in Austin. The only reason she could give for this change of course was that she enjoyed working with people and liked figuring things out. Geology failed on the first but prepared her well for the latter. Louise began medical school at the University of Texas Medical Branch in Galveston the next year.

Louise remembered her resolution to read up on dengue. Plus, she had to get the guest room ready for Marnie. Better get after her research while her caffeine levels were still high. The guest room preparations could wait.

She wandered inside and sat at her desk, taking a minute to gaze out the window toward the bay. The early fall light was indirect. A soft breeze made the tall grasses lining the inlets dance and carried a salty aroma to Louise. Herons stalked through the muddy flats looking for breakfast. Even if Didier considered them common, they looked stately to her with their measured pace.

She turned her attention to her computer and got to work. Dengue was caused by a mosquito borne virus. Her reading reminded her it was most commonly an unpleasant but self-limited illness with symptoms of fever, headache, rash, with muscle and joint pains. The joint pains were severe enough to earn its common name, break bone fever. The fever would come and go twice over three to seven days. She had seen cases in the Emergency Department, mostly travelers returning from south of the border. Although rare, some patients developed severe dengue after the initial fever. Blood pressure dropped, platelet counts plummeted resulting in bleeding from multiple areas, the liver and kidneys could fail, the heart muscle was attacked, and even the brain could develop the dreaded state of disease known as encephalopathy. Diego was clearly on that trajectory. *Poor boy.*

She switched her computer to the hospital electronic medical record and searched for Diego in the ICU. He had the entire calamitous clinical picture. Specialists were doing their best to preserve the function of the organs for which they were responsible. Supported by IV fluids and powerful medications, his vital signs were decent. She imagined the poor kid with tubes everywhere. Thinking about the scene in the ER, she hoped a social worker had been consulted to help

Diego's mother navigate this nightmare.

Looking at her screen, Louise realized why she hadn't seen severe dengue, aka dengue shock before this case. It was rare; only 0.3% of cases developed it. She reviewed the manner in which the disease was diagnosed. The immunological blood test results varied with the phase of the illness. They had all been ordered. The infectious disease consultant was confident of the diagnosis. Unfortunately, he was also not optimistic about Diego's prognosis. It was a virus without a specific treatment.

The Island had had its share of mosquito borne illnesses since it was populated. Malaria and Yellow Fever were scourges into the 20th century. In the case of dengue, it had been recognized in South Texas for years, predominantly in underserved immigrant communities with inadequate sanitation facilities. A single mosquito of the Aedes aegypti family may bite several unsuspecting family members and transmit the disease from one infected subject to others.

As Louise read on, the bad news continued. The current vaccine was not very effective and could lead to more severe symptoms in some cases.

So why were they seeing this cluster of dengue shock patients if it *was* so rare? Climate change had invited multiple tropical diseases to the southern U.S. And here, her thoughts drifted back to Gen again. She had worked at the lab in the Insectary Division. She would've had some theories to spin.

Not letting herself get emotional, Louise took a quick look at her hospital email just to be sure she hadn't overlooked any of her medical staff requirements. There was always something due.

"Damn it," she muttered. Her flu shot was due by the end of the week. Unless she received it, she would be locked out of the electronic medical record and placed in email jail. It was best to get it today before Marnie's arrival.

She dressed in her favorite jeans and a fitted oxford

cloth blouse, an outfit comfortable enough for grocery shopping and nice enough for a visit to the hospital's occupational medicine clinic.

After efficiently administering the shot, the clinic nurse applied the sticker to Louise's ID badge announcing that Louise had received her flu shot for the season.

"Let's hope it works better than last year's shot," the nurse added pessimistically.

A severe influenza epidemic had overwhelmed resources last winter. The surge of cases nearly doubled the ER census at times. The thought of viruses and vaccinations brought Louise back to Diego and dengue. She decided to check on him in the ICU.

The intensive care unit was never a fun place to visit. She remembered all the times she ran up three flights to respond to a code blue in the wee hours of her night shifts. That was before intensivists and hospitalists covered the in-house crises. Today, as she took the elevator, she ran into Dr. Navin Prakesh, an infectious disease specialist. She had seen his consultation on Diego's chart.

"Well, hello, Louise," he said kindly, holding the door open for her. "By the way you're dressed, I can see you're working when you're not working."

Navin was half a generation ahead of her. As an infectious disease specialist, he was often consulted on the thorniest cases in the hospital. Despite long days and calls at all hours, he was consistently polite and helpful. Louise couldn't say that about many members of the medical staff.

"Good morning to you," Louise greeted him. "It looks as if you have your hands full today."

"I tell my son to hurry up with that MBA so I can retire, and he can take care of me." He laughed.

Louise smiled, as this was his common refrain. "Give me a break. What would you do with all that time on your hands?"

"I would sleep like Rip van Winkle for twenty

years straight, then I would finally be rested up for my retirement. But for now, we will keep working. Did you come to visit the young man you saw in the ER? One of my four patients with dengue shock, I'm afraid."

"Four?" She nodded. "Yes. How's he doing?"

Navin caught her up on Diego's case. He had stabilized over the last eight hours. Now, it was a question of time to see if his kidneys, liver, heart, and central nervous system would be permanently damaged.

They left the elevator together, and then Navin sat at a desk to start his rounds on the computer.

Louise approached Diego's room. She was relieved to see he was still breathing on his own, without the help of one of the ventilators purring away in the unit. Among the IVs supporting him, one contained blood. His platelet count was so low he had hemorrhaged into his GI tract.

He was awake and smiled at her. That was a good sign.

"You probably don't remember me," Louise said. "I'm the doctor who treated you in the ER a few days ago when you came in. I wanted to see how you were doing."

Diego nodded, then closed his eyes.

"*Doctora! Yo le recuerdo.* I remember you!" said Diego's mother from a chair in the corner. "Thank you for coming. I think he's a little better. The doctors, so many doctors, say we have to wait and see if the infection caused damage. I keep praying." She was clutching rosary beads.

"I'm so glad he's doing better," Louise said. "This must be a nightmare for you. Are you getting some help from social services? I know it must be impossible to keep up with it all."

"Oh, yes. Ms. Anita has been so helpful. She tries to explain everything. She called my boss, too, and explained why I was missing work. There was also a man who came to talk to me. He asked if I had other kids. I told him three. He wanted to give me money to send them to my sister in Mexico. He said, so they don't get sick like Diego. I asked Ms. Anita about him after he left but she didn't know who he was."

"Did he leave a card or phone number?" It sounded odd to Louise. She thought this guy should be reported to security.

"No. Nothing. And how did he know about my sister in Mexico? I didn't say yes or no, and he left."

Louise was sure that Mrs. Jimenez had enough experience to smell a *raton*. She looked like a survivor. As a Mexican immigrant in Texas in 2018, you had to be. Louise was glad she never needed to ask her patients about their legal status. In the ER, everyone was treated the same once they crossed the threshold of the double doors. Ms. Anita, on the other hand, might have plenty of trouble getting the teenage Diego emergency Medicaid insurance for his ongoing treatment if he turned out to be undocumented.

Louise told the woman that she'd continue to follow up on Diego and assured her that he was in good hands. She caught Navin across the unit as he was donning a paper gown to enter a room with isolation precautions.

"So, you have four cases of dengue up here?"

"Sadly, yes, Louise. We let the city health department know about the cluster of cases and I hope they go up the ladder to the state. My brother in Corpus Christi says it's the same down there."

He'd told her once that his brother was an internist 200 miles south along the coast.

"Global warming, right?" Navin said. "The mosquitoes are immigrating faster than our current leaders can stop them. These bugs are the criminal element we should be denying entry to, not the people looking for a better life. But our current administration still seems doubtful about the existence of climate change. Don't get me started…"

He was well beyond started. Louise couldn't help

finding pleasure in a camaraderie based on mutual disgust with the current administration's abysmally anti-intellectual approach to just about everything.

She looked at her watch. After placing a call to hospital security about Mrs. Jimenez's visitor, she headed out. She had enough time to get to the grocery store before picking up the kids from school. The guest room was still a mess.

***

Rotterdam Titan Oil Rig

After crossing off two full days of work on his calendar, Travis was up in time to see the sunrise over the Gulf on day three. The morning haze cast a spectacular rosy light show across the eastern horizon. The old rhyme "Red sky in morning, sailors take warning, red sky at night, sailors delight" always haunted him on sunrises like this. Though he was settling in, he couldn't get the image of Dr. Drake's escape from Suzy-Q out of his mind. *What a fuck up.*

Even after twelve hours of heavy-duty work, Travis had a hard time getting to sleep. He knew it was risky, but he kept a few tabs of Oxy, some Fentanyl patches, and some heroin in a secret pouch in his duffle. He needed just a little something to maintain his equilibrium. So, the night before, he opened a patch and chewed up a little bit of the contents. He relished the rush of well-being and ended up sleeping like a baby.

After a hearty breakfast of eggs, bacon and Texas toast, he reported to his safety and crew meeting and received his work assignment for the day. He wasn't happy to learn that Maples had joined his team. The way Maples glared at him in the mess hall and around the rig, made it clear the guy hadn't forgotten about the previous run-in.

Travis kept his cool and headed off to the container they were working on. Once the oil was extracted it was pumped into enormous reservoir tanks, which would be loaded onto oil tankers and transported to shore for refinement. The tanks were always coming up for inspection and repair as needed. As a welder, Travis had been doing this work since the first day he set foot on a rig. He was a dry welder which meant that he worked on the surface. Wet welders worked underwater, making repairs that required diving equipment. Needless to say, the wet welders earned more than the dry ones. The differential wasn't enough for Travis to want to get the training. He'd seen too many underwater accidents, in the navy and on the rigs.

Today's assignment was to continue work on the seams of a tank. Since the tanks were huge, the welders had to use ladders to cover the entire length of some seams. Travis was up about six feet with his welding arc in one hand and his chipping hammer in his apron pocket. The pointy chipping hammer was used to remove rust and slag. He kept it in his front apron pocket for easy access. Travis bent to the left to get a good view of what needed to be done. As he bent at the waist, his hammer fell and glanced off Maple's welding arc, causing sparks to fly and knocking Maples off balance. He fell against a tank of muriatic acid used for rust removal.

"What the fuck!" screamed Maples. "You trying to kill me, you clumsy yahoo!"

"Oh, grow a pair! It was an accident. The tank's still sealed. Nobody got hurt," Travis replied as he rolled his eyes.

Maples immediately left to make a report to the foreman. He made it sound as if he was a boy scout, reporting a near miss just like they told them to in the safety meetings. It was standard operating procedure for Travis's foreman to request a drug screen on both men.

Travis failed, as he knew he would. There were no extenuating circumstances to a failed drug screen on the rig. Per his contract, he was to be shipped off the rig immediately. After the meeting with his supervisors, he agreed to follow through with all the requirements to return to work. Counseling, Narcotics Anonymous meetings, random drug screens all loomed ahead. As if a return to shore, with his loss of income, wasn't bad enough, things got worse.

When he went to pack his gear, he was met by Tibo and two supervisors right there in his room. Tibo sadly shook his head, "Listen Travis, you really messed things up for yourself. You should just be grateful that nobody got hurt. You know that with a positive drug screen we were going to search your room, right? We found your stash. We had to notify Gulf County PD. They're gonna meet you when you get to shore. You gotta kick this thing, son."

Travis wasn't surprised to see Maples leaning against the wall outside his room. He was chuckling.

Chapter Nine

September 30, 2018

Galveston, Texas

After another quick hotel stop in Dallas, Marnie called Ellie Jean and brought her up to speed about Gen. She told her where she was headed and why. Ellie Jean was distraught but said she had a friend with her for support. She reassured her mom that she'd be okay.

Marnie walked the dogs before hitting the road. From the car, she called Louise and gave her an estimated arrival time. Driving down I-35, Marnie knew she was back in Texas. The highway baked in the autumn heat, daring a person to fry an egg on it.

Five hours later, she arrived at Louise's house—hoping the guest suite was up and working. Her own place would be ready tomorrow.

As Marnie pulled into Louise's driveway, Louise came down the long staircase to meet her. Her athletic friend looked good with her loose blonde hair pulled back and out of the way. She was a few inches shorter than Marnie.

After an embrace, Louise took a good look at Marnie and was glad to see her friend had some animation in her expression. "It's been a hard year," Louise said.

"You've always been a master of understatement,"

Marnie replied sadly. "Until recently, Gen competed with you. Funny how much you can miss someone you probably only communicated with once a month or so."

Louise squeezed her shoulder. "Come on inside."

After admiring the newly painted living room, Marnie continued. "I miss Adam like a dull ache, but I'm not convinced he's gone. I guess that's one reason it made sense for me to go live somewhere else for a while. I need to stop looking at the door, waiting for him to come through it."

During the conversation, Harlee and Jack had been trying to run circles around Chico, Louise's Chilean rescue dog, Chilean by birth, Heinz 57 by breeding. Chico felt more comfortable with Harlee, who at only twenty-five pounds was more his size, but Jack, at sixty pounds, was not to be excluded.

"Okay, let's take this dog circus out into the yard," said Louise. "You know you could have stayed with us instead of renting your own place."

Marnie raised her eyebrows and looked at the dogs making loops around Louise's yard. It looked like a racetrack. "Seriously, how long before Didier shot my dogs and dumped them in the bay?"

Louise laughed. "Okay, point taken."

"Did you get a chance to go by the place yet? Is it an honest representation online?"

Louise gave Marnie the "mom" look. "I had an extra shift this week and barely got clean sheets on your bed."

"That's okay. I'm just ribbing you. I had Nancy check it out right after I rented it. I love abusing your mom more than you. It reminds me of all the help she gave me when Ellie Jean was a baby. I send her yellow roses on her birthday to let her know that I remember."

"I know," Louise sighed. "She sends me a picture of her two dozen roses just in case I forget it's her birthday. Come on, let's get you settled."

Louise walked around to the other side of Marnie's

car. It looked like something out of *The Grapes of Wrath* if they had been driving BMWs. There wasn't a square inch of space left in it. "Where did the dogs sit?"

"Jack had the front seat and Harlee sat in my lap or Jack's. I think Harlee was the one most offended with the arrangement. Don't worry. It's very organized. The only things I need are on the floor of the back seat and the dog bed on top. Not like they need the bed for sleeping, but it's a good security blanket for them."

Louise shook her head.

"Oh, come on, Louise. Forty percent of people sleep with their dogs and at least another twenty percent lie about it. You and Didier are the outliers. I remember when I first met Adam and his surprise that Tonya, my original dog, slept on my bed. Because his family had never had indoor dogs, he was hesitant about the arrangement. Then, he became such a pushover.

"These dogs are something else. Jack's been trainable but getting him to sleep on the spare places on the bed hasn't been easy. Even now, with more spare space," Marnie said wistfully as she grabbed her belongings from the car and trudged behind Louise.

Louise and Didier had wondered how Adam and Marnie had had sex. Marnie knew that they were curious, but she never let Louise know that, of course, the dogs got shut out.

After getting settled in the guest room, Marnie joined Louise on the back porch. It was one of the best times of the year to sit outside in Galveston.

"We have about twenty minutes before Didier gets home with the kids," Louise said, handing Marnie one of her favorite beers.

Marnie asked, "Any word on the autopsy?"

"Definitely looks like foul play. I've been getting bits and pieces from Iliana Sudhan. Remember my detective friend? Strictly off the record." Louise gave Marnie a meaningful look. "There's more. Did you know that Gen was transgender? It's getting to be common knowledge here."

Marnie paused a minute. "Yes, I've known for quite a while, but it was never my secret to share. Gen felt strongly about her privacy in this area. I only found out when Ellie Jean was born. In medical school, there were things Gen said that only made sense if she wasn't born with female anatomy. I got to wondering about her being transgender. It seemed to explain a lot of things—her estrangement from her family, her lack of a past, and her resistance to dating."

Taking a sip of her beer, Louise nodded.

Marnie reminisced. "A week after Ellie's birth I started hemorrhaging and couldn't reach Adam—the 90s remember—no cell phones, and pagers didn't always work inside the research lab. Gen stopped by to check on me and found me in a pool of blood. I would have bled to death if she hadn't come by."

"I remember," Louise said.

Marnie continued, "Gen looked at the situation, immediately called 9-1-1, and, as I was fading in and out of consciousness and babbling about Ellie Jean, she said, 'Thank you for sparing me this!' It was one of the few things that stuck in my brain. Weeks later, those words still came to me."

Marnie took a sip of her beer. "At first, we never talked about it. I was on maternity leave for three months and she visited often. Outside of Adam and Nancy, she held Ellie Jean the most. I often think the scents babies and caretakers share in the first few months of life seal their relationships forever."

"It's possible," Louise said.

As Marnie continued her story, she was transported back to that time. It had been so scary. The doctors had recommended a hysterectomy, but Marnie had resisted. She had been determined that Ellie Jean not be an only child like herself—a situation she'd hated.

After another sip, Marnie continued, "Back to Gen. One day when she was over, she asked if I remembered the details of my near-death experience and what she had said. I told her yes. Then, she told me about growing up with her gender dysphoria in a small town in Iowa. She got to go to college on a basketball scholarship. It was during college that she learned about and came to grips with being transgender. At the time, her parents couldn't come to terms with her pursuing re-assignment."

"Man, that must have been so hard for Gen," Louise said.

"Yes. I think it scared her from telling anyone else. Over the years, I tried to convince her that times had changed and that she didn't need to take any guff about her status. I was unsuccessful. She felt strongly that no one know. I do think in the last few years she was becoming more confident. Garrett had done a lot to reassure her. Do you think her death was related to her transsexuality?"

Louise's eyes were fixed on a point on the horizon as she answered, "I don't know. The only thing that has come up is that it seems she fought with her attacker. It's hard to tell if her bumps and bruises were from a drowning—getting rolled about in the ocean can be pretty brutal. But she wasn't in the water for very long. She was found about ten hours after her last credit card charge at the grocery store. They think she had some skin under her fingernails."

"Wow," Marnie said.

Louise continued. "It correlates with Garrett's story. He told me that he was planning to cook a special dinner after closing the restaurant for the night. They were going to celebrate her decision that her transgender status didn't need to be a secret anymore. She had run to the grocery store for some last-minute ingredients and wasn't home when Garrett got there. He had a creepy feeling—a Born-on-the-Island intuition—that something was wrong. He filed a missing person complaint immediately, but the police didn't begin looking into it before her body was found the next morning."

"Damn, damn, damn," Marnie mumbled. "It seems

unfathomable that this happened. None of it makes sense. Louise, someone dragged her out there. Hard to believe it was a hate crime since so few knew about her sexuality. Do you think it was related to her work?"

Louise looked hard at her friend. "I think we need to find out what the full autopsy shows before we worry about why she was murdered."

"You and I both know she didn't go into the water willingly."

Louise reached forwarded and patted Marnie's hand. "I know…"

"The memorial is in two days," Marnie said. "After that, I'll talk to Garrett and get a look at her computer. What are your plans tomorrow?"

Louise thought for a moment. "I have a day shift tomorrow and then I'm off for the memorial. Why don't you get settled? Dinner here tomorrow?"

"Sounds good," Marnie said. "What's your work schedule for the week?"

"I'm back on days starting Thursday. You could come by the hospital and let me know what you find out at Gen's. Our old friend, Mrs. Riley is in the hospital making a slow recovery from hip surgery, complicated by pneumonia. You could see her, and then after my shift, we can grab a drink. Didier has a work meeting that night, so my mom will be here to watch the kids."

"I'm so glad you told me about Mrs. Riley. I would love to stop in and see her. After getting through this week, we will need a happy hour," Marnie said. *Life moves too fast. Death moves even faster.*

***

"The kids were so excited to see Aunt Marnie and her crazy dogs that I didn't think we'd ever get them settled down for the night," Louise said to Didier.

He was reading in bed as she slipped into her Houston Astros nightshirt, a Mother's Day gift from the children. She stood at the window for one more look at the bay, now offering a rippled reflection of the full moon.

He looked up. "How do you think Marnie's doing? I wasn't expecting her to be so animated, if that's the right word. She gave me an earful when we were doing the dishes."

Louise went to her side of the bed and climbed in. "I know what you mean. She seems driven to get to the bottom of Gen's death. And she's in a hurry to do it. It's almost manic."

"I guess it's her way of coping with another loss, but seems kind of extreme," Didier said.

"Then, today I find out that Marnie has known for years that Gen was transgender. I'm not sure how I feel about being left out of that secret between them."

She filled him in on Marnie's revelation and continued. "Did Gen think I'd have been judgmental? Not that it matters now."

"It definitely doesn't matter now. And no, she would not have. You were always a good friend to Gen. It sounds as if she was about to let all of us know, if only…" Didier said, shaking his head.

"It's been a long day. Let's turn off the lights," Louise said softly and snuggled next to him.

Chapter Ten

October 1, 2018

Galveston, Texas

Marnie woke early the next day. She had a lot of things to get done. She needed to check into her house and make sure it was clean enough to unload. To accommodate her mild OCD, she had paid for an extra cleaning service. Not that it would stay clean once she had introduced the dogs to the beach. It was her need for a fresh start.

Stretching out in bed, she organized her plan for the day. She would start with a run with the dogs on the beach. Then shower, load the pups and go to her rental. It shouldn't take her too long to unpack.

She thought she'd call Nancy to meet her for lunch. It would be good to see her again. Nancy filled the part of Marnie that missed her own mom terribly. She made herself pop out of bed and get dressed in her black running gear. She was done moping around.

The dogs were thrilled to see the leashes in Marnie's hand. Luckily, from the guest room of Louise's house, Marnie could sneak out the back and not disturb Louise's breakfast-get-to-school-and-work routine. She could hear the sounds coming from the kitchen as Louise got ready for the morning rush.

Marnie headed out the back, down a quiet alleyway

and out to the beach to look at the sunrise. A few people were running or walking on the beach. Several dogs were off leash, which thrilled both Marnie and her pups. Soon, they were running at their own breakneck pace—back and forth from her to the water.

After her run and shower, Marnie peeked her head into the chaos of the kitchen. The kids ran over and gave her hugs before Didier urged them to get in the car. Marnie said she would see them that evening.

Marnie looked at Louise, who looked as if she had already put in half a day's work.

"I remember those days and I only had one," Marnie said. "I loved raising Ellie Jean, but it isn't something I'm tempted to repeat. It was so non-stop. I think about the play *Hamilton* and the description of him being 'non-stop.' That song is really a mother's anthem." She took a breath. "After some coffee, I'm going to head over and get settled. Then, I thought I'd call Nancy and meet her for lunch."

"I envy you time with my mom. She will be thrilled. I mean to make time for the two of us but there never seems to be any time to make."

"When the kids are older," Marnie said, "you'll have more time."

"Let's hope. Lately, it seems the future is not guaranteed."

***

Marnie pulled up to her "new home." It was a small mint green beach house with darker sea green shutters and white trim. It perched on a quiet block between the beach and the town and featured a large front porch. She was looking forward to sitting on it—if she ever sat.

The pups seemed thrilled. They ran in and out, smelling everything.

Letting them investigate on their own, Marnie methodically unloaded her car. She felt like a turtle, able to move her home around whenever she needed. She marveled that she still had the knack after twenty years.

Shortly after organizing her bungalow and getting the dogs comfortable, Marnie went looking for a coffee shop. While enjoying her latte, she noticed a bulletin board with people offering a variety of services—including one for pet sitting.

When the proprietor saw her take one of the slips for pet sitting, she said, "That's my cousin. I'll vouch for her."

Marnie arranged to meet the sitter soon and was glad to have that housekeeping chore completed. She had time to clean up again before meeting with Nancy. They emailed frequently and talked some on the phone, but Marnie could count on one hand the number of times that the two of them got together without children or husbands.

Not a problem I have anymore, I guess.

***

"Oh, Nancy," Marnie exclaimed as she rushed to join her at the corner table. "It's so good to see you in person! I love meeting up at the Mariposa Café. Good choice!"

As they exchanged hugs, Marnie thought that Nancy looked great. Working for thirty years as an educator and principal in the Texas public education system should have drained her, but she looked as if she had enough energy to work another thirty.

As usual, Nancy had on the perfect outfit. Today she was dressed in casual island chic, neat and pressed. White pants that were still white. Island tropic shirt. Marnie was glad that she had brightened her own black outfit with a white shirt.

97

"Oh Marnie, it's so great to see you. The last time was so sad. I wanted Louise to bring you home with her, but she said you wouldn't come."

Marnie took a deep breath. "That time's a memory surrounded by fog. I do remember you coming. I needed to settle too many things in May to leave home. And I've been functioning at a snail's pace, so it's taken me a whole five months."

The waitress came by and took their orders.

"How are you feeling now?" Nancy asked.

"Better. When my parents died, I never took the time to grieve," Marnie said.

Nancy nodded in understanding. "Our traditions surrounding mourning are based on the need to step back from our lives," she said as she took Marnie's hand.

"Back then, I was in my junior year at Yale and my world literally fell away from under my feet. I can recall that emotional devastation so sharply. That they died in a commercial plane crash was so unlikely it made the event seem ludicrous. This time, with Adam, I knew I had to take some time."

After taking a sip of water, Marnie asked, "So how is it to be retired in Galveston?"

"We love it. It is so nice to be close to Louise's family and able to help out. I finally have time to pursue my real passion. Painting. I love the concentration and I enjoy the local art fairs—being a seller and not just a buyer. I'm getting a bit of a reputation in the Galveston art scene."

"I'm so happy for you. Even if you're not BOI, you can claim IBC status."

Nancy laughed. "Yes, Island-by-Choice."

"I'm eager to see your work. Ellie Jean will join me and spend most of her winter break here. We're hoping you'll have time to show us the new and improved Galveston."

Nancy laughed again. "Definitely on my calendar."

"How's Claude?" Marnie asked.

"Busy. We did a lot of remodeling to move permanently to our Galveston beach home. Then Claude got bored, so he found a part-time job at the local community college. Lucky for me. As all my friends say, I married for better or for worse but not for lunch. How's Ellie Jean?"

"She's doing as well as can be expected. We spent the summer together, hiking and enjoying the pups. We watched old family movies and talked about Adam. With me on sabbatical this year, it took some effort to get her to go study abroad as planned. I helped her get settled in Amsterdam. Then, I came back to my empty house and slept as much as the pups would let me. I think I'm finally finding my equilibrium again."

Their meals arrived and they ate with relish.

After a bit, Marnie continued. "The loss of Gen feels different. Somehow, it's galvanizing me into action. I have this magical feeling that if I can figure out what happened, I can bring her back. I know better but I can't shake the feeling. If we can find out how and why it happened, I know it will bring me closure."

"Sounds like you're convinced there was foul play."

"There has to be," Marnie said. "Gen wouldn't have gone willingly out in a boat that night, not when she and Garrett had plans. It doesn't make any sense."

"I agree. But the *reason* for the foul play is what we have to focus on. Who would benefit from Gen's death?"

As always, Nancy zeroed in on the key question.

"That's the thing. I'm not sure. I think it must be related to her research. I can't imagine her making personal enemies. She was excited about her latest data correlating tropical disease cases in the U.S. to climate change. That might threaten some industries, especially oil and gas."

Nancy nodded. "I have a friend from college who works in the EPA. Maybe I should give her a call. It's always good to crowdsource a problem."

Marnie shook her head. "EPA? Didn't I read they

were directed to avoid the use of the words "climate change" recently? But, yeah, I agree. Let me know what you find out."

After lunch, Marnie headed to her place. She had to plan what she was going to say for the memorial. And then, she was going to sit on her porch with a cold drink.

Chapter Eleven

October 2, 2018

Galveston, Texas

Garrett looked at the crowd gathered for Gen's memorial. It overflowed from the restaurant into the street and onto the seawall. He had no idea so many people had known Gen. He sensed there were a few curious spectators in the crowd, but mostly those present kept coming up to him and saying how sad they were—not for his loss, but for their own. They all had little stories to tell him.

The cashier from HEB said how much she missed Gen's late-night stops for the things Garrett needed. Then, she started to cry, thinking she was one of the last people to have seen Gen alive.

A gas station attendant said he looked forward to Gen's rare stops to put gas in her Prius. She was so polite, and her smile made the sun come out. If he wasn't twenty years younger than her and had his own family, he would have asked her out. He indicated that neither of those factors stopped him from thinking about it. Despite his sadness, Garrett had rolled his eyes after the man left.

Kathy Walsh, Gen's division's administrative assistant had come. She had been so proud of Gen's accomplishments at the lab. And Gen, recognizing

Kathy's talents, had treated her as a valued member of the team. Garrett saw other coworkers, including her assistant, Billy. Even her boss, Roy Williams, had made an appearance.

Garrett thought back to his first meeting with Gen. She had been friendly but distant during the years she had come into his restaurant. It wasn't until two years after his divorce that she had even *hinted* she would consider seeing him. Their time together had been way too short. God, he missed her.

Garrett got a nod from his sound technician that the system was ready to broadcast for the large crowd. Usually, he used it only for local bands that played at his restaurant.

All of his waitstaff were crying. They weren't serving until after the ceremony. He'd given Marnie and Louise, Didier, and their family space around the bar near the microphone. Like Marnie and Louise, he was trying to be stoic. They planned to speak briefly about Gen and then open the restaurant for the real celebration. Marnie had wanted to go first, and she walked to the microphone.

"Hi, everyone. Thank you all for coming today. Gen would have been so honored to see such a crowd. For those of you who don't know me, I'm Marnie Liccione, the only non-local allowed to speak," Marnie said. "I lived in Galveston twenty years ago and this is where I met Gen. We went to medical school together. Both of us needed a family, and in the next four years, the female students in medical school filled that role."

She paused. "Gen often acted like a mother hen to the group. She was only a little older than us but wise beyond her years. She advised and comforted us and kept us laughing. She was a hoot. Nothing got her down except cruelty, and she was a fighter against that. She was the older sister I never had but always wanted."

Garrett realized about this time that Marnie needed to wrap up her talk because tears were streaming down her face. He smiled sadly and nodded to her.

"So again, I want to thank you for Gen, who is probably waiting impatiently to raise a beer for a toast. The biggest thing she wanted at her funeral—though it should have been forty years from now—was a party. Cheers to Gen when the bar opens."

Garrett saw Didier give his wife's hand a squeeze as Louise walked up to the mic.

"Good morning. I'm Louise Finnerty. I count myself fortunate to have been a member of the medical school family that Marnie just described. Gen knew I had a fear of public speaking. She helped me when I had the misfortune of presenting a case at Grand Rounds as a third-year med student to an auditorium full of potential critics. She practiced with me over and over and told me to find one person in the audience who looked kind and to talk to that person. Luckily, she was in the audience that day. Today, I see nothing but kind faces, which makes this easier." She wiped away a tear.

"When it hits me that she's gone," Louise said, "I try to remember how funny Gen was. I remember her after-dinner parlor tricks. Once, she used a scarf to create new identities for our dog. Chico as a nun, Chico as a gypsy, Chico as an aviator. And our dog actually liked it!"

The crowd laughed.

Louise smiled and went on. "She was there for me and my family so often. When I had to miss another field trip with my son's kindergarten class, she would pinch-hit for me so he wouldn't feel left out. There was a visit to the zoo Noah still remembers. Aunt Gen showed up in a safari suit, complete with a pith helmet. We'll miss you, Gen." Louise looked up at the ceiling, then back at the crowd. "Serious Gen, accomplished Gen, beautiful Gen, loyal Gen, loving Gen, and funny Gen. We'll miss all of you."

Garrett approached her, and Louise gave him a smile and a hug as she passed the mic to him.

Garrett stood closer to the mic. He had thought a lot

about what he wanted to say. Gen had always said to keep things short and sweet. She liked goofing around, but she was no nonsense about excess chatter.

"Like everyone here, I knew Gen a long time before I really *knew* Gen. The last two years with her were some of the best years of my life." A tear slipped down his cheek. "What can I say about my true love? She was a magnetic person. She knew me better than anyone. She was kind and generous. And what an athlete!"

He grinned. "She made aging into the middle years look easy. As a roommate, Gen bordered on the obsessive-compulsive side, though I was beginning to wear her down a bit."

The crowd laughed and he could see many people smiling.

"She had a cat to keep life real. She told me once that she was convinced cats protected a person from allergies—their dander got everywhere. Gen was a big believer that some germs and pollen keep us healthy. She always had a lot of science to back her up."

Garrett took a breath and slowly let it out.

"Gen struggled with a part of her identity that she was unwilling to share during her twenty-five years here on The Island. I have debated mentioning this today in deference to her privacy, but I think she would have wanted me to share it, especially since it is likely to become public knowledge in the next few weeks. She would have wanted to tell you the story herself so as to get it straight. I will do the best I can."

Garrett looked out into the sea of faces.

"As some of you may know, Gen was born in Iowa. What you may not know is that she was born a male. In our current understanding about gender, we are more accepting today of some fluidity about the subject. But thirty-five years ago, that was not the case. Gen told me that when she was growing up there were boys and girls. For her, this made no sense. Something told her that she was a girl but when she looked at her body, it had the wrong parts. For years, Gen played the role of her assigned gender. She worked hard on the family farm. She got a basketball scholarship to a state university."

He smiled, pulling himself together. "It was during college that she first heard the word *transgender*, and suddenly, she began to understand her situation. This led to a course of action that caused a painful separation from her family. Luckily, in the last few years, she was able to reconcile with her parents. Her sister and her family are here today to honor Gen. They've agreed that Gen was ready to come out, to stop being afraid. Understanding her gender identity allowed her to understand other people and their conflicts better. She enjoyed working with people, but her passion was research—especially of viruses. It was less confusing than the inner workings of the human mind and heart, she said.

"In the next few months, Gen planned to quietly let it be known that she was transgender as a way to help people break down their prejudices. We had begun to plan our lives together. Someone took her from all of us prematurely. If it was related to her being transgender, she would've wanted it known."

Garrett paused to collect himself before continuing. He cued the waitstaff to pass out the drinks.

"Right now, though, I want us to celebrate the life of Dr. Gennifer Drake. Everyone, please join me and raise a glass to toast the memory of a remarkable woman."

The sound technician started playing music. The opening notes of "One Love" began playing. It was Gen's all-time favorite song in medical school. The lively beat helped to lift spirits.

Garrett watched as a flock of magnificent frigate birds soared overhead, out to sea.

***

José Torres attended the memorial to honor Dr. Drake. Police suspect a murderer might make an appearance at such a ceremony. He saw Detective Sudhan and suspected she was also there for multiple reasons.

When he walked back to his car, he spotted Roy Williams. While chatting with him, he noticed the frigate birds take flight over the Gulf and met Louise Finnerty's intense gaze. When Williams walked off to his car, José sat on a bench along the seawall and gazed at the breaking waves.

Dr. Drake's reluctance to disclose her LGBTQ status saddened him. He understood it, though. He remembered his early years as a cop. Having gotten through the police academy in Dallas, where it wasn't at all accepted to be openly gay, he lacked a plan to get ahead. People had suspected his status, but nobody said anything. As the years went by, he couldn't help but think he was passed over for assignments that might lead to promotion. Nonetheless, he enjoyed being a cop.

He made a few weekend trips to Galveston with friends and decided that he liked the atmosphere. He'd settled here fifteen years ago. He met his partner, George, and they had made a life together in the vibrant and welcoming community. Opportunity for advancement seemed better in the Gulf County Police Department than in Dallas.

Scouting the area five nights ago, he had been at the beach before the paramedics got there. The weather had turned out to be horrific. He was questioning his decision to go rogue as he crouched down in the dunes, scanning the shoreline for activity.

As he was about to give up, he spotted something near the water. He tried to get a better look with his binoculars. *Shit, is that what I've been waiting for?*

Coming back to the present, he scanned the sunny beach for answers. None came.

Chapter Twelve

October 2, 2018

Norman, Oklahoma

Bert Springer had a full schedule when he returned home to Norman, Oklahoma. Despite the fact that the head of his department wanted the faculty to be visible in outside professional endeavors, Bert wasn't granted any additional administrative time for these responsibilities. Ernie had forwarded his checklists and summaries of his staff interviews shortly after the survey, but not his completed report of Dr. Drake's research. Bert wanted this off his desk. Even though surveyors often went over their forty-eight-hour deadline for report submission, Bert realized it was only a matter of days before the U.S. Biosafety Association would be calling.

On that warm October day, he could hear the band practicing for the next football game through the closed windows. Having grown up in New York, Bert never thought he would end up in a place like Oklahoma, but here he was. He had graduated from S.U.N.Y. Stony Brook on an ROTC scholarship, followed by three years of active duty at Fort Sill in Oklahoma. He found living here easy. Housing was affordable. The people were friendly. The lady at the DMV actually *smiled* and called him "Sugar." Plus, he'd met his wife, a native Sooner.

After obtaining his Ph.D. in microbiology, the University of Oklahoma offered him a position as an adjunct and then, relatively quickly, promoted him to assistant professor on tenure track. With his uncomplaining attitude, solid research skills, and good evaluations from students, Bert aimed to become head of the department.

The band was still at it when he put in a call to Roy Williams. Because his calls to Ernie had gone unanswered, he wanted to let Roy know about the delay on recertification. The ever-helpful Kathy Walsh answered.

"Kathy, hello, this is Dr. Springer—Bert."

"Yes, so nice to hear from you," Kathy replied.

"I was hoping to speak to Mr. Williams about a little snag we ran into. Certification may be delayed."

"Well, you just missed him. He's headed to an off-campus meeting. Looking at his schedule, hmmm, he's going to be off campus for several more meetings this week. Best to send an email. But thanks so much for letting us know about the delay. I'll pass your message on to the staff so they don't panic. We all worked hard to get ready for the inspection."

Bert left his contact information and hung up. He wondered again how on earth Roy managed to have such a capable assistant in this age of cutbacks. Everyone else had to work off their email, cell phones, and Outlook calendars.

He was correct about the U.S. Biosafety Association. Their call came an hour later, inquiring about the report. Not wanting to blame Ernie directly for the tardy submission, he made excuses about workloads from their primary employers. Then, he redoubled his efforts to locate Ernie.

They had previously communicated by cell phone and email. Both methods had proven unsuccessful. He remembered that Ernie worked at Invotech in St. Paul, and with help from the internet, he found the main number. He was transferred three times to

Ernie's voice mail, only to be told it was not accepting messages.

After placing one more call to the receptionist with a plea to speak to any human in Ernie's department, Bert finally got to a lab tech.

"This is Ronald?" said the voice at the other end of the line.

Bert introduced himself and explained he was trying to reach Dr. Pedersen.

"Dr. Pedersen? He's on vacation, right? Down in Texas? He called to say he was taking a few more days' vacation. Some R&R in the desert? It's already been cold and wet up here but now it's sunny again?"

That the young man would turn all his sentences into questions irked Bert. Maybe it was a generational thing. He persevered. "I need to get a message to him. It's important. Do you have any way to get in touch with him other than his cell phone?"

Ronald said the caller would have to go through HR for that information. "But I doubt they'll give it out?"

Bert left Ronald his contact information and signed off. He didn't care about the weather report in Minnesota and was not hopeful that Invotech HR would help him. He decided to call the Gulf National Laboratory again later in the day. He wanted to speak directly to Roy Williams before he called the U.S. Biosafety Association back.

***

Saint Paul, Minnesota

Allison Pedersen took her morning coffee and phone out to the deck. It was unseasonably warm for a fall day in St. Paul. After the first cold snap, the temperature was back in the 70s again. She looked at the sky when she heard a flock of geese overhead. They were in a perfect V formation, heading south. They knew winter was coming soon.

She checked her phone for at least the tenth time that morning. Still nothing from Ernie. It had been nine days since he had left for Texas and his U.S. Biosafety Association survey. His phone message on September 26th said that he was going to take a few more days in Texas and meet his college buddy, Carl. They planned to spend time in Big Bend National Park on the southern U.S. border. He told her he would be home by September 28th. Just needed a few days to clear his mind, he had said, sounding worn out.

Allison understood completely. Ernie had been working overtime between his job at Invotech, U.S. Biosafety Association surveys, and other freelance assignments. He referred to the assignments as "consultations." She knew he was trying to earn extra money any way he could. He'd confided to her that he felt like a failure having to scrimp and save to cover his daughter's tuition. Allison tried to reassure him that it would all work out. They could economize. Even take out a home equity loan.

Theirs was a second marriage for both. It had been working out so well. Allison had learned from the failure of her first marriage that both parties needed space and respect. She vowed not to hover and act suspicious as she had with her first husband.

Allison met Ernie when he came to a book signing where she worked. They started to chat as she was tidying up the desk and chairs after the event. He came again for a workshop or reading every week. He feigned interest in topics like container gardening, slow cooking, and calligraphy to run into Allison. Finally, he asked her out. They became best friends and fell in love. Neither knew that was possible.

She tried his phone again. Today it was dead. Not even a click over to voicemail. She tried a text. Undeliverable. She had assumed cell service would be spotty in the wilds of the Rio Grande Valley, but it was now four days past his expected return. She decided to call Carl.

When she hung up, she sat still, waiting for her head to clear. Carl was home in El Paso. He hadn't heard from Ernie in over six months. He wanted to help Allison, but, as he blathered on, she just wanted to get off the phone. She promised to call him back when she knew something.

She called the hotel Ernie had told her he was staying at. They told her he had checked out on September 25th.

She calculated that Ernie had been missing for seven days. She decided to call the police in the last place she knew he had been. He was now a missing person. She dialed and cleared her throat, ready to make her report.

"Gulf County Police," a young female voice chirped.

"I need to report a missing person," Allison began.

"Please hold. Let me transfer you to…"

Allison began to worry that she would get nowhere. The next voice on the phone was another young voice, this one male. He identified himself as Kevin Briggs, Communication Division. He listened to her without interrupting.

Briggs explained he needed to ask a series of questions. Some of them might seem personal, but it was only so that the police could focus the search. Allison described her husband as Briggs posed the questions. Age forty-five. White. Five-eleven. About 185 pounds. Short brown hair, light brown eyes, no facial hair, and a scar on his chin. No tattoos.

"Mrs. Pedersen, are you sure your husband was in Galveston before he disappeared? Could he have gone somewhere else, some place he didn't want you to know about?"

"Yes. I'm sure it was Galveston, Texas. The Third Coast Hotel said he had checked out on September 25th."

A few more questions. "Do you think your husband was in any kind of trouble? Does he have any problems with drugs or alcohol?"

"Only that he's been worried about money lately."

"Okay, your report's on its way to the Criminal Investigation Division. I'm going to give you a case number and an email address. The next thing we'll need are some photographs of your husband. We recommend you talk to friends and family to see if anyone else has heard from him. You can expect a call from us in twenty-four hours with an update. One more thing, a hard thing. Try not to worry. My grandpa went missing last year, and our police department tracked him down in a day."

"Thank you for the reassurance," Allison said.

Despite the horror that was enveloping her, she hadn't expected the kind words at the end of her call.

***

Galveston, Texas

Kathy Walsh looked out her window at the tankers moving up the ship channel to Houston. She kept thinking about the recent events happening at *her* lab. Something was off. *Seriously off.* Dr. Drake's death and the loss of some of her research suggested malfeasance. She wondered if she had a responsibility to let someone outside the lab know. She hated the thought of casting a shadow on the lab's reputation.

Just then another call came in from Dr. Springer.

"Oh, Dr. Springer, let me put you through to Mr. Williams," Kathy said. "You caught him."

Kathy connected him to Roy Williams, placed her phone on mute and listened. "Mr. Williams, this is Bert Springer from the U.S. Biosafety Association. You're a hard man to track down."

Williams took so long to respond that she thought the line had gone dead.

"Yes," Roy eventually replied.

"I wanted to let you know we've run into a complication completing your report. The U.S. Biosafety Association won't be able to rule on your recertification until we get it turned in. I wanted to let you know about the delay."

Another pause, then, "Okay."

"While I have you on the line, I wonder if you could help me out here. What's missing is Dr. Pedersen's evaluation of the proposed research. I can't seem to get in touch with him."

"And?" Another monosyllable from Roy.

"And I was hoping, with your approval, that I could go over the proposal with Dr. Drake by phone and finish this up."

"No. I don't think so."

"Let me explain this again. If we don't finish the report, your division of the Gulf National Laboratory will not be recertified and will have to reapply and pay for a new survey in six months. I assume you report to someone at the lab who would be disappointed if that happened."

"You misunderstand the situation, Dr. Springer. We won't be submitting the research Dr. Pedersen reviewed. We've had to make some changes and will put you in touch with another of our division's investigators. I'll get back to you."

Bert stammered into the phone, "But, but… That will mean a significant revision of our report."

Roy said, "Please alert your supervisors. We'll be in touch." The phone went dead when Roy hung up abruptly.

Kathy was stunned. *What was going on in her lab?*

***

After his conversation with Dr. Springer, Roy Williams decided to go off campus. He was on the verge of a panic attack. He exited the security checks, got into his car and headed down Harborside Drive. He drove past the cruise ship terminal and turned right onto the causeway to Pelican Island. Although it was in the high 80s, he rolled the windows down to get some air.

He parked along the waterfront at Seawolf Park. It was a grassy picnic area on a spit of land that jutted out into Galveston Bay. Its lack of shade, struggling foliage, and rickety tables were witnesses to the harsh weather it withstood.

Roy had been coming here for as long as he could remember. He discovered it when he was in medical school. At the right times of day, he could see the Mosquito Fleet of shrimpers scuttle past. It was a popular spot for land-based fishermen to cast their lines. Roy thought the folks fishing that day wanted to be alone as much as he did.

It was at times like this that Roy let himself ruminate. It had been such a grand and successful plan for years. He grew up in West Texas. His dad worked on the oil rigs that sprouted from the prairie. Roy was a good student and a good-looking young man. When his hairline receded in his late twenties, he shaved his head and still looked strikingly handsome. After college in Lubbock, he had no intention of returning to his windswept hometown and getting his hands dirty in the oil patch.

He was accepted to medical school and entered U.T.M.B. a year ahead of Louise, Marnie, and Gen. His plan was to get a residency in ophthalmology or dermatology, having calculated that these specialties had the best reimbursement/misery ratio. In his second year, his grade point average dropped. Without a 4.0, he would not gain acceptance into his preferred specialties. He started to cheat on exams and was promptly caught. As a powerful object lesson for the rest of the students, the dean of the medical school let it be known that Roy Williams had been expelled for cheating.

After his expulsion, Roy decided to regroup and played his last trump card. He had been having an on-again, off-again affair with a married professor of microbiology. His partner, Ellen, had wanted to end it, but she was addicted to their affair. Roy enjoyed the sex but had little emotional investment in the relationship.

Still playing a long game, he used his connection with Ellen to get into the microbiology program. She pulled some strings, and, in a year, he had his masters. Roy demanded a job as a researcher in exchange for his continued silence about their affair. Over the following years, he worked diligently and climbed the professional ladder.

When the Gulf National Laboratory opened in 2008, he was handed his position as Chief of the Insectary Division. Even as he was on a prestigious professional trajectory, the government paycheck didn't match the goal he set as a medical student.

He stayed on the fishing pier with his elbows on the railing above the rocky shore and continued to try to calm his jangled nerves. *What the hell am I doing?*

Chapter Thirteen

October 3, 2018

Galveston, Texas

After the memorial, Marnie pondered the essential question. *What could be a motive for killing Gen?* Gen's research was a threat to the status quo. Though, of course, ironically its suppression was a threat to everyone in South Texas. *Not like the current administration was interested in the big picture. They might be a little more invested if it posed a threat to their golf courses.*

Marnie recalled Gen's excitement about her latest research on dengue fever. Gen hadn't felt supported by her superiors at the lab. Was something else going on this time? When Marnie had first seen Garrett, he was so overwhelmed with grief that she hadn't been able to bring it up. Now, it was time to have a heart-to-heart. She dialed Garrett's number.

After he answered, Marnie said, "Hi Garrett. It's Marnie. How's it going?"

"It's going. I'm hanging in there. None of this seems real yet."

"It can take a while. Half the time I still look for Adam to come through the door and it's been five months. Do you have some time to get together? Are you back to work?"

"You know the restaurant business. There's never any time off. I've had my cousin covering for me the last few days, but he has his own restaurant. I said I would be in today after the lunch crowd."

Garrett Mancinelli was "Born on the Island" and came from a long line of restaurateurs. He was a distant relative of the Maceo family which dominated the underworld of Galveston from the 1920s until the 50s. After The Great Storm of 1900, the family dove into bootlegging, gun running, gambling, and prostitution. Galveston, known as the Free State of Galveston because of its tolerance for diversity, alternative lifestyles, and crime, was the perfect location for these well-behaved criminals. They grew legitimate businesses, mainly restaurants and nightclubs. When underworld murders went unsolved, the family members were suspected, but never convicted. Once Garrett told Marnie that the Mancinelli arm of the family had inherited the hospitality gene. His goal was to serve good food to the locals and tourists alike. His menus featured Sicilian classics and Gulf Coast favorites. It had been a winning combination.

He was happiest cruising through his restaurant, greeting customers, and giving approval for new dishes. The five days he had taken off for the trip to Colorado with Gen had been his first vacation in six years.

"Would it be possible for me to come by to look over Gen's stuff from work? Maybe look at her computer?" Marnie asked.

"Yes, I'm planning to be here until 2 p.m. The police just returned her computer. They didn't find anything. I've looked at it, too. There doesn't seem to be any secret files on it."

"Well, I'm sure you were thorough. But she was so excited about her latest research. I think she might have left a clue to what was going on. Maybe it's something a friend and a fellow doctor could pick up on."

"Sure, stop by. I'll make us some lunch. It will be

fun to cook for another person again. Gen and I had been living here together for a while, though keeping our own places. She felt like she needed the surety of her own place. I could move home, but right now I feel more comfortable here. I miss her, Marnie…" His voice cracked before he regained it. "I've adopted her cat, Skeeters."

Marnie thought about how intensely Gen had worried about her cat. It was her first pet since leaving farm life.

"That's great. She'd want to know that you had him," Marnie said.

"I'll have to decide soon about what to do with two homes. Funny how even though we hadn't made an official commitment, Gen had wanted us to be powers of attorney and executors on each other's wills. Something about turning fifty later this year. Her parents' deaths a few years ago shocked her. Dealing with her parents' estate was a mess. They died without wills."

Marnie remembered Gen's grief.

Garrett continued, "I was so happy for her when she reconciled with them. Shortly after we started seeing each other seriously, I encouraged her to make one more effort. They had been older when Gen was born—she was their youngest. She visited them a few times the first year we met. They were in their eighties.

"At first, they'd been unable to understand how their son was now their daughter, but after a few visits they realized that she was still their child. Call her Jim or Gen. Still their child with a wicked sense of humor and a big heart."

"Oh man, I know too much about unexpected death," Marnie replied. "I think I've become compulsive about keeping wills up-to-date."

Marnie felt Garrett's shock at coping with a sudden loss. She was still too raw to be able to handle the details, but she had empathy for a friend in need.

"Okay if I come over around noon?"

"Perfect," Garrett said. "See you then."

Arriving a little before noon, Marnie stared at the porch where Gen should have been sitting. Gen had said she bought the place for its classic Galveston porch. Garrett must have seen Marnie drive up because he was on the porch before she got out of the car. They embraced.

It was amazing how much this group of friends seemed like siblings. They had all jelled so well. Garrett had fitted in perfectly. Three couples—four physicians, one tour guide, and one restaurateur. They always joked that if they were marooned on a desert island, they would survive, but mostly thanks to the naturalist and the restaurateur.

"We're having sauteed local flounder with lump crab meat and braised leeks. Ready in thirty minutes. I took a quick look around Gen's office and it's pretty much how she left it, despite the police intrusion. I thought you might like to look at it before lunch. It does seem like she's still there."

Marnie salivated at the mention of a Garrett lunch. It might be hard to concentrate on her task at hand with the savory smells coming from the kitchen.

She started by sitting in the room at Gen's desk, feeling her friend's presence. She thought about her last email from Gen.

It had started out asking about how she was, her mood, and activities. Then, it had morphed to a discussion of the dismal political situation the country was in and how science was now being dictated by politicians. Gen said that her latest research was uncovering some current threats to human health caused by global warming. She had mentioned how much she hated leaving the world so messed up for **Liz**'s generation. That was the weird part. Nobody called Ellie Jean, which was short for Elizabeth Jean, Liz. It hadn't meant much at the time, but Marnie wondered why Liz? Why in bold? Maybe it was an attempt at a joke. Now she wondered.

Marnie wandered over to the bookshelves. She glanced at the eclectic selections—chick lit, and mysteries mixed in with non-fiction. *Both of us had loved The Hot Zone.* Then, she scanned the photo albums. Old albums from Gen's childhood were now proudly sitting next to all the others. One album was from their early days at medical school.

And there it was.

One red album amongst a bunch of navy-blue ones. Inside the album were pictures of Ellie Jean's first year in Galveston. On the outside was the title "Liz."

Marnie picked up the album and started looking through it. Halfway through the album she found a letter addressed to her.

Dear Marnie,

If you are reading this, then I'm not nearly as nutty as I feel writing and hiding it. Garrett would say I have the heebie-jeebies. I hope that soon I'll be sharing this letter with you and laughing about my cloak and dagger moves. But honestly, I would be too embarrassed to share this with you in person. So, if you are reading it then it means I'm probably dead. Very strange to write a letter that might be read after you die.

First, and most importantly, I want to tell you what it has meant to have you, Ellie Jean, and Adam in my life. You were the first person that I told about my situation. The fact that my story didn't faze you, or in any way change how you thought about or acted towards me, was my first inkling that coming out was a possibility.

While I was growing up, I always felt so off center. Every part of me wanted to be a girl. In a small farming community, there was only male or female. I felt that my body was made wrong.

I was born in 1968 when the women's liberation movement was coming into its own. People forget that, at that time, a woman could be fired for getting married, or if the workplace was advanced, they would only fire her after she became pregnant. It didn't matter if she needed the job. She had no rights.

I grew up in the 70s and 80s, and by then, there was a backlash against women's liberation and the proposed Equal Rights Amendment. Oh, the horrors of single sex restrooms! The Texas Legislature was still fighting over the Bathroom Bill in 2017! Nowadays, many restrooms are single use with both signs on them. Funny how this doesn't make the world stop spinning.

But despite the obvious workplace disadvantages of being a woman, I knew I was one. I didn't know it was an old problem which many civilizations had coped with in various ways. In India, there are Hijra, who consider themselves neither male nor female. Though frequently born male, they act and dress female. The first known "woman" physician in the military was James Miranda Steuart Barry. He was born Margaret Ann Buckley in Ireland in 1789. He rose to Inspector General in charge of Military Hospitals in Britain before his retirement. It wasn't discovered until his death that he was a woman—who had even had a child.

Now in our generation, transsexuality has been acknowledged and the process of reassignment has been improved. I was able to take advantage of these changes. When I first walked the street as a woman, I was sure I would be ridiculed. But few people took any notice. By the second year of my transition, I was getting appreciative stares from men.

It was an incredible feeling. I felt whole.
Coming to Galveston was like being reborn—
or at least finally being allowed to be the
person I always was. At the same time, I could
pursue the career I dreamt of.

Falling in love with Garrett was like the
end of a long journey. I had discreet and brief
relationships in the past, but Garrett is the
first person I let into my heart. And now, we
are being threatened by mean, petty men. I
don't know how they found out about my past.
I can only think they dug around in my college
transcripts and found a discrepancy. But it's
time to quit worrying about this secret now.

So, now we come to the cloak and dagger
part of this letter.

In the last two days, our division had an
inspection. As part of the process, I had a
meeting with a surveyor, Dr. Ernie Pedersen.
He informed me that I had to change my
research. You would have thought that he
wasn't a scientist! After years of study and
research, we don't change our results on
request. Especially since my research directly
affects the people I live and work with, as well
as the public health of the country. There was
something creepy about the way he acted.
Right after our meeting, I got a strange and
threatening phone call.

After that, I went to the lab and backed
up my research on a thumb drive. At the last
minute, something happened in the lab and
I was afraid to walk out with the drive. I
stashed it in a hiding place and was unable
to retrieve it before the end of the day. So
hopefully, this letter is totally unnecessary, but
if you are reading this, I'm going to hope you
can figure it out. I'm afraid to be too specific
in case you're not the person reading this.

*As we always joked, the best hiding place is
in plain sight but not in plain view. Marnie,
I'm not sure why this is happening. There
have to be some decent people in government
agencies who have maintained their integrity.
Someone needs to see my data. NIH, CDC,
and EPA come to mind. Please help.*

Love, Gen

Marnie sat silent for a few minutes. Her mind was
racing. *What to do next?*

She needed to get into the lab to search for that
thumb drive. She decided against asking Garrett for
help. She didn't want to add to his burdens right now.
Maybe Louise would have an idea. *What had Nancy
said about a friend at the Environmental Protection
Agency?*

Chapter Fourteen

October 4, 2018

Minneapolis, MN

Allison picked up when she saw the Gulf County Police Department on her caller ID. "Hello, this is Allison Pedersen."

"This is Detective Iliana Sudhan, Gulf County PD speaking. I don't know how to say this any other way, Mrs. Pedersen," the detective said. "We have an unidentified murder victim here that *could* match the description you gave of your husband."

"Could match? I don't understand," Allison said, trying to keep her voice from breaking. "I sent a picture."

"Yes, and thank you for that. The victim we have has had some trauma that makes recognition difficult with just a photograph. We're going to need DNA confirmation to rule him in or out."

Allison only heard the first part. "Trauma?"

"Unfortunately, yes," said Sudhan. "If we could get a sample of your husband's DNA, we could get a result in two hours. The quickest way is for you to bring it here."

After Detective Sudhan told Allison which items would most likely have her husband's DNA and gave general directions to the Gulf County Police

Department, Allison said she would get on a plane as soon as possible. She got up slowly and walked to the bedroom. The horror that she had dreaded enveloped her. She placed Ernie's hairbrush and extra toothbrush in a Ziploc bag beside her own toiletries and booked her flight to Houston.

***

Galveston, TX

Detective Sudhan hung up the phone after speaking to Mrs. Pedersen. She thought that it was likely that her John Doe was about to get identified. The motive for his violent murder remained elusive. It seemed that whoever killed her John Doe tried and succeeded in slowing the identification process.

It was time to call it a day. Two murders in her town drove up the year's murder rate. A 200% increase.

She headed home. Bob was working the evening shift in the ER and wouldn't be home until after midnight.

She marveled at how they had managed to stay married, employed, and raise their son by alternating shifts until she worked her way to detective and he, to head nurse. Their son, Ben, was now at Rice University. He was a real blend of their coloring and could easily fit in with all the shades that filled the cosmopolitan city of Houston.

The last eighteen years seemed both grueling and gone in a flash. She sometimes wondered if they had ever stopped to smell the roses along the way. She thought of her parents who, after their marriage, had settled on the eastern edge of Texas and run a convenience store. They had managed to get their four children through college.

Iliana Sudhan was the youngest child and the last to leave. She often thought her interest in law enforcement was rooted in the anxiety she had felt behind the counter of her parents' store. Her dad had a shotgun under the cash register and was insistent that all the kids were comfortable using it. He was clear-eyed about the risks of a convenience store in East Texas. Being Brown was only one step up from being Black, and while, for the most part he was deferential to the White clientele who ran the town and frequented the store, he wasn't going to die without a fight.

The day Sudhan graduated from college, her parents sold the store and headed to Pakistan for a long visit. When they returned, their next stop was buying a little place near her to help raise their grandchild.

"And to garden and see the sunlight," her dad said.

Born in America in 1947, his family's American story preceded that of many Americans. His grandmother's family had lived in Texas when Texas was still part of Mexico. After Texas gained its independence in 1837, her family was one of the prominent Tejano families that, along with prominent Anglos, governed Texas during its nine years of independence before it joined the U.S. in 1845.

His grandfather came from Kashmir in 1907 to help build the Western Pacific Railroad. Falling in love, he had married Sudhan's great-grandmother and moved to San Antonio. Feeling guilty about not returning home for an arranged marriage, he had insisted that all of his male heirs return to Kashmir for their brides.

When Sudhan's father went to Kashmir for his arranged marriage, he fell in love with the sister of his betrothed. They eloped, bringing shame to their families. For defying her grandfather's wishes, her parents were banished from San Antonio to East Texas.

When Iliana had fallen in love with Bob, who was studying nursing in Houston while she studied criminal justice, her parents had been thrilled to have their last child happily married.

Bob's family came in 1960 from the Netherlands and he was born in Texas in 1970. He was considered a "real American" even though he was only second generation. Nobody ever gave him a lecture or told him to "go home." It was a lecture which Sudhan heard frequently. She had learned not to give in to the temptation to tell her critics that her ancestors were in Texas when theirs were still on the plains of Europe.

***

After a hard shift, Louise hung up her white coat, collected her lunch bag, and was heading to the ER exit door to look for Marnie when she was stopped by a question.

"Dr. Finnerty, do you have a minute?"

Unlike the usual last-minute question, the person posing it didn't work in the Emergency Department. Her antenna went up immediately when she saw his ID badge.

"Sorry to ambush you. My name is Chris Hill. I'm from the Bay City Daily and wanted to talk to you about Dr. Drake. You were here the night she was brought in, correct?"

Initially, Louise didn't say anything, remembering the frequent bad press the paper had provided about her ER.

The man saw her hesitancy but plowed ahead. "I already got the facts from Dr. Torson, who was the treating doctor. She said you were a friend of Dr. Drake and I hoped you could share your thoughts as to why she was murdered? Do we know if *murdered* is even the right word? You must have some theories."

He doesn't waste any time. No preliminaries. And yes, I have some thoughts, if not theories, about the motivation. But she was unlikely to share them with him. It was then that Marnie appeared from the

127

elevator. Marnie had finished her visit with Dorothy Riley, their sweet neighbor from the old days. They credited Dorothy with keeping them alive through harrowing weeks of finals and board exams with baked goods and vegetables from her garden.

They were headed to happy hour at O'Bryan's. There was no lack of happy hours on The Island. The watering holes had learned the benefit of extended hours to service the shift-working staff at the medical center as well as the tourists who had lingered on the beach past sunset. Didier had a meeting with the Galveston Island Nature Council, so Louise's mother was spending the evening with the kids.

Marnie glanced at Chris's badge and smiled. "It's about time one of you guys showed some interest in Gen's murder. I'm Marnie Liccione, another friend of Gennifer Drake."

Of all of Marnie's assets, that open smile made everyone, male or female, putty in her hands. It was clear to Louise that Mr. Hill would be joining them for drinks. Despite her reservations about talking to reporters, she was happy to see Marnie's interest in the handsome journalist.

It was a short walk to The Strand, Galveston's historic main drag, and down a side street to O'Bryan's. The three of them set off on foot. The night was a bit cool for once.

Louise loved this time of year, when there were hints that the siege of summer was coming to a close. The tourists would thin out, leaving the beach an open expanse for exercising and family outings.

Louise, Marnie, and Chris settled themselves into a booth at O'Bryan's on Post Office Street. The women sat next to each other. Chris slid into the other side of the booth. Louise and Marnie ordered Causeway Kolsch. Chris ordered Knob Creek on the rocks.

When Chris pulled out an old-fashioned notebook and ball point pen, Louise continued her assessment. Mr. Hill was easy on the eyes. Mid-forties, tall and slim. His dark brown hair was shaggy and a few weeks overdue for a haircut. He wore a blue oxford cloth shirt, untucked, with gray slacks and Birkenstock sandals. This was Galveston, after all.

"Thanks for agreeing to talk to me, Dr. Finnerty," Chris said.

"Dr. Finnerty works fine for the record, but we're on a first name basis at O'Bryan's. Call me Louise."

After a few preliminary questions about how long the women had known Gen and in what capacity, Chris Hill dove in. "The paper is going to run a follow up story about Dr. Drake the day after tomorrow. As you know, the police are saying that she died under suspicious circumstances."

"Yes, like murder," Marnie interjected.

Chris glanced at Marnie and continued, "Have you received any word on the autopsy results, Louise?"

Louise had to take a deep breath before responding. It was unreal to her that she was in a bar discussing her friend's postmortem.

"I don't have anything official. I wasn't the treating physician, so I don't have access to the details. Plus, the report hasn't been finalized. I did hear that she showed signs of trauma with what appeared to be defensive injuries and blood and skin under her fingernails."

"Do you have any idea, any theory, about why someone would want to kill Dr. Drake?" Chris asked. "Any enemies? History of abusive relationships? She worked at the Gulf National Lab. Was there any hint that she might be mixed up in some sensitive research there? Something that somebody would kill for?"

Louise was glad that the drinks had arrived and all three took big sips. This was getting stressful. She knew she was limited in what she could reveal about a patient, even the deceased.

"That's a lot of questions," Marnie said, as she glanced at Louise.

Louise nodded to let her friend know it was fine with her if Marnie chimed in. She had called Louise earlier to explain about finding the letter.

Marnie continued. "No enemies or abusive relationships that we know of. We think there's some connection to the lab."

Chris quit taking notes. "Why is that?"

Before there was time to answer or stall, Louise stood up and waved to a couple of women on their way out the door. "Hey, Connie and Tina!"

Louise had worked with Dr. Connie Garcia for five years. After having a set of twins, Connie left the ER for more civilized hours. It happened all the time in emergency medicine. She and her sister, Tina, knew all the best places for happy hours on The Island. The fortuitous coincidence at this happy hour was that Dr. Tina Garcia was a pathologist in the medical examiner's office.

"Can you join us? I still miss you, Connie. How are the girls? You remember Marnie?" Louise asked.

After more introductions, the sisters said they could stay for a few minutes. Both had husbands on duty at home. "This is our monthly sisters' night out," Tina said.

Louise brought the conversation around to Gen.

"She wasn't my case," said Tina. "But I heard the results. They came out this afternoon. I'll tell you, at least what I heard. Off the record." She shot a stern look at Chris.

He held up his hands, palms facing the group in a posture of surrender. He was outnumbered and besides, he probably didn't want to antagonize his sources.

"The autopsy confirms that Dr. Drake was murdered. Although she had been in the water for at least 30 minutes prior to her mortal injury, she didn't drown. There was no water in her lungs. She had evidence of strangulation and blunt trauma. Her liver was lacerated, and she bled out internally."

Tina's description was unvarnished and presented as one physician would relay the information to another physician.

Around the table, everyone took another big sip

of their drinks. Marnie and Louise were horrified to realize that their friend had been able to make it to shore only to be killed in such a brutal fashion.

After seeing their reaction, Tina said, "Oh, sorry to be so graphic. I forgot that this was personal for y'all. There is more."

"Please go on," they said in unison.

Tina said, "Her toxicology is preliminary, but it was positive for opiates."

Marnie and Louise were shocked into silence. Louise regained her composure as the sisters started leaving. She thanked Tina for the information. As she gave Connie a hug, Louise promised to get together again soon.

"Okay, then," said Chris, sinking back onto the worn booth. "That was more than I expected to learn tonight. Can I ask a few more questions?"

"Shoot," Marnie replied, even more resolute to figure things out.

"Opiates? Do either of you suspect she had a drug problem?"

Louise shook her head.

Marnie said, "Absolutely not. Aside from the fact that Gen was super conscientious about taking care of the body she had worked so hard for, she was always a straight arrow. Her research is the thread we need to follow to figure out what happened." Marnie explained to Chris their suspicions related to the missing flash drive.

"Louise and I are sure there's information on it that Gen wanted protected. The question is where she hid it. I haven't asked Garrett about it yet—he's still pretty raw."

"Who's Garrett?" Chris asked.

"Garrett Mancinelli is, was, her boyfriend. They were about to move in together. Do you know Garrett's Seawall Trattoria? He's the owner."

"Yeah, his name is familiar. I think I know Garrett from somewhere in my past. High school? Sports?

I don't know. Somewhere. Probably an old Island family thing."

Marnie wasn't interested in the "Born On the Island" relationships that constantly cropped up among the descendants of Galveston's A-list families. She forged ahead. "So, Chris, do you want to help us find it? The flash drive? We think she hid it in the lab. Do you know how we can get into the lab with your newspaper connections? Do you know an investigator who could help us?"

"Well, yes, maybe, and yes. Let me sleep on it." He gave them each one of his cards so they could reconnect.

Checking her watch, Louise said, "We've got to get going. You two can talk tomorrow. I think we need to find this thumb drive, but we need to be careful. If Gen was murdered, there are some powerful forces at work here."

"I'll be in touch," Chris said.

***

Chris walked slowly back to his car, thinking about the interview. He had obtained much more information than he had expected. He had the makings of a big story. Marnie's intensity about the investigation drew him to her. *Among other things—like her good looks and obvious intelligence.*

Clearing his mind, he noticed The Grand 1894 Opera House and thought about its history. Opened as an opera house with stars like Sarah Bernhardt, it had descended into a vaudeville theater on its way to becoming a seedy movie house. Now it was being resurrected and restored as a performing arts center.

He turned north to continue his walk on The Strand. Originally named B Street, it was renamed The Strand after an enterprising jeweler insisted on copying the name of the famous street in London. The name stuck and the five-block stretch was a booming commercial center during the latter half of the 1800s. Banks, cotton exchanges, wholesalers, and newspapers were housed in iron fronted brick buildings. The Strand became known as "The Wall Street of the South." Throughout the nineteenth century, Galveston was the biggest city in Texas.

The Great Storm of 1900 demolished The Island and left 6,000 dead. This devastation combined with the ascendency of a safe, deep water port in Houston brought an end to Galveston's status as a commercial center. After the hurricane, most of the old buildings were replaced by hulking warehouses. It wasn't until the last half of the next century that Islanders restored and revitalized the area.

It was a short drive to his home. Well, he *wanted* it to be his home. Right now, it was a work in progress. He had purchased the house on 18th Street from his cousin two years ago. Hurricane Ike had done serious damage to the Victorian mansion in 2008, but the place had been in the family since it was built. Originally, his family's money came from the Galveston Cotton Exchange, which one of his ancestors had founded after the Civil War. Much of the man's financial success allegedly came from cheating the farmers, as well as the buyers, and the state of Texas at each step in the process.

When the port of Galveston lost its dominance to Houston, his family branched out into oil and gas. They also owned and ran the Bay City Daily until the mid-sixties, a bit of family history that had fascinated Chris while growing up and eventually led him to choose journalism as his major.

He padded up the steps to the garage apartment, which served as his living area. He could see a light on in the big house and knew Rosa, the Hill's retired seventy-five-year-old former housekeeper, and now Chris's maintenance coordinator, was getting ready for bed. When he reached the top of the stairs, Chris wasn't surprised to see a covered plate of chile rellenos on his doorstep.

It was getting late. He had one more thing to accomplish before watching the last few innings of the Astros game and piling into bed with a book.

He had told Louise and Marnie that he might have an investigator. Savannah would be perfect. He made a call, left a message, and followed up with a text. After warming up the plate of food Rosa had prepared for him, he flipped on the TV. The Astros were beating the A's 8-0 in the seventh.

Chapter Fifteen

October 5, 2018

Galveston, Texas

The sun woke Chris as it filtered through the curtains that Rosa had embroidered for his bedroom. His phone started to hum. He was pleased to see it was Savannah returning his call.

Savannah Hargrove was a youth minister at First Baptist Church. Her title always gave Chris a laugh. She had been an investigator for Reliable, a giant insurance company. With girl-next-door looks and big Texas blonde hair, she could get anyone to talk to her. She had saved a lot of money for the company by ferreting out false claims. Eventually, she became disgusted with both the lying "victims" and the greedy insurance company that denied even legitimate claims. She made a one-eighty and took a job at the church. She loved her work, and the Baptists loved Savannah.

At a bar favored by the newsroom staff, a coworker of Chris introduced them. Any bar was an unlikely spot for a Baptist, so Savannah could enjoy a few drinks without fear of exposure. In the course of the conversation, Chris learned that she did some work on the side for his colleagues, off the books for both the paper and the church. Her IT skills and resources, maintained after parting ways with Reliable, had become legendary in his office.

"Mornin' Sugar. Did you miss me after all?"

"Every single day," Chris answered. He wasn't fully awake and regretted his playful response immediately. He and Savannah had hooked up once, several years back. It turned out she was looking for more than he had to offer. Since then, she either pretended to or still carried a torch for him. He couldn't tell which anymore.

He sat up and tried to assume a more businesslike voice. He explained that he wanted her to investigate a few people at the Gulf National Lab.

"Does this have anything to do with the murder of the doctor who worked there?" Savannah didn't miss a beat.

"Can't say yet. But I need to know if Dr. Drake's colleagues are involved with anything outside of work that might smell strange."

"Shouldn't be too hard. You're lucky. Our mission trip to The Valley isn't for another week."

Chris knew the valley in question was actually the flats of the Rio Grande floodplain, a destination with plenty of misery for a youth group to alleviate. Chris confirmed her hourly rate and made an appointment to see her at the watering hole the next day.

He showered, then dressed while eating the remaining rice and beans from last night's meal. When he left, he waved to Rosa, who was being trailed by four young men and their painting gear. She was handing out shoe covers and barking orders as he pulled out. After Chris's parents retired and moved to be near his sister and the grandkids, they had left Rosa with a small stipend and a bungalow without a mortgage. What she didn't have was the family to whom she had devoted her life. She was a *solterona*, a more pleasing word than the English word spinster. About that time, Chris acquired this disaster of a mansion. Knowing he would get nowhere with the endless lists of repairs and keep his day job, he hired Rosa, whom he had known and adored since childhood, as his foreman.

Rosa came to live in a corner of the big house during the interminable restoration. Her Cristobal preferred to live in the garage apartment, which was renovated, and, more importantly, re-wired, so that he could be connected to the media 24/7. She oversaw painters, plumbers, and electricians with an iron hand. Since the majority of the labor force was Hispanic, she was able to give them tongue lashings that reminded them of their abuelas. Chris and she made sure that the kitchen was the first room to be completed. From there, she was able to create meals for the workers, which took the sting out of her frequent chiding.

As he got into his car, he pulled out his cellphone to dial Marnie.

She picked up on the first ring. "This is Marnie," she answered briskly.

"Chris Hill here. Uh, from last night. I think I can help you on your mission to get into the lab. Can you meet me for lunch to discuss a plan?"

"Sure."

After they arranged a meeting, Chris smiled and dropped his phone on the front seat. He realized he was looking forward to more than a front-page story. There was something interesting about this woman.

Chris pulled into the parking lot of the newspaper at 8:30. The office was in a 60s building close to the causeway connecting The Island to the mainland. He was dismayed to see that someone had beaten him to his favorite patch of shade. He should get a sign reserving it for The Editor. He had earned that honor.

He'd always thought the current home of the paper didn't do justice to its history. The paper started in a grand iron-fronted brick building on Market Street where it had been published for eighty years. That elegant structure was the first building in the country built solely for a newspaper. It was the first newspaper in Texas to have a telephone. The Bay City Daily was founded in 1842 back when Texas was still a republic and Sam Houston was its president. It had been in continuous publication, not even missing an edition after the Great Storm. During all those years, it endorsed scoundrels and heroes, made and ruined political careers, and kept on printing.

Chris hurried to his desk where he still kept a Rolodex. It was an anachronism but every time he thought about tossing it, he hesitated. He had never systematically gone through it and transferred contacts into his electronic address book. Today, he was looking for Englebert Salinas. That name was hard to forget. "Sal" Salinas was in charge of public relations for the Gulf National Lab. As he worked tirelessly to get the community to support the lab, Sal confronted growing skepticism about the wisdom of placing a biosafety level 4 lab on a sandbar that was regularly ravaged by hurricanes.

Chris had written a few positive articles about the lab before it opened in 2008 in the face of public safety concerns. The lab remained unscathed by Hurricane Ike that same year. Chris played this up as well as the financial benefits the lab contributed to The Island.

Ten years later, Chris was glad that Sal had not changed his number. Chris explained that he was doing a follow up on the unfortunate murder of the Gulf National Laboratory researcher.

"I'd like to visit the lab and her department to get some background," Chris said.

Sal agreed, with conditions. "Yeah, Chris, I can make it happen. You need to know we can't afford any negative press about safety and security. There have been some articles lately about biosafety lab mishaps around the country. Not here, mind you. We could use some good publicity before we open our new BSL4 lab wing. It's actually great you called, because I've been trying to figure out how to get this into the news. I can set you up for a full tour and they'll let you suit up and everything."

"Sounds good. I'm mostly interested in finding out more about Dr. Drake as a person. Maybe I could chat with her coworkers and look around her office? I think touring the new lab would be interesting, and I promise not to let any bugs escape."

"You better not."

After a pause, Sal added, "The police have been by already, you know."

"Yes, I would imagine they have been. I'm more interested in the soft side of the story. I'm bringing a very attractive doctor, a friend of Dr. Drake, to help navigate the science. So, is it a go?"

Apparently, that did the trick. Chris's deposit in the good will bank in 2008 had held its value with accrued interest. He worked out the details with Sal for a visit starting at 4:00 p.m.

"Send over your identification credentials asap so we can get you cleared to come to the lab," Sal said.

"Will do."

Chris hung up, called Marnie, discussed ID requirements for clearance, and changed their lunch date to a meeting at 3:30.

Chapter Sixteen

October 5, 2018

Washington, D.C.

Anne Hallam walked purposefully through the call center of the Environmental Community Access Hotline, a division of the EPA. She had just returned from a managers' meeting and was replaying the uncomfortable commentary in her mind. She strode past the twelve employees in her section. They were at their stations, headsets on, typing as they took calls from the hotlines. This center was one of twenty hotlines that could be accessed by anyone. Some of the lines had clear titles such as Asbestos Hotline, Drinking Water Hotline, or Lead Information Hotline. The Environmental Community Access Hotline, however, welcomed calls from anyone concerned about an environmental threat to their community. There was never a dull day.

Anne cast a glance at Susan. Her workstation was a mess, as usual. Sensing that she was being observed, Susan kicked her overflowing tote bag under the desk.

Anne continued to her office and sat at her gunmetal gray, government-issued desk from the 1970s. A dinosaur, just like Anne. At seventy-three, she was one of the longest serving EPA employees. She had joined in 1978, only eight years after the agency was established by Richard Nixon. She recalled the enthusiasm and sense of purpose they all had. An agency to protect the environment! The original staff of 5,000 had swelled to 17,000.

Anne had been a career employee since the Carter administration and was now on her seventh president. She lost count of the number of agency directors who came and went. It had been a wild ride. With her experience in multiple divisions, it was no accident she landed at the hotline. It was her job to sift through the call reports and decide what merited further investigation. She relied on her staff's attention to detail, experience, and sixth sense to enable her to do her job.

Anne could tell that Susan had a story to tell when she came into her office. Despite her unruly workstation, Susan was among the best in the department. Anne saw her as a potential successor. But then again, she had no plans to retire.

"This is a strange one," Susan started. "I had two calls today about Gulf National Lab. It's Region 6."

Anne accessed her memory bank. Texas Gulf Coast. Lots of calls from community members, folks in the tourist trade, and fishermen had poured in before the opening of the BSL4 on that hurricane prone island. She had fielded many not-in-my-backyard concerns about all sorts of facilities—nuclear power plants, strip mines, and chemical waste dumps. But the uproar on Galveston Island calmed down when the Gulf National Laboratory withstood Hurricane Ike in 2008.

Anne was up and pacing behind her desk at this point. "Go on, Susan."

"The first call came from Dr. Bertram Springer. He's a microbiologist at the University of Oklahoma and a surveyor for the U.S. Biosafety Association."

"U.S. Biosafety Association," Anne repeated as she made a quick turn towards the opposite wall.

Susan, like all the hotline employees, was familiar with Anne's habit of pacing through a report. It meant she was listening.

Susan continued. "Dr. Springer said he was afraid research was being suppressed. Research related to climate change. In this case, the emergence of a disease. Let me check my notes. Dengue. A new variant. It's transmitted by mosquitoes. The warmer it gets, the further north these mosquitoes invade and transmit the disease. This variant of dengue is killing people in South Texas."

Anne drew in a deep breath. *God that hits a nerve.*

"What's this about a second call?" Anne asked.

"So, I'm on Region 6 today. A woman called and said she was concerned about research being destroyed at the same laboratory. She said it was related to that disease, dengue. Then, and this is where it gets weird, she said she thought it was related to the murder of a researcher!"

"Did she give her name?"

"The caller? No. But she said the researcher who was murdered was Gennifer Drake, M.D., Ph.D."

"Thank you, Susan. Good work. Drop off your report when you have it completed. Put these two calls on the top of the list. I'm going to need to put this in front of someone upstairs."

The two women exchanged meaningful looks before Susan left the office. Since the election of the current president, the EPA's mission seemed to have gone into reverse. The agency was actually *cheering* for repeal of regulations on polluting industries. The automakers had a green light to produce more gas guzzling, hydrocarbon spewing SUVs. Despite being economically nonviable, new coal powered electrical plants were in the works. Today's managers meeting had been about rolling out a retraining module for the call center employees. The EPA Director had proposed a policy which required calls from all twenty hotlines that related to climate change be sent to a "tactical group" made up of new hires. Anne and her fellow career employees knew what that meant. In her four decades, Anne had never seen anything like it.

Sure, the EPA staff grumbled through some administrations. But flat-out denial of scientific facts was another thing. In his last job, the director described himself as a leading advocate against the EPA's activist agenda. He was appointed by a president who said that global warming was created by the Chinese. If even half the stories about the director were true, he should have been fired months ago. First class travel, living in a lobbyist's luxury condo, having his staff keep a secret calendar of his meetings with industry magnates, and a $43,000 soundproof phone booth for his office! And that's just what's been in the news. The insiders at EPA knew more.

Anne realized she was ruminating. She knew to whom she could speak frankly, but she would need to proceed carefully. She didn't want to implicate Susan or any other employee. Anne could take a hit if need be, but these kids needed their jobs.

She didn't tell Susan that she had also received troubling news from Galveston. The night before, her old friend from college, Nancy Finnerty, had called her out of the blue. Normally, they just exchanged Christmas cards. After catching up on friends and family, Nancy asked if she could give Anne's contact information to her daughter and her daughter's friend. One of their classmates from medical school had been murdered and they thought it might be related to her research on climate change and emerging diseases. She worked at Gulf National Laboratory. After Susan's report, Anne needed to talk to these women.

Where there's smoke, there's fire. Time to get to work.

She pulled up the EPA organizational chart. Since she worked better on paper, she printed it out on several sheets and taped them together. The jackass director was on top, but she was starting at the bottom. She started circling names. The ones she identified had served in the agency for over twenty years. Since the last election, they had all commiserated with Anne at one time or another regarding the current state of affairs. She smiled when she came to Dave Yardley, Deputy Regional Director of Region 6. She knew she could count on him.

She connected the names in a zigzag line that led to Acting Director, William Oakes. He was a career employee who had to hold his nose to continue in his current post. He was doing his best to mitigate the damage done by the current administration.

Casting a motherly look over her employees, Anne closed her office door and went to work. She felt the rush she got when she was doing something meaningful, something that mattered, something morally right.

Chapter Seventeen

October 5, 2018

Galveston, Texas

Louise walked briskly down the busy ER hallway to Room 11. She had started the swing shift, 3 p.m. to midnight. It'd been busy when she arrived, and she knew it would be busy when she tried to extricate herself. As she passed room 9, she heard a voice call out over the hum of activity in the department.

"Hi Dr. Finnerty, did you change your hair? Looking good!"

Louise didn't need a visual to recognize the voice of Vance Smith. He was a frequent visitor to the ER. On this day, he was accompanied by a police officer and was handcuffed to the gurney. This was a common presentation for Vance. Louise and her colleagues had cared for him numerous times over the years. In a city the size of Galveston, and in a state like Texas, an uninsured drug addict had few options for health care. On this occasion, Vance definitely had no other choice, as Louise's hospital was the designated hospital for the emergency care of inmates.

Louise had cared for Vance's multiple injuries and resisted his blatant drug seeking for conditions that could never be fully diagnosed. She also recognized his legitimate medical emergencies. She diagnosed his case of appendicitis when the jail staff, as well as Louise initially, thought he was malingering. Since then, he seemed to seek her out for his medical care when he could.

None of the doctors in the ER had regular schedules, so it was hit or miss, but he did seem to turn up more often when she was on duty. Over the years, Louise had tried to help him with his addictions. His most recent drug of choice was tramadol. He got hooked on it after extensive dental work for his methamphetamine damaged teeth. She made referrals to rehab programs and enlisted social workers. Vance was never able to kick his opiate addiction.

Louise stopped outside his cubicle. A beefy, redheaded constable was sitting on a plastic chair with thin metal legs. It was straining under his weight and stabilized by his splayed legs. His nametag said Tudor. He looked content to be at rest for a few hours, maybe more, and was engrossed in his word jumble paperback. Louise knew it made sense to take care of the formalities with Vance now. She would have to pass his gurney many times before he was treated and returned to jail.

"Hi, Vance. What's going on?" Louise said, declining to acknowledge his compliment.

"Oh, it's that same chest pain I get, Doc. Dr. Forrest did an EKG and said he'd be back in a bit."

Vance gave Louise a gap-toothed smile, evidence that the dental work was never completed. He looked thin, but his eyes were bright that day and his blonde hair was cut stylishly and looked clean. She knew that chest pain was a sure way to get out of jail for several hours. After being successfully sued for several bad outcomes, the jail administration no longer ignored an inmate's complaint of chest pain. The ER staff took good care of the inmates, but once an emergency was ruled out, they were not a high priority.

"Well, I'm sure Dr. Forrest will figure it out for you," she said. "Take care, Vance."

She felt no need to find out why he was in custody. Constable Tudor never looked up from his brain training.

Scanning her laptop as she walked, she continued to her original destination, Room 11. Mrs. Betty Howard, age ninety-three. Chief complaint of fever and altered mental status. Louise had already looked at her medical history. Mrs. Howard had been in the ER three times in the last four months and admitted for a complicated urinary tract infection each time. This was the first time Louise had cared for her.

She introduced herself to the 70ish woman who was close to tears as she stood next to Mrs. Howard's bed. She had fluffy white hair and blue eyes that matched the light denim jumper and Keds she was wearing.

The woman spoke, "I'm her daughter, Dottie Howard. I don't know how much more of this either of us can stand, Doctor."

Understanding that Dottie was exhausted by the ER visits and hospitalizations, Louise confirmed the recent course of events. She gently performed a quick physical exam on Mrs. Howard, who appeared to be sleeping restlessly, muttering unintelligibly. Afterwards, Louise suggested to Dottie that they speak outside the cubicle. She reminded herself that patients in Mrs. Howard's state could still hear.

"Your mother is critically ill right now. The lab tests we did show her kidneys are failing. Her potassium is dangerously high, putting her at risk of serious heart rhythm problems. Her blood pressure is low, and her heart rate is high. She's on the verge of sepsis."

"That's what I thought, so I brought her here. Her doctor, Old Doc Pope, died himself last year, so she hasn't been seen except when she comes here."

"We'll take good care of her, but I need to ask if your mother made her wishes clear about end-of-life care. Did she let you know what she wants?" Louise asked.

Dottie sniffled a bit before she collected herself.

"She said she didn't want to die hooked up to a machine with all those tubes like Daddy did. What happens is that every time she goes into the hospital, my sister flies in from New Mexico and tells the doctors she wants everything done. When Mama gets better, I guess we're not in the mood to talk about it."

Louise saw a version of this family drama every shift. She had been a doctor for twenty years and still didn't know the definition of "everything."

Louise explained that there were plenty of things that could be done to make her mother feel better without putting her on machines. She would get Mrs. Howard admitted to a hospitalist who gave a damn about this kind of situation. She promised to contact the hospital chaplain and social services to help Dottie negotiate the next few days.

Unfortunately, during their conversation the hallway was crowded and noisy. Louise and Dottie were pressed against the flimsy barrier between Rooms 9 and 11. By the end of the conversation, Dottie was sobbing and had grabbed Louise's hand. Louise knew the least she could do would be to stay by Dottie's side until she regained her composure.

As she stared down the hall, Louise could hear Vance's voice from the next room.

"Officer, can I please at least get up and use the restroom?"

"You know the rules," replied the officer. "You get the fancy urinal."

When, as if by divine intervention, two members of the Howard's church appeared with coffee, donuts, and words of comfort, Louise extricated herself. She started down the hall, checking lab results as she walked.

"Dr. Finnerty!" Vance called out from Room 9. "I know you're busy, but I need help with a situation."

Louise stopped, still looking at her laptop's screen. "Yes, Vance," she said with poorly disguised irritation.

"It's not medical, I mean, maybe it's adding to my chest pain and all."

He stopped talking until he saw Louise turn her attention to him from her computer.

"Long story short, Doc. I need a good lawyer and wondered if you could recommend one."

"Don't you have one appointed to you?" Louise asked.

"I need to talk to a real lawyer about some information I have. A lawyer who can help me get my charges reduced. It relates to murder."

Vance drew out the last sentence dramatically. Constable Tudor snorted.

"Did you know the lady doctor who was killed last week? I heard the nurses talking last time I was here. Someone said she was your friend. That broke me up, about her getting killed and being your friend and all. I need to talk to someone about some stuff I overheard in the showers last week. There was a new guy in there. He looked like he was kind of jonesing. He was talking to himself, trying to calm down, and said something about a body, a woman. He said that he thought she was dead. She went in the water. It wasn't making sense. It was the guy they brought in from the rig last week."

Vance had her attention now. "I'll see if I know someone. In the meantime, you need to bring this to the attention of the lawyer you have and ask to talk to the detectives on the case."

Tudor broke in at this point. "C'mon, Smith, leave the good doctor alone. She's too busy to listen to your BS."

Louise used this as an opportunity to keep moving. Vance was still talking.

"Shit, man, can you at least hand me the bottle to pee in?"

Before seeing her next patient, Louise cleared off a patch of counter space for her laptop and placed a call to Detective Iliana Sudhan.

"Hi Louise, are any of my family members in the ER again?" she asked.

"Not today, as far as I know. Hey, listen, I've only got a minute. An inmate told me a jailhouse story that might relate to Gen's murder." Louise gave Sudhan the gist of Vance's story.

"Sounds like a prison snitch trying to trade information for a get out of jail free card. Happens all the time."

"I know, but what if this guy's telling the truth?"

Louise didn't let Sudhan know how unreliable and manipulative Vance could be. She told her that Tudor was the escorting officer.

"Okay, I know you're still upset about your friend. I get it. Let me talk to the guys tomorrow. I'll track down Tudor."

Louise thanked her and hung up. She was dismayed by Sudhan's lack of urgency but assumed the detective's days were as busy as her own and involved constant prioritization. That was exactly what she did when she looked at her list of patients. She was off and running until the end of her shift.

Chapter Eighteen

October 5, 2018

Galveston, Texas

At 4:00 p.m., Chris and Marnie appeared at the Gulf National Laboratory on the campus of U.T.M.B. Since they had submitted their identification, the campus police had their visitor badges ready. As they waited for their guide, they studied the handsome mural in the lobby which gave a brief history of infectious diseases in Galveston. They were relieved that plague, yellow fever, and malaria no longer threatened the city. There was also a model of the lab with its new addition.

Since her office was off the main lobby, Kathy Walsh greeted them.

"Hi. So good to see you again, Dr. Liccione. I remember when Gen brought you for a tour right after we opened."

"Marnie, please. I meant to say hi to you at the memorial, but I lost track of you in the crowd. This is Chris Hill, from the Bay City Daily," Marnie said.

After shaking hands, Kathy said, "Dr. Salinas asked if I would start showing you around. I thought you might want to see Gen's office and lab, where she used to work. We've been moving personnel around since her death. Her boyfriend came by the other day and picked up her personal belongings. I've been keeping my eye out for anything we missed but haven't seen anything."

As Kathy guided them through the maze of hallways, Marnie was struck by how little the lab had changed. When she had visited Gen here ten years ago, Gen had been as proud of it as a new parent. Despite the panoramic views of the bay and gulf, which Marnie glimpsed out of certain windows, the lab felt like a prison to her. She got the creeps when checking in and out. With its submarine-like doors, the structure was claustrophobic.

Marnie smiled at Kathy and said, "We're grateful for you helping us look around. I'm still trying to grasp that Gen isn't going to come around the corner and show us around herself."

Kathy nodded. "It's like her spirit is still here. She was very dedicated and anxious to get her latest research validated so it could be used to help people."

"What happened to the project she was working on?" Marnie asked.

After glancing around to make sure no one was within ear shot, Kathy replied, looking pointedly at Chris, "Off the record. It was very strange. We had a power outage the day Gen's body was found. The emergency power came on immediately but there was a little bit of a panic. All of the data was found to be in place. A couple of days later, members of her team noticed that the raw data was there, but the report Gen was working on was missing. Unfortunately, no one has been able to find her analysis and conclusions."

Prior to proceeding to the upper levels of the building, Kathy showed Chris and Marnie the model by her office. She explained that Level 1 labs were open to administrative personnel as the agents being studied were not known to cause disease in the average person. The joke was that they were safer than hospitals. Level 2 labs were designed to work with moderate agents that could cause severe diseases but were not easily transmittable. HIV and hepatitis viruses were in this group. Level 3 labs, which are the type of labs that housed insectariums and where Gen primarily worked, involved microbes which can cause serious, and potentially lethal, disease. Researchers must wear protective gear called "bunny suits" that provide head-to-toe coverage, along with respirator masks and goggles. Work was conducted in biosafety cabinets. Foot traffic was restricted. Research on agents like West Nile, tuberculosis, and dengue fever was conducted there.

Seriously dangerous diseases like Ebola were studied in Level 4 labs. The agents studied in this level were easily transmitted through air and had no readily available vaccines or treatments for their infections. Since the Level 4 lab that Chris and Marnie were going to see was not yet operational, they would not have to undergo all the training usually required. They would be able to get into a full hazard suit to experience what the researchers go through.

Kathy led them to a small office.

"This was Gen's. Her main assistant, Billy, is moving in here."

Marnie looked around. It was full of a clutter of boxes, half unpacked. Nothing in the space suggested Gen's obsessive neatness.

"Any chance we can see her lab?" Marnie asked.

Kathy nodded, "Dr. Salinas said that he would be here shortly. He's going to give you a tour of the new lab and let you suit up there. Then, he will take you down a level to Gen's lab."

Right on cue, a middle-aged man dressed in a polo shirt with a GNL logo appeared in the doorway.

"Welcome back to the lab, Chris," said Dr. Salinas, moving in for a handshake. "It's been a while."

Chris greeted him with a smile and introduced Marnie.

"I'll take it from here, Kathy. Thanks." Sal nodded at Kathy in a way Marnie felt to be dismissive.

"Let's get this show on the road. You two are lucky with your timing. The new wing of BSL4 is ninety percent complete. Follow me, and we can talk on our way over."

The three set off at a brisk pace down a long hallway. On the walk, Sal explained BSL4 lab procedures. "Personnel must wear a protective suit supplied with positive air pressure, or more commonly called a 'space suit.' All personal clothing must be removed in the changing room and replaced with laboratory clothing, including undergarments, pants, shirts, jumpsuits, shoes, and gloves. When leaving the laboratory, a researcher must take a thorough shower. Used laboratory clothing is treated as contaminated materials. After the laboratory has been completely decontaminated, necessary staff may enter and exit."

Marnie said, "The procedure does sound thorough. It's every researcher's nightmare that something would escape from a lab."

"No joke," Sal said, taking a deep breath. "Since the new lab is not operational at this time, we can skip the showers and undergarment changing but I thought it would be fun for you to put on the space suit. Maybe you can use it as background in your next piece, Chris. Right now, it's the only place you can go six feet without needing a security badge."

After clumsily getting into the suits, Sal helped them guide their hoses through the lab. The positive pressure hoses were quite powerful and had to be carefully tended.

"Man, I could never do this. These masks are horrible," Chris said.

Marnie laughed. "I can't stand it, either. I even had trouble in surgery with the masks and gowns. I thought if I was going to stitch and sew, I would rather be doing it from the comfort of my recliner."

"At least here the air conditioning is top notch," Sal said. "People suited up to work on the Ebola outbreak in West Africa in 2014 were passing out from heat exhaustion."

After seeing the new lab and removing their suits, Marnie and Chris followed Sal to Gen's lab. Most of the staff had left for the day. Sal said that he would be leaving them there and Billy would show them the lab. He would be able to do all the security badge openings required to guide them out.

"Hey, Sal, thanks for the tour. This is great background for the story about the opening," said Chris.

"I'm counting on a good review, man," replied Sal over his shoulder. He was gone as abruptly as he had appeared.

A gangly young man approached from the other end of the corridor. Marnie looked up and gave him one of her smiles.

"Hi!" Billy stammered. "I'm Billy Stanton. I used to be Gen's right-hand man."

Marnie and Chris introduced themselves as they walked to Gen's lab.

Billy said, "I can't tell you how much I miss her. She was such an amazing researcher. She taught me more in the last year than I learned in graduate school. She was so precise and thorough. If you stopped by her old office, you can see that neatness is not my strength. But I have maintained her order in the lab."

Marnie looked around. This place did seem to hold Gen's spirit. Everything was labeled and in its place. She immediately looked for anything with "Liz" on it.

"Where did Gen keep her thumb drives?"

"There's a row of the current ones here. But I've looked through each one carefully and there isn't a final report on any of them. Some older ones were kept in her office—but again, I searched them before the police took them last week. It doesn't make sense. I'm sure she finished it, but it seems to have been erased. I'm trying to recreate it, but I don't have a full grasp of the research in the same way Gen did."

Marnie and Chris exchanged glances. After looking around the lab carefully, they could see Billy was fidgeting with his keys.

"Sorry," Billy said. "I have an eighteen-month-old and a newborn at home. I promised my wife I'd be home by 6."

"No problem," Marnie said with a resigned smile. "I think we aren't having any better luck finding Gen's report than you are."

On their way back to the main lab, Billy started babbling.

"I keep thinking about the last day she was at work. We had the surveyors here. She had a meeting with one of them around three. I don't think it went well. But by the time she left she was upbeat. Triumphant. There seemed to be a glow about her. She smiled and gave me a thumb's up."

He looked nervously in Marnie's direction as if gauging whether to go on. Marnie nodded reassuringly and he continued.

"She told me that all of 'this' was going to work out. She congratulated me on my new son. She said she was going to talk to Kathy, and then head out for the day. The word around the lab now is that she was transgender. I both would never have guessed and feel that it fits perfectly. It seems irrelevant now."

Marnie stopped him. "She spoke to Kathy before she left?"

"I gather that Kathy wasn't actually in her office when Gen got there. She said that she saw Gen in the hallway as she was leaving. Gen said that she would talk to her later and left."

"Thanks, Billy. We've kept you long enough," Marnie spoke softly, calming him.

Having opened and closed all the security doors, Billy left them in the hallway to Kathy's office.

Marnie whispered to Chris, "I need to get a good look around Kathy's office. If she's there, you need to distract her."

"Got it," Chris replied.

They spotted Kathy in her office, getting ready to leave for the day.

"How was the tour?" Kathy asked.

Chris took the lead. "Great. It was good to see the new lab and Gen's space. Do you think you can answer some questions for me about the model?"

"I only have a few minutes but, yes, I'll try."

As Kathy walked to the model with Chris, Marnie meticulously scanned every inch of Kathy's office. It made her think of looking at a chest X-ray. Start with the general picture, and then look line by line, quadrant by quadrant for an outlier—trying to see not only what the test was ordered for, but for what you don't expect. *In plain sight*, Gen had written.

Going down Kathy's bookshelf of manuals and code books, Marnie saw it. A big binder. Citations. *In plain sight/cite? Is that what she was trying to tell me?*

After opening the manual, Marnie saw it there in an inside pocket. A thumb drive. Carefully taking it out, she put it in her pocket and put the binder back on the shelf. Then, she wandered over to where Chris and Kathy were.

"I think that pretty much answers my questions," he said. "Can we walk out with you?"

"Oh, I'm parked in the back. If you go through the main exit with a security badge, the alarms will go off. I'll have you wait here in the atrium for a security guard to take you out front. Let's get together sometime soon and have a drink to Gen."

As Chris and Marnie waited in the atrium, they examined the displays which told stories of researchers making historic breakthroughs.

From the reflection off the cases, Marnie saw a disguised figure coming at them down the hall. As he got closer, Marnie could see that he was inappropriately dressed in a bunny suit and mask. There was something menacing about his approach. She didn't want to be caught with the flash drive in her pocket.

Turning to Chris, Marnie said, "I don't like the look of this. Let's get out of here."

They turned down the hall but were quickly blocked

from going forward without one of the magic badges. Looking up a side hallway, they spotted the new BSL4 lab entry on the right. Not needing to use a badge there, they ducked in.

They heard the man behind them. They picked up their pace to a run.

Marnie and Chris tried to get their bearings. They were now in the suit up alcove, where they had connected their suits to the oxygen line. Their pursuer approached from across the wide room.

"What are you two doing here? Don't you know that snooping around isn't good for your health?" the man snarled.

Chris signaled Marnie to move to the room's other exit thirty feet to the left. Chris turned to face their pursuer.

"What are you talking about? And why the hell are you slinking around after us?" Chris demanded. At close range, Chris saw that the man's respirator mask obscured his face.

As Marnie headed to the exit, Chris grabbed one of the oxygen hoses, flipped the switch to start its flow and aimed it at their pursuer's face. The strong blast of air knocked back their attacker.

When he tried to get up, Chris swung the hose as hard as he could, landing a solid thunk on the side of the man's head. He tore the man's security badge off his neck.

Using the badge to make their way to the public access area, Chris and Marnie ran out the door, leaving their pursuer stranded.

Composing themselves, Chris examined the badge. It was totally unhelpful, having only a barcode on it. No name. Tossing it in a nearby trash can so that it didn't set off the buzzer, they calmly walked out the main exit, waving to the state police. They hurried through the picturesque campus of the medical school and headed straight to Chris's car.

Settling into Chris's Saab, Marnie exhaled. "I need a drink."

"My place?"

"Sounds good. Let me call my pet sitter to take care of the dogs. I'm eager to see what's on this flash drive."

Chris nodded in agreement, enjoying the knowledge that this woman could rob a Level 4 biosecurity facility one minute and the next minute propose cocktails and arrange her dogs' dinners.

***

A minivan parked three rows behind Chris and Marnie sat idling. Billy Stanton was in the driver's seat, clutching the steering wheel with white knuckles. He needed to calm down before going home. His anxiety was through the roof after an intimidating phone call informed him that he was being monitored. His subsequent involvement with Gen's data was strongly discouraged. Plus, by the tone of the caller, he didn't think he had a choice if he wanted to stay employed at the lab.

Chapter Nineteen

October 5-6, 2018

Galveston, Texas

After they settled into his Saab, Chris and Marnie peeled out of the Gulf National Lab visitor's lot and took a quick right, coming to an abrupt stop in front of a police car blocking the road.

Officer Torres approached the car and said, "Sorry guys, this road is closed. Sinkhole collapsed earlier today and left a six-foot crater. You'll need to do a detour through the medical center. Oh hi, Chris, I didn't recognize you at first. Did you just come from there?"

Looking up and recognizing Torres from some previous reporting, Chris laughed. "Yep, just got a tour. Pretty much gives you the creeps. We're eager to get as far away from those diseases as possible."

"Well, I'm sure that they won't attack you on the street. Just go back a ways and take a few lefts and a right, and you should be fine."

Chris slowly and deliberately did as he was told. Driving to his home, he parked outside the garage of the imposing main house.

"Welcome to my humble abode, or rather I should say, humbling abode."

"Wow, this is something. Are you planning on a

large family?" Marnie asked, almost giggling at the immensity of the project.

"I think most of these restored mansions have two people living in them," Chris replied. "The problem is, what to do with the history? During the late 19th century, the nouveau riche competed to build the most elaborate homes in this neighborhood. The mansions have turrets, spires, columns, and whatever flourish was considered de rigueur for the times."

When they'd pulled up, Marnie saw a small, older woman come out the front door. As they got out of the car, Chris made introductions. Rosa smiled approvingly at Marnie.

Rosa asked, "Cristobal, do you have a minute? I need to show you our latest progress."

Chris glanced questioningly at Marnie.

"I would love a tour," she said. "I can see your house withstood the Great Storm." Marnie indicated the diamond-shaped plaque that was issued to other survivors around town. "I remember admiring these mansions when we lived here, but never got inside one."

Rosa ushered them into the gleaming modern kitchen with brushed steel appliances, white flecked quartz countertops, and rich grey cabinets.

"We're trying to keep much of the beauty of the mansion but not its inconveniences. The kitchen's designed to be efficient and functional," Chris said.

As they continued into the dining room, it felt like traveling back in time. The original oak wainscoting had been refinished. Stained glass filled the half-moons above the Palladium windows, sending multicolored beams across the floor. Chris and Rosa escorted Marnie through several parlors to his favorite work in progress, the library. The floor to ceiling bookshelves seemed to cover an acre. A vintage rolling ladder was in the corner ready to be of service when he had a chance to arrange his stored books. Chris punched the antique push button light switch which turned on most of the bulbs in the chandelier.

"Not the best light for reading, but my historian friend says it's a fine specimen of turn of the century lighting. Our Island forefathers were keen to show off their new electricity."

Back in the kitchen, Chris complimented Rosa on the progress as she handed him a plate of enchiladas, easily enough for two. After the attack at the lab, Marnie found the craziness of Chris's work-in-progress mansion was a welcome distraction. It evoked images from all the Victorian romances she'd read as a teen. She loved the way Chris and Rosa interacted. Such love and respect.

They left the main house and went to Chris's apartment. She was impressed with its clean efficiency. Not messy but comfortable. It was a light airy space. Glancing into the bedroom, she noticed that the bed was made.

In the corner of the dining area, Marnie reviewed Chris's selection of bourbons.

"I have a great collection of bourbons and not much else," Chris declared.

"My husband, Adam, was a huge fan of bourbons. Knob Creek is fine for me."

"You're married?" Chris asked.

"I was," Marnie said, saying no more. Chris looked away.

After getting the drinks and warming up the enchiladas, Chris put the flash drive in his computer. Marnie took the desk chair with Chris leaning over her. The closeness of his body and his warm, earthy smell made Marnie's heart beat faster. She hadn't felt like this in months. At least while she was awake. Her dreams of Adam pressing up against her could awaken her in a full-fledged orgasm. She thought such things only happened to teenagers.

"This is definitely what we were looking for. It's what Gen wanted me to find."

At first, she couldn't concentrate on Gen's report. Marnie's breaths were quick. Scrolling to the conclusion section, it became clear what a dramatic find Gen had made, and she forced herself to slow her breathing.

With Chris still reading over her shoulder, Marnie asked, "Can you follow what she's saying?"

"I'm getting the drift of it. This is major. This new strain of dengue isn't only a local threat to South Texas. The entire southern U.S. is vulnerable."

"Look at this." Marnie scrolled down and Chris leaned in closer.

"Gen seemed to have been working on the preliminary stages of a vaccine. This needs priority funding," Marnie said.

Glancing up at Chris, she took in his strong jawline, slight stubble, and his warm "bourbon breath" as Adam used to call it. Chris's eyes met hers and he bent in for a kiss.

Marnie met him willingly. Drinking in his kiss with a hunger she didn't know she had. She stood up, folding into Chris's arms.

"To the bedroom?" Chris asked.

Marnie was already headed that way.

Before she undressed, she hesitated. She hadn't undressed for anyone but Adam for twenty years. It all felt a little intense. She didn't even know Chris's relationship status.

"So, you're single?" she asked.

"At the present time, yes. I'm hoping to change that shortly." He smiled as he took her in his arms. "We could take this slower. There's no rush."

Marnie was thinking about how hot and bothered her body was and didn't agree. "Well, let's see how it goes," she murmured.

As they lay in bed side by side, Marnie thought how nice it was to be next to a real person and not a memory. Chris rolled over on top of her, supporting his weight on his elbows. She could feel his strong lean muscles lined up with hers. He wasn't much taller than she was but just enough. He had said he was an avid rower and Marnie could tell. Strong but lean. Matching her runner's body perfectly. Every inch of her felt alive.

"We can go slow," Chris repeated.

Marnie gave him a smile. "I've always kind of liked it fast."

***

The next morning, Marnie lay quietly in the bed, feeling Chris's warmth beside her. She slowly got up and stretched. Something she had learned from the pups. Stretching was the best way to start a day.

Chris rolled over, and seeing Marnie smiling at him, said, "You know you have the best smile of anyone I have ever known."

"I feel like I've smiled more in the last forty-eight hours than in the last six months. Get up lazy bones. We have to figure out what to do with Gen's report."

As Chris pulled on clean jeans and a t-shirt, Marnie felt envious.

"I don't have any pants that will work for you, but here's a clean t-shirt," Chris said.

"Thanks." Marnie started laughing. "It must be twenty-five years since I've found myself in this situation. I'll take a quick shower and put on my new 'outfit.' I'll be out in a minute."

Padding his way to the kitchen, Chris took out a few items. He cracked fresh eggs, added some leftover sausage, and made each of them a delicious scramble. They went out to the porch to enjoy the morning sun.

Marnie thought how much she had missed a man cooking for her. Adam had been a great cook.

After savoring her contentment, Marnie broke the silence. "So, any thoughts about our next step? We now know that Gen's death is related to her research. Since all of the results seem to have been deleted—

even on Gen's home computer, it's up to us to make sure the right people get this thumb drive and take the appropriate next steps. It's hard to know how high up the cover-up goes."

Chris hesitated. "I agree with you, but I don't think we have enough proof. With the blackout at the lab, they can claim ignorance. We have a motive, but not enough data to convince the police."

"Okay, back to my question. What is our next step?" Marnie asked.

"Yesterday morning I called a friend, an investigator, to get a little scoop on the people at the lab. Savannah thought she would have some data for me tomorrow afternoon."

"Savannah, huh. I hope she's sixty-five and married to her work."

"Yeah, not quite. But she is quite good."

"So, this morning we should eliminate other motives for her murder. Just to help nudge the police along. Who benefits from Gen's death? I don't know who is in her will but let's assume no one particularly benefits. She wasn't married, she didn't have any kids, and she wasn't that close to her brother and sister. They would be unlikely to know how to orchestrate a murder from Iowa, especially since they might not benefit. Garrett might be the beneficiary, but no, I can't go there. I know he loved her."

Chris started playing along. "If not inheritance, then a hate crime? Did anyone know she was transsexual? It seems like a pretty tightly held secret until after her death."

"Yeah, and as far as I know, she wasn't hanging out with the LGBTQ crowd," Marnie agreed. "The most likely person to benefit is someone at her lab, someone who didn't want her research released. Or maybe, someone who would gain an advantage if she wasn't working there? If we consider that the person who committed the murder might've been getting paid, the question remains, who would orchestrate it?"

Chris nodded in agreement. "The lab is the key. Hopefully, Savannah will have some new angles for us to look at. What should we do today?"

"I need to get my dogs and go for a morning walk. With the help of their grandmother, Nancy, Louise's kids, Noah and Cora, are going to start walking them after school. Louise and I are going to have another girl's night out."

Chris smiled. "Sounds like fun. I'll head to the newspaper this afternoon and get a preliminary article out about Dr. Drake's murder. Maybe it will flush out some information. I wonder if we shouldn't rest a bit more before starting our activities. It looks like we might be busy for a few days."

Marnie answered his smile. "I do feel a little tired after that delicious breakfast." She wandered back to the bedroom, with Chris following.

***

With the noise of construction at his house fading into the background, Chris and Marnie headed to her little cottage. The day promised to be warm, but it still held a hint of the morning's freshness. As they pulled up to Marnie's, Chris realized they were neighbors. Not that Galveston was very big, but this was close even for a town of 50,000. He admired the little green house tucked into the row of older homes.

"How did you find this place?" he asked.

"How does anyone find anything?" Marnie said. "The internet. I felt like I recognized it. I used to walk my daughter, Ellie Jean, up and down this neighborhood. We lived closer to the hospital but not so far that I couldn't walk these streets."

By this time, the dogs were barking relentlessly.

"We better go in before they come through the window."

Harlee and Jack greeted Chris like a long-lost friend and ran around the furniture. Jack's tail was going around in circles so fast he looked like a helicopter about to take off. Chris asked if this is what Marnie meant by well-trained.

She reached down to pet Harlee. "They're trained in the things I care about. I started off trying to train them not to get on the furniture but Adam, my husband, who had never had dogs in the house, liked to pet them on the couch in the evening. I despaired teaching them they were welcome on the furniture only when invited."

She shrugged. "I don't care too much about excessively nice things. Couches are replaceable. I was clear to the owner of this cottage that I would replace anything damaged.

Chris bent down to give both dogs some pets and looked up at Marnie. "I feel like I need to know a little bit more about your life. The oblique references to a husband and a daughter make me nervous."

"Sorry. My husband died last spring in an accident. My daughter is twenty and studying abroad this year. She'll probably come for a visit this winter." Grief was etched on Marnie's face.

Chris took a deep breath. "I'm sorry for your loss," he said.

Marnie gave a weak smile. "I can't really talk too much about it." She bustled around as an excuse to compose herself. "Let's take these puppies for a walk."

"I know some hikes on the bay side at Galveston Island State Park that allow dogs," Chris said.

"I like the plan. Let me get into my own clothes and we can head out. We can pick up lunch after we tire these guys out. I'll text Louise and tell her that we found the thumb drive and what's on it."

After a short drive down Galveston Island, they watched the dogs frolic in the surf. Looking at bits of tar stuck to the dogs, Marnie began thinking that what she most needed to find was a dog spa somewhere close by. She also thought she was way too smitten with Chris Hill. She didn't know anything about him. *How old was he? Had he ever been married?* She thought about dancing around these subjects. *Shit, I'll just be myself and ask outright.*

"Hey Chris, I feel like I've told you some basics of my life, but I don't know anything about you. Which is my way of saying, spill your beans."

"Okay, sounds fair," Chris said. "I'm forty-two and grew up here, went to the local high school. My family has worked at or owned the newspaper in Galveston since it was founded. My dad discouraged me from staying in the business since the digital age has been hard on small newspapers. I went to the University of Texas in Austin and dutifully took some computer science classes. But my interest in technology only extended to improving the newspaper."

"What did you do after college?"

Chris smiled. "My dad gave up on me doing something else when I moved back to Galveston and became a reporter. Over the last twenty years, I've been slowly taking control of the paper and working to make it relevant to both the local population and to the state of Texas. Trying, anyway."

More self-consciously now, he went on.

"I've had several long-term relationships but am pretty married to the paper and few women want to play second fiddle. I will confess that turning forty makes a man think about the future and where a family would fit in."

"Oh whoa," Marnie protested. "I wasn't looking for a marriage proposal. But if you haven't guessed, I'm a rather intense person. Falling into bed with a stranger really isn't my style."

She looked away and bent down to pick up a shell before continuing.

"Which is something I clearly needed and enjoyed. I guess I want to make sure that our relationship isn't complicating your other life. I don't want to be cornered by someone telling me something 'for my own good' or by an angry—and armed—girlfriend."

"Oh, I can't swear that those situations won't happen, but I'm a straight shooter. No current attachments." He took her hand and went on. "I'm an employed man with my own teeth and I've been told that's the going requirement on a dating app these days."

Marnie grinned. "I haven't had the pleasure of consulting a dating app but it's nice to know there are rules. Okay, what about hobbies besides breaking and entering Level 4 labs?"

Chris thought a minute. "I work out and row some just to clear my head. I play a poor game of golf to socialize with the important people at the Bayside Country Club."

"Oh, that's way more important than teeth for me. I love a man who plays a poor game of golf. I love to win."

They spent the rest of the morning talking about the news and whether a Democrat had a chance in Texas. After a walk, Chris introduced Marnie to his favorite food truck where they thoroughly enjoyed tortas. They took the pups to a local pet shop for a quick rinse and then landed them back at the cottage for their nap.

Chris said, "They're your babies, aren't they? I have to admit that they've charmed me. Jack is such a doofus. He's so big but incredibly funny."

"Yes, they are my *kids*." Marnie laughed. "Terribly more spoiled than my daughter ever was. I'm going to clean up and then sketch down what we've learned. Think about what we need to look into."

"I'll head to the newspaper and try to get a story out about Gen. Touch base tonight or tomorrow?" Chris asked.

Marnie's phone vibrated. "It's a message from Louise. She's changing the plans for tonight. She wants to meet sooner to talk about some information she got from the EPA. I'll let you know what we find out."

"Sounds good. Talk soon." Chris gave Marnie a kiss and headed out the door.

Chapter Twenty

October 6, 2018

Galveston, Texas

At Houston Hobby Airport, Allison Pedersen made her way from the gate to the car rental desk. As she glided along the moving sidewalk, she wondered if anyone else in the busy airport was traveling to identify a body. Her mind was taking her into uncharted territory. Once in the rental car, her GPS gave her the simple directions for the forty-minute drive. She pulled onto I-45 and headed south. The interstate transitioned into a boulevard shortly after crossing the causeway onto Galveston Island.

Before she could adjust her speed, she missed her left turn onto 54th Street. Seeing a cemetery on her right, she slowed to orient herself and noticed the above ground mausoleums and tilting monuments. A low wrought iron fence surrounded the cemetery. A few palm trees broke up the expanse of jumbled grave markers. She wondered how often she had passed cemeteries without any thoughts of the dead. Today was different.

She rerouted herself the few blocks to police headquarters. After the chaotic Houston airport, she was relieved to see ample, open air parking.

Getting out of her rental, she realized the air was

fresher here than it had been in Houston. Noisy seagulls were swooping overhead, catching updrafts in the sea breeze.

She stared at the metal detecting equipment as she entered the nondescript building. It seemed so final, so real. When she stated her business, a uniformed officer directed her to the Criminal Investigation Department. She had called Detective Sudhan before her drive from the airport and had confirmed a time for their meeting.

***

Sudhan observed Allison approaching the detective's office and braced herself for the task at hand. Mrs. Pedersen was of average height and delicately built, her blonde hair pulled back in a simple ponytail. She was dressed in corduroy jeans and a cardigan sweater that were a bit too heavy for early fall in Galveston. *Yes, from Minnesota.*

She met Allison at her office door and guided her to a chair. Though it was far from the first time the detective had shepherded a distraught relative through an identification process, each time was different. The department had an overextended chaplain, who was at the hospital for an injured officer. Knowing she would need an empathetic colleague present, Sudhan had invited young Briggs from Communications to help. The three of them sat at a round table in the corner of Sudhan's office.

"Hello, Mrs. Pederson. I'm Detective Sudhan and this is Officer Briggs. Thank you for flying down today. So sorry for the circumstances." Sudhan paused. "I want to ask you a few questions about your husband's trip to Galveston."

"Oh yes," Allison said. "He was doing a survey for the U.S. Biosafety Association at the Gulf National Laboratory. He does them occasionally for extra income."

"Do you know where he was staying?"

"He told me he was at the Third Coast hotel, but they said he checked out on the 25th."

"Did he tell you if he was working with someone?"

"Let me think. Oh yes, his partner was named Bert something. He said it was always funny to introduce themselves as Bert and Ernie."

"Did he mention where he ate or if he did any sightseeing?"

"No, we only talked once, and he laughed about a place called Fisherman's Folly Bar and Grill which barely had a bar and no grill in sight. Mostly, we just left a few short messages on our cellphones. He was only supposed to be gone for two nights."

Sudhan nodded. *A few leads to follow up on. Now for the hard part.*

Briggs handed a manila folder with photographs to Sudhan.

Sudhan began, "Mrs. Pedersen, we no longer bring people to the morgue and pull back the sheet the way they do on TV. We will be showing you photographs. As I mentioned, the victim sustained traumatic injuries that resulted in his death. The injuries are extensive on his face, skull, and hands. I didn't want to upset you with too much information when we talked by telephone. We'll let you know what you will see before we show you the picture. We can stop at any time if it becomes too much for you. Are you ready?"

Allison nodded almost imperceptibly and put on her glasses.

They started with the torso, front and back.

"It's hard to tell, but, yes, that could be my husband," she whispered.

Moving on to the man's legs and genitalia, she gave the same response.

Sudhan warned her that the next photograph would involve the face. It was of the neck, chin and mouth.

Allison gasped at the sight of shattered teeth and lips torn past recognition. Her eyes fixed on the underside of the chin.

"Do you need a break?" Briggs asked. "Some water?"

Allison was looking at a crisscrossed scar. "Oh god, this is Ernie. I used to joke that I would always be able to identify him with this scar from a series of hockey puck injuries. A perfect triangle. Oh god, oh god..." She started sobbing.

Sudhan stayed by her side. She nodded to Briggs and glanced at the Ziploc on the table. He stood, grabbed the samples for the forensic lab, and crossed paths with Chaplain Ross who was hurrying through the door.

The chaplain met Sudhan's gaze, nodded, and took a seat next to Allison.

Sudhan explained softly that the DNA results would be available in the morning.

Chaplain Ross introduced himself and assured Mrs. Pedersen he would be by her side throughout the rest of the process. For the wife and family of a victim, the trauma was far from over.

***

"Thanks for meeting me earlier than planned," Louise said to Marnie as they settled on the coffee shop's patio. "Remember when Mom said that she had a friend in the EPA? Well, they finally managed to connect. It turns out that Anne Hallam, Mom's friend, is in charge of the Environmental Community Access Hotline. They take calls from all over the country when people are concerned about an environmental threat. Anne was aware of two recent calls about the Gulf National Lab. Both concerned research meddling and one discussed Gen's murder."

Marnie leaned back in her chair. "Wow. Looks like we aren't the only ones kicking a hornet's nest. Did Nancy learn who called the hotline?"

"One was anonymous, but the other person said he did a lab safety inspection there for some other agency," Louise said.

"That must be one of the surveyors that Billy mentioned. I think I should call Ms. Hall and let her know what I learned about the research. Gen wanted us to get this information to the proper authorities. It was her final request. This is a start," Marnie said.

Louise nodded. Then she looked at the quiet street in front of the coffee shop. It was hard to believe that her quirky little hometown might be an epicenter of disease.

Marnie continued, "Let me tell you about the adventure Chris and I had at the lab."

"Adventure?" Louise met Marnie's gaze with a quizzical look.

When Marnie finished relating the events that culminated in stealing the thumb drive and a chase through the unfinished new wing, Louise's expression was full-on alarm.

"I think we should go see Sudhan, Marnie. We may be getting in over our heads."

"You're probably right because the chase by that mad man wasn't the end of the story."

Louise just shook her head.

"As we were leaving, not two blocks from the lab, we were stopped by a police officer. He checked us out and redirected us because he said the road was closed due to a sink hole. I'm not sure if he was suspicious, but luckily, Chris knew him from crime reporting for the paper. Hispanic guy, Bermudas, slicked back hair, José Somebody? When we left, there were smiles all around."

"Sounds like José Torres. I know that cop. We've been crossing paths in the ER for years." Louise thought for a minute. "He was at the scene when Gen was found on the beach. He turned up at her memorial, too. Definitely time to talk with Sudhan."

"Do you think she would tell us more in an unofficial

setting? Maybe have her join us for dinner?" Marnie asked.

"Maybe. Let's split up for a few hours. You call Anne. Here's her cell number. I'll call Sudhan and badger her to come to dinner. Let's meet at 6 at the Saucy Enchilada on Market Street."

***

It was 3 p.m. when Marnie got back to her house. *I think I'll try to track down the surveyor before I call Ms. Hall. Maybe Kathy will be willing to share his information if it's to help us find Gen's killer.*

Marnie tossed her purse on the table and dialed Kathy Walsh as she greeted the dogs with pats and treats.

"Kathy? Marnie here," she dove right in. "Listen, we're tracking down a new lead on Gen's murder. I don't have time to go into detail, but we think something happened during that safety survey Billy mentioned. I need to talk to the surveyor."

"Hmm. Yes. Gen left just before the surveyors finished up. Gosh, I guess I can give you the name of the one in charge," she paused, clearly concerned about giving out confidential information.

Marnie sensed her reluctance and added, "It's all we've got to work with right now, Kathy."

Kathy sighed. "Okay. Try to get in touch with Dr. Bertram Springer. He's a professor at the University of Oklahoma. I have his number." She rattled off the number for Marnie.

"Thanks, Kathy. This helps a lot. I'll keep you posted."

Marnie's phone call was answered quickly.

"Dr. Springer here," he said.

"Hi, Dr. Springer. This is Dr. Marnie Liccione. I understand that you did a survey in Galveston recently." She paused.

"Yes, that's right," Dr. Springer said. "Are you with U.S. Biosafety?"

"Uh, no, I'm not. This is more a personal than a professional call. Kathy Walsh thought you would be willing to speak to me," Marnie said. "I think you met my good friend, Dr. Gennifer Drake during your visit."

"Yes, she has some very interesting research we are going to use as an example in our survey."

Marnie took a deep breath. "That's why I'm calling. She was murdered ten days ago, and I think it was related to her research."

Silence came from the other line.

"Oh, my god," Dr. Springer said. "That is terrible news…"

He paused and Marnie wondered what he was thinking about. "It does explain some things, though. How can I help?"

"I'm wondering if you noticed anything suspicious during the survey."

He thought for a moment. "No, not really. Dr. Drake didn't attend the last meeting, which seemed a little strange. Her assistant was there. He might have seemed a little nervous but that was understandable if he was filling in for her. The odd thing for me happened after the survey. I can't get a hold of my partner. He was the one who reviewed Dr. Drake's research proposal. I'm still waiting for his report on it."

Well, that is some new information. I don't think I will mention the thumb drive right now. No need to put Springer at risk.

Marnie said, "I haven't heard anything about that. If I learn anything, I'll let you know."

"Likewise," Dr. Springer said. They exchanged cell phone information and said good-bye.

It was almost time for Cora, Noah, and Nancy to appear to start their new job of walking the dogs after school. When they arrived, Harlee and Jack were ecstatic.

"So, two dollars a mile. Here are your pedometers,"

Marnie said. "I'm going to leave around 5 p.m. to do some errands and meet your mom. After the walk, give Harlee and Jack their dinners and let them in the backyard for a bit. Then, you can leave them in the house until I get home. Thanks again, Nancy, for being the best grandmother ever. Louise and I appreciate this time together."

"Glad to do it," Nancy said. "Did you call Anne yet?"

"Going to do that after you guys leave. I spent some time this afternoon organizing my notes. I'll share with Louise this evening and have her pass the word to you."

After the crew left, Marnie sat at the kitchen table and called Anne. The bungalow was unnaturally quiet without the dogs. Her first call went to voicemail. She left a voice message and then texted Anne her name and connection to the Finnertys. Five minutes later, Anne called.

"Hello," Marnie said. "This is Marnie Liccione. Thanks for calling me back."

"I'm so glad you called. Nancy said you might," Anne said. "I understand you're looking into Dr. Drake's death."

"Yes, it has been ruled a homicide."

"Oh my," said Anne.

"Gen left me a thumb drive with her research on it," Marnie said. Anne didn't need to know the details of the lab raid. "It's pretty conclusive that we could have an epidemic of a virulent strain of dengue fever here that could spread through the southern U.S. Her research shows a clear correlation to rising temperatures."

"Can you get that to me? You can overnight it to my home address in Alexandria, Virginia." She gave Marnie the address.

"Sure. Is there anything you can tell me now?" Marnie asked.

"We're working under the radar with this information. I'm putting together a group of people I trust to figure out how high up the orders are coming to bury this research. I was afraid that it could affect some employees' jobs, but if murder is involved... Be careful."

"Point taken," Marnie said.

"I'll let you or Louise know what I find out."

The first of Marnie's errands involved making several copies of Gen's thumb drive and mailing one to Anne, one to herself in Colorado, and one to the Bay City Daily care of Chris.

When Marnie got to the Saucy Enchilada, the hostess looked up and smiled. "You must be meeting Dr. Louise. We gave her a quiet table in the back room."

Louise and Iliana were already sipping their margaritas. Marnie was envious.

"Hi, Iliana. I'm so glad you could come tonight," Marnie said.

"It's good to see you again. I remember your last trip to Galveston—a wonderful dinner at Garrett's restaurant. Tonight, Louise wouldn't take no for an answer. She knew Bob was on evenings."

"Louise always tells me how much she likes working with your husband," Marnie said.

"I do. Were you able to talk to Anne?" Louise asked.

Marnie relayed the information she had learned that afternoon. She told Iliana about the thumb drive.

"Thanks for the information. I agree that silencing Dr. Drake was the motive. I learned today that a John Doe is probably the missing surveyor you mentioned. You two need to be very cautious. It seems like some of the players in this game are playing for keeps. I think you should let the police handle it from here," Iliana said.

Louise and Marnie nodded in agreement but neither thought they would be able to bow out until Gen's murder was solved. Marnie steered the dinner conversation away from murder and epidemics.

After saying good night, Marnie headed home.

Pulling up to her little green house, Marnie smiled to see Chris's car there.

As she walked into the living room, the dogs could hardly get up. They were fast asleep on Chris's lap and by his feet. "The pups and I missed each other," Chris said. "I got the story about Gen's murder into the paper for the morning. Left hanging the mystery of her research disappearing. Maybe we'll get some leads. Then, I thought I deserved some time off."

"Great," Marnie said. "I have some information to share about the surveyors who came right before she was murdered."

"All ears," Chris said.

After bringing Chris up to speed, Marnie looked at the dogs, still sound asleep. "They'll keep in the living room for a bit," Marnie said as she took Chris's hand and walked him to the bedroom, closing the door after them.

Chapter Twenty-one

October 7, 2018

Galveston, Texas

Roy Williams went up to the 5th floor for his biweekly meeting with Dr. Thomas Thatcher, M.D., Ph.D., Director of the Gulf National Lab.

Dr. Thatcher's office suite was considerably more upscale than Roy's rather utilitarian space in the Insectary Division. The walls were painted a muted gray. Sleek black chairs and a sofa were arranged on a geometrically patterned Kilim rug in the anteroom. A striking floor to ceiling abstract painting hung on one wall. On further inspection, visitors with a background in biology recognized that it was a representation of a cell nucleus. Non-scientists saw a pleasing tableau of colors and shapes.

Roy knew Dr. Thatcher must have at least one administrative assistant, but today, as always, none were present for their meeting. He knocked on the door leading to the office proper.

"Come in." Dr. Thatcher's tone was customarily curt. "Have a seat."

Even though the meeting had been scheduled, Roy got the feeling he was interrupting something more pressing on the director's agenda.

"So, where are we?" Thatcher demanded, without

making eye contact. He closed his laptop and turned his attention to Roy.

Roy reviewed the events in the Insectary Division, including the recent visit of the surveyors.

"How is your team holding up after the tragic death of Dr. Drake?"

"We're hanging in there. It's been damn hard to keep everyone on track, even with the help of the grief counselor you arranged for us," Roy said. "Everything else is going as planned."

Thatcher nodded. "Anything else?"

Roy knew that meant the meeting was over. He was dismissed.

***

Washington, D.C.

"You can't make this stuff up," Anne Hallam muttered to herself as she had studied the organizational chart for Region 6 in her tiny office. A quick online search revealed that the regional director was Bella Smithers. She had previously worked for the George W. Bush administration, where she toiled to tone down regulations on the oil and gas industry. Bella was "unsure of the extent that humans impact climate change." No background in science. Sworn in December 2017.

Ugh! Luckily, Dave Yardly had stayed on. He started at EPA in D.C. in the nineties, had been in Clean Air and was an early proponent of wind energy. He was now stationed in Dallas as deputy regional director. *Okay, that's a start.*

By 7:00 p.m., long after the call center had turned the phones to voicemail, Anne had hobbled together a tight group of career employees whom she knew she could count on. She was damn lucky she could find that many. Since the election, 700 employees had fled and 200 of them were scientists.

She called everyone in her group one by one. Each call required several minutes of catching up and comparing war stories. All the locals agreed to a meeting on October 10th at Anne's home in Alexandria. She saved Dave Yardly for the last.

"Hi Dave. How're the Texas winds blowing?" Anne asked.

"Keeping our turbines turning, at least as long as we don't get a severe freeze like in 2011," said Dave. "What's up?"

"I've had some calls about your region concerning the Gulf National Laboratory. Anything going on there?"

"Funny you should mention that," Dave said. "The Dallas paper reprinted a story about the murder of a researcher down there."

"We had two tips on our hotline. One from a surveyor who just finished a safety inspection and one from an anonymous source which mentioned the death. Both calls mentioned concern for suppression of scientific data. I'm putting together a group of some trusted people to look into what's going on," Anne said. She filled him in on the meeting time and agenda.

"Count me in," said Dave. "I'll join by video. See you on the 10th."

***

Dave Yardly looked out his 7th story window at the EPA, Region 6 headquarters in downtown Dallas. He noted the construction of an addition to the Fine Arts Museum and a new hotel being built. These buildings overlooked the ten-block green space that had been miraculously created atop the I-35 freeway when it was routed underground. The cityscape was always changing.

He had come to appreciate the nervous energy of his adopted hometown. It had an optimism that never let up, despite the roller coaster economy which was driven by the energy industry. He was going to miss it. At sixty-seven-years old, he was preparing for retirement. He needed to make good on the promise he'd made his wife twenty years ago. She wanted to move back East to be close to aging parents and old friends.

His career had been satisfying. There had been ups and downs that were the natural consequences of a career in the public sector. *What's going on now, though, that's another kettle of fish.*

Chapter Twenty-two

October 7, 2018

Galveston TX

Chris and Marnie arrived at Bubba's Sports Bar ten minutes early for their appointment with Savannah. Located across the causeway on the mainland, on a patch of sand named Tiki Island, the bar was a five-minute drive from the newspaper. The clientele included some regulars from the nearby refineries, newspaper folks, and curious tourists. Outside, the smell of the Gulf bordered between earthy and dead sea life.

Inside, the smell was of fresh seafood and deep fat frying. The walls were a random display of aquatic animals, nautical paraphernalia, and Texas license plates from the 1950s. A stuffed alligator head wearing an Astros cap and a grin greeted guests at the entry. Marnie noticed that its tail was mounted above the bar, curled around a Shiner Bock. A thin young woman in Island attire looked up from her phone and welcomed them from behind the bar.

"Nice spot," Marnie said as she took in the eclectic décor and patrons. Her stomach growled in anticipation of some fried appetizers.

They slid into a booth by the window with a view of

I-45, with Galveston Bay as a backdrop. Patches of sea grass dappled the shallow water in a cow print pattern. The sun was still high, lending a silvery sheen to the still surface. Chris stole glances at Marnie, rerunning the conversation from on the beach. He grinned and was rewarded by her smile.

"I hope I'm not interrupting anything," Savannah said as she approached their booth.

Chris stood up to welcome her. She gave him a hug and a kiss on the cheek. He quickly introduced Marnie and the women shook hands. Big blonde hair, full face of makeup and a healthy bust line. Savannah looked as tough as nails.

The young woman behind the bar came to take their order. Three draft beers and a fried appetizer plate. Savannah pulled a folder out of her oversized purse.

"Okay, then," Savannah said once the drinks arrived, and the barkeep had drifted back to her stool and cell phone. "Let's start with Dr. Drake's research assistant, William Stanton, who goes by Billy. He's on the Gulf National Lab payroll as a half-time employee and receives a stipend from the National Institutes of Health, altogether bringing in a total of about $60,000 a year. With his now stay-at-home wife, he's let it be known that he would like to be hired full-time and get benefits and funding so that he can pursue his own research." Savannah stopped for a sip.

"He sure seemed broken up by Gen's death," Marnie added. "Rudderless, I'd say."

Chis nodded in agreement.

Savannah continued, "I did a little more digging. Billy Stanton hasn't always been an eagle scout kinda guy. He played a bit fast and loose with his undergrad funding and did some double dipping. The financial aid folks let him off the hook under the condition that he pay the overpayment back with interest. This is how his credit rating got trashed. I'm sure he'll be paying for quite a while.

"Then, there's the division's administrative staff.

All are full-time employees of the lab. Kathy Walsh is an administrative assistant to the division chief, Roy Williams. Ms. Walsh has been at the lab since it opened. From what my sources tell me, she's the go-to person to get anything done. Ms. Walsh is married to Glenn Walsh, a local realtor. Glenn has taken some big financial hits over the last ten years, especially after Hurricane Ike. There's not much appetite for vacation homes on The Island these days. It looks like he wants to diversify but if something doesn't happen soon his business will go under."

"I know Kathy pretty well," Marnie said. "There is no way she would jeopardize the lab's success. It's more than just a job for her."

Savannah raised her eyebrows, then continued. "Then we come to Julia Green, the division's IT support. I found out she's getting treatment at U.T.M.B. for some kind of blood problem. She has to get transfusions every month. She's a full-timer with benefits. She definitely needs those benefits. Apparently, she's been overheard talking about stem cell treatments that cost big dollars.

"Still with me?" Savannah said, looking up.

Chris and Marnie nodded in agreement.

Chris was jotting some notes.

"You're not going to need those notes, Sugar. I'm going to leave you this whole packet," said Savannah.

Chris looked up. "Old habit, I guess."

Savannah continued, "Maria Gallegos is the division's finance supervisor. She basically lays the budget out for Williams before it's submitted upstairs. Then, according to my guy, she holds onto the purse strings pretty darn tight after it's approved. Staff joke about how stingy she can be, even when it comes to basic office supplies. Maria is past full retirement age but still working full-time. It looks like she's supporting her granddaughter and two great-grandbabies. Lord, may that not happen to me!"

"Second that sentiment!" Marnie said.

"I'm leaving out a string of grad students and postdocs who are on the part-time payroll of the division and/or any number of funding agencies. Some of these organizations are…let me see," Savannah said as she shuffled some papers. "Yeah, NIH, already mentioned, CDC, the Environmental Protection Agency, several outside universities including Louisiana State, Texas A and M, Woods Hole Oceanographic… The list goes on."

"That's a lot of folks," Chris interjected. "Many of whom could use cash infusions."

Marnie nodded in agreement. "Good work bringing all the actors more clearly into focus. I'm trying to wrap my head around all the ways messing with Gen's research could lead to financial gain. Any ideas about that, Savannah?"

"Beats the hell out of me. You hear a lot about theft of intellectual property in certain circles, Big Pharma, competing government agencies, foreign actors. But that's above my pay grade."

"Thanks, Savannah, this helps. You probably guessed that this is about more than a headline story," Chris said.

"I'm starting to catch on. You two are working on something. I don't need to know any more. It's better that way. I've got more, but before we go on, let's review the terms of our agreement, hon."

Chris groaned. Since quitting her job as an insurance investigator, Savannah preferred to be reimbursed in a way that benefited the youth group activities at First Baptist.

"You owe me a field trip to the Daily headquarters for my middle school group and a week of vacation bible school next summer for the Pre-K group. A deal's a deal, Sugar."

Marnie burst out laughing. "Vacation Bible School! You better get cracking on your scriptures."

"I'm a man of my word," Chris muttered, and the three clinked glasses.

"Let's move on," Savannah resumed. "I have a few more lab folks to go over with you."

Savannah's report was interrupted when Marnie's phone hummed.

Chapter Twenty-three

October 7, 2018

Galveston, Texas

*S*econd day on the job. They had enjoyed an early dinner at a local burger joint to prepare for the responsibility. Nancy smiled. With Harlee and Jack in the lead, Noah, Cora, and Nancy were enjoying the crisp autumn day, a rarity in Galveston this early in the fall. She loved this island but living here had always been a challenge for someone who grew up in the Northeast. Smiling to herself, she remembered her conversation with Marnie.

"Oh Nancy, it's so good of you to supervise the kids walking my pups. Jack is such a goof, and it's impossible to get him enough exercise. These Colorado dogs don't know what to do with the waves of the beach. Harlee is pretty sure she's supposed to chase them. I think Jack would drink the whole bay up if it wasn't salt water."

"It's a great way to motivate all of us to go for a walk. Noah and Cora are excited to have their first paying job."

"Oh, it's money well spent. Louise suggested twenty-five cents a mile. I laughed and told her it was 2018. The going rate is two dollars a mile."

As they completed their second mile and circled

back to Marnie's, they passed through Darragh Park. It was decorated with a wrought iron gazebo and benches, which were anchored with huge chains to prevent them from wandering off. One person in a hoodie sat quietly on the bench.

Jack, totally out of character, started growling.

Nancy quickened her pace to draw level with Noah. That's when she noticed the hooded figure stood up and turned to face them. When she looked closer, all she could see was a gun pointed straight at Cora.

Nancy shrieked. The children dropped their leashes as Jack lunged at the person, getting a piece of his leg. The gun went flying and landed several feet away.

The man stumbled backwards, and Jack went for his face.

Nancy commanded the kids to run to the car, grabbed the dogs' leashes and followed the children. She clicked the car door open as she ran.

Once inside, she locked the doors, started the car and drove off—for once, not checking if the kids were buckled in.

***

Sitting on their family room couch, Didier and Louise were enjoying a few minutes of conversation after an adult-only dinner.

Didier was recounting a "sighting" for Louise. He loved to tell her about the birds he had been lucky enough to see each day, along with any details he found interesting about his clients.

"I was with my group today, three sisters and a sister-in-law, on their annual sisters' trip. We were looking north from Seawolf Park on Pelican Island, out to the Selma shipwreck. It's a magnet for brown pelicans and laughing gulls this time of year. The birders were more interested in the view of that half-submerged WWI concrete battleship than the birds,

I think. I was having a hard time convincing them that concrete could float…"

Before Didier could finish, they heard footsteps pounding up the front steps. As Chico dashed to investigate, the door flung open, and Cora and Noah ran in and attached themselves—Noah to Didier and Cora to Louise. They were both crying. As they were trying to learn what had happened, Nancy came through the door with Marnie's dogs. Her cheeks were flushed, and her hair was uncharacteristically plastered to her scalp with perspiration. At seventy-three, she was in excellent shape, and Louise was shocked to see her so breathless.

"Mom, sit down. Let me get you a glass of water. What on earth happened?" Louise went to the sink with Cora still glued to her, her head pressed into Louise's neck.

It was Noah who spoke up next. "He pointed a gun at us!"

Didier got up holding Noah, scanning the street outside and locking the doors. All three dogs were circulating the room, trying to figure out what was going on. Nancy had collected herself enough to speak.

"We were walking Marnie's dogs. Noah had Jack and Cora had Harlee. We were circling the park near Marnie's bungalow when I spotted a man—I mean, I think it was a man—sitting on a bench and appearing to read a magazine. He stood up when we passed, dropped the paper, and pointed a gun right at us."

"Oh my god!" Louise said.

"At first, I froze," Nancy said. "When he took a step toward us, Jack lunged at him. Noah let the dog go and I think he bit the man's leg. The man fell back, rolled over, and we ran to the car. Here we are."

By now, the dogs were settling down. Jack sat facing the group, looking from one to another. Noah climbed down from Didier and gave him a hug.

"I'm calling the police," said Didier. "We need to find this guy. Why would he threaten our family?" He dialed 9-1-1.

Louise's mind was racing. It wasn't only their family, but what was left of Marnie's family as well. *Was this attack related to Marnie's and Chris's trip to the lab?* She transferred Cora to Nancy's lap, found her phone, and dialed Sudhan.

"Detective Sudhan? Iliana?" Louise continued breathlessly, unable to assume the calm demeanor she displayed in the ER. "It's Louise. We need your help. My mother and our kids were just threatened at gunpoint. They got away and we're all fine now. Didier's on the phone with 9-1-1. I think this is related to Marnie finding the thumb drive and Gen's murder."

"Okay, slow down. Everyone's okay? Did they get a good look at this guy? Never mind, I'm on my way. Sit tight," Sudhan said.

Louise's next call was to Marnie.

***

As Savannah discussed the remaining staff members, Marnie, seeing that Louise was calling, answered her phone. The color drained from Marnie's face as Louise filled her in. She gestured to Chris that they needed to go and headed for the door.

"Oh my god! Are the kids okay? Nancy?" Marnie asked.

"They're all still shaken up, but yeah, safe and sound. We called the police and Sudhan. They're on their way. I think this is all connected to Gen."

"The dogs?" Marnie half sobbed the question.

"Don't worry, your kids are safe and sound, too. Turns out Jack was the hero. I'll explain when you get here."

Before following Marnie, Chris dropped some cash on the table and made a quick apology to Savannah.

She thrust the folder at him. "Take this with you."

As they pulled out of the parking lot, their car

churned up a white cloud of dust from the shells and silt. Marnie could feel her heart pounding. *Please God, not another tragedy.*

Chapter Twenty-four

October 7, 2018

Galveston, Texas

On the drive to Louise and Didier's place, Marnie was holding herself together, literally. Her arms were wrapped around her chest and she was rocking in her seat.

"Everyone's okay, right?" Chris asked.

Marnie seemed to come from somewhere far away. "Yes, kids, pups, and Nancy, Louise's mom, are all fine. This investigation has gone from the cerebral to the visceral. To threaten *them* means that whoever is involved in Gen's murder is vicious. Not that that wasn't obvious from Gen's death, but he or she is sending a message directed to us. It's not a problem of the past. It's a current threat."

Chris took her hand as she continued.

"Ridiculous how I hadn't sensed the danger involved. To think that Noah and Cora could have been hurt makes me sick."

Chris understood. He reported on loss and tragedy all the time, but it was someone else's loss. When you knew the victims, it was different.

When they reached the Finnerty/LaSalle place, Marnie was out of the car and up the stairs as soon as the car stopped. She swooped into the house and scooped up Noah and Cora in a big embrace. The shock of the threat had worn off and they were flushed with excitement. They both started talking at once.

"Oh, Aunt Marnie, you should have seen Jack. He was so brave. He jumped at the guy and made him fall down. We've never seen Jack so mad!" Cora said.

Noah said, "We would have been toast without Jack!"

Jack and Harlee were not to be left out of the excitement. They were jumping up and down. While Harlee was jumping all over the couch—much to Didier's disapproval—Jack threatened to knock Marnie out by jumping up when she bent over to pet him.

Marnie spoke to them soothingly. "You pups are okay. Settle and lie *down*."

Emphasizing the down, both dogs got off the couch and lay on the floor. Looking at Marnie, the pups army-crawled with excitement but stayed down.

"Good pups," Marnie said as she calmly petted them, and then released them from the position of down. "Quiet now."

Chris was stunned to see the dogs obey. Clearly, Marnie had done some serious training. He now understood that, as she said, the pups would obey when she meant it.

After the dogs settled, Marnie looked at Noah and Cora and said, "I am proud of Jack but also of the two of you. I'm glad you did what your grandma said. You kept your heads and that helped all of you come home safely."

Didier glanced up. "I've called the police and Detective Sudhan will be here shortly."

Chris put his hand on Marnie's tense shoulder. "Are you okay?"

Marnie replied, "Getting there." She reached up and took Chris's hand.

By this time, Harlee had managed to wiggle onto Marnie's lap and Jack was at her feet. The rhythmic stroking of Harlee calmed all three of them and seemed to have a calming effect on the whole room. Chris took a seat next to her, still holding her hand.

***

Louise watched the exchange between Marnie and Chris. *Holy cow! Those two have been knocking boots!* She couldn't believe it.

Deciding that she needed a few minutes to digest this situation, she took the kids up for baths, hoping that a semblance of a routine would help them get through the evening.

After baths, Louise and Didier swapped places and Didier continued with the bedtime routine. Seeing Detective Sudhan arrive, Louise met her at the door and thanked her for coming.

***

Sudhan stood near the door and said, "I'm sorry that the tragedy of Dr. Drake may have spread to involve your children. I hope that we can get to the bottom of it quickly."

"How should we start?" Louise asked.

"Let's begin with what Mrs. Finnerty can tell me," Sudhan replied, looking at Nancy.

Having regained some of her composure, Nancy outlined the event.

Sudhan turned to Marnie. "Any additional information since we spoke last night? Did you notice anyone watching your house?"

"I haven't seen anyone suspicious around," Marnie said. She glanced at Chris. "We've been getting some background information on Gen's coworkers."

Sudhan gave Chris a quick glance with skeptical eyes. "I'm sure your involvement wouldn't have any relation to breaking news by your newspaper. What did you learn?"

Marnie said, "There are plenty of people she worked with who could use some cash."

"As could most of us," Sudhan said.

"Yes, but these people may have had an easy opportunity to make some. Someone destroyed Gen's conclusions, and permanently silenced Gen," Marnie said.

Detective Sudhan looked at the room of smart, determined civilians. Chris looked thoughtful and observant. Marnie was on high alert. Sudhan had known Louise for a long time. She knew that the doctor could take command of an ER. The detective had seen Louise handle a mass casualty triage when a ferry had overturned in the bay. She didn't know how well Louise could handle a direct threat to her family. Detective Sudhan hoped it wouldn't come to that. It was her job to prevent it.

"I feel like we could all use a glass of water or some caffeine and something sweet," Sudhan said.

Nancy stood up. "I would love to have something to do. I'll leave the kitchen door open so I can hear. I need to call my husband and let him know what's going on."

Having returned from upstairs, Didier offered to help her.

"Let's find a comfortable place to sit," Sudhan said. She ushered the group into the dining room and took a seat at the head of the table. Sudhan gestured to Chris and Marnie. "Okay, let's start with you two."

Dining room tables were the best place to take interviews. Something about gathering around the table made people want to share their stories. If she had designed police interrogation rooms, she would have had such a table in the rooms. She set her phone to record.

Marnie and Chris related the tale of their last forty-eight hours, including what they had learned from Savannah.

"Gen's division has plenty of potential suspects if financial gain was the motive," Chris offered. "But who's paying? And why?"

As the group sipped coffee and ate cookies, Sudhan could feel the cohesion building and the tension lessening. She glanced at the dogs who were calmly sleeping off their busy day in the adjacent room. Her gaze traveled up the stairs to where she saw the children eavesdropping on the conversation.

She gestured to Louise and Didier, who smiled and decided that eavesdropping was acceptable given the events of the day. They would take their children to bed and answer questions after everyone left.

Settling around the table, Nancy chimed in. "Now that my nerves have calmed down, I can recall the person more clearly. Although the hoodie obscured his face, I could give a pretty good description of the person's general build and aura. My artist skills may prove more useful than I thought."

Sudhan said, "Tomorrow, Nancy, I would like you to come to the police station and work with a sketch artist. Is there anything you would like to add, Louise?"

Louise took a deep breath and looked around the table. "From what we know, Gen was murdered after she reached the beach. How she got there and who did it are two unanswered questions. Why it was done is a third." Turning to Sudhan, she continued. "I think a link may be the jailbird who was babbling about a woman in the water. The guy I heard Vance talking about in the ER. His arrest fits in our timeline."

Sudhan nodded. "I've scheduled an interview with Vance tomorrow."

"Also, I saw Officer Torres with Gen's boss at her memorial," Louise added. "He was at the scene when Gen was found on the beach."

"And *he* was the cop who stopped Chris and me after our visit to the lab. A coincidence?" Marnie asked.

Sudhan said, "I have no idea."

She looked from one to another to see if anyone else had more to add. "So, my next step is to locate Vance's jailbird and see what he has to say. I will be in touch with you tomorrow. In the meantime, I will have our patrol cars come out this way more often."

After she left the Finnerty/LaSalle house, Sudhan headed back to the police station. She wanted to get her notes from the meeting on the record. Bob was still on the evening shift.

Sudhan turned her attention to tonight's assault. As a senior detective in Galveston's fourteen-person detective squad of the CID, Criminal Investigation Division, she was already in charge of Drake's murder. This assault was most likely linked to it. She would be talking to the snitch, first thing in the morning. She better talk to Torres as well.

Chapter Twenty-five

October 8, 2018

Galveston, Texas

When Sudhan arrived at work, she conferred with her fellow detective, Paul Lacroix. He would start digging into Vance's background.

While Paul was investigating, Sudhan called Officer Torres in for an interview. Louise's comment from the night before had been nagging her.

"Hi José, I want to review the way you found Dr. Drake one more time." She nodded towards a chair facing her desk.

José took a seat and a deep breath. "Detective Sudhan, I've been trying hard to think of a way out of this, but a confession looks to be the best option. I was on the beach before the call came in through Dispatch. I'd heard chatter about a load of Chinese fentanyl coming in. Enough to ruin thousands of lives…"

He looked up to meet Sudhan's stern gaze as he continued.

"I thought this would be my chance to shine. My dream has been to become a detective. I've admired your skills for many years. I thought this could be my big break. I saw something that I thought could be the "drop." Just then the couple walking the dog discovered the body and called 9-1-1. I guess I didn't know how to explain my presence at the beach when I was off duty and still in uniform."

Sudhan stopped to analyze this confession. Although she understood José's quest to belong and to succeed, she was stunned that an officer would not be forthcoming earlier in the investigation. "You know that omissions in a report are a serious offense. I've also heard that you spoke with someone from the lab after Dr. Drake's memorial."

"Yes, when I saw Roy Williams at the memorial, I took the opportunity to chat him up. I wanted to see if I could do a little detective work, even though I wasn't officially on the case. He's a strange bird." José paused. "He intimated to me that a person who worked at the lab, a Billy Stanton, might have benefited from Dr. Drake's death. He didn't say how or why. I was going to dig around a little more. I didn't want to get Stanton in trouble on the word of Williams."

Detective Sudhan nodded. Galveston was a small town and rumors spread. "I appreciate your concerns, but you should have come forward with this information. We still have Billy as a main suspect. If you learn anything else, please let me know. We will talk later."

Sudhan knew she would have several more conversations with Officer Torres. He had crossed several lines. His behavior would require sanction. It could wait for now.

After that unsettling meeting, Detective Sudhan joined Paul. Within two hours, they had enough to start the jailhouse interviews.

First, Vance was brought into the interrogation room. After offering him some coffee and kolaches, always a good ice breaker in an interview, Sudhan started. "How is your stay at the jail going?"

"Oh Detective, always interesting. I'm so glad you asked to speak to me." Vance went on, rapid fire. "I need to tell you about this guy in here, fresh off an oil rig, who was talking nonsense about a boat and a woman who may be dead. Then, at the hospital I overheard some talk about Dr. Finnerty's friend coming into the ER dead. I think I can really help the police with this investigation."

Sudhan smiled. "Well, you already have. And what is the inmate's name?"

"Well, you know that I've got a bum rap pending against me. I found that gun on the beach and was trying to get a few dollars to feed myself. I didn't mean to peddle it to an undercover cop. I ain't ever used it. I had nothing to do with those robberies. I have no idea who owned it."

Detective Sudhan looked at Vance with a blank face. She didn't need him to get the name of the inmate. Only one person had been brought in from the rigs recently, Travis Jones.

"The only problem with that story is that the gun had no sand in it," Sudhan said. "It hadn't been lying on the beach. So, I'm thinking someone wanted to get rid of the gun and left it where you found it or gave it to you to fence. I need to know where you actually got it."

Vance thought for a minute. "So, look. I found it in a Dumpster on Harborside Drive. I was rummaging around looking for something useful. I don't know any more about it than that."

Sudan paused. "Well, thank you for your information."

"Hey, wait, is there some way of getting some help with my charges? Can I help anymore? I hate that a friend of Dr. Finnerty was murdered."

Sudhan had originally thought about moving Vance into Travis's cell as an informant but now decided he would never be able to keep his mouth shut.

"I'll get your cell assignment changed to be closer to Mr. Jones. You keep your ears open and let me know if you learn more."

The next interview with Travis Jones started as soon as Vance had been safely escorted back to his cell.

"Good morning, Mr. Jones. How are you today? Would you like some kolaches and coffee?" She'd heard Jones was still suffering from the late effects of opiate withdrawal. He was itching all over and having cramps and chills.

"Sure, Detective, don't mind if I do," Jones replied.

"It looks like you have gotten yourself into trouble on the rig. It must be hard to see such a well-paying career go away."

Jones shrugged. "Oh, they can't kick out people who have a little health problem like addiction. I just have to rehab myself and they'll be glad to have me back."

"Maybe. The problem is, you had a little trouble keeping your mouth shut while you were detoxing in our jail. You seem to have gotten involved in something more serious than possession of drugs. We've traced a timeline on a murder which occurred the day before you went out to the rig. The murder of Dr. Gennifer Drake. With court orders, we looked at your properties and bank account. It looks like you came into some money around then as well. Coupled with those facts, we're building a pretty good case against you."

Jones choked on the kolache. He started scratching his forearms. "Wait a minute, I just inherited that money. I ain't had anything to do with a murder on the Gulf."

"I didn't say the murder took place on the Gulf. However, we're going over your boat, Suzy Q, with a fine-tooth comb. I'm sure we will find some evidence. The money in your account was wired from an offshore bank. Not a typical inheritance route. Another thing that you might want to think about is that whoever hired you might not be so happy to have you walking around. You could be a lot safer here in the jail than you know."

"Look, I don't know anything about a murder. I was asked to take a heavy duffle out to sea and drop it there. The guy offered a lot of cash and littering seemed worth it. I don't know his name but could give a description of the man. He met me at the dock and gave me the duffel. I took it out to sea and dumped it. That's all I know."

"Let me get the artist here to get a picture of the man," Sudan replied, thinking she had him for the attempted murder.

She dismissed Jones and he was escorted back to his cell. Building a strong case against him wouldn't be hard. There was bound to be evidence on his boat and his DNA might match the evidence from under Drake's nails. The first link in the chain was in Sudhan's hands. Now she needed to find the man who wanted to have "a duffle dumped."

As Sudhan was gathering her thoughts and planning her next move, Paul came in.

"Hey, I thought you would want to know the DNA match was positive for our John Doe. It's Ernie Pedersen."

With this information, Sudhan gathered her team and shifted all resources to find the connection between the murders of the microbiologist surveyor and the laboratory researcher. It was unlikely to be a coincidence. Now, with a positive identification, Sudhan could put her foot on the gas. Both victims had connections with the Gulf National Laboratory.

***

Possessing current photographs of members of the staff at Gulf National Lab including the surveyors, Bert Springer and Ernie Pedersen, Sudhan called Jones back in the interview room after lunch.

"Good afternoon, Ms. Detective," Jones said sarcastically while he scratched whatever part of himself he could reach. "Hard to believe I'm missing my afternoon repast for another interview."

Sudhan let the attitude slide. *No need to assert my*

authority yet. "I appreciate your time. You were so helpful this morning that we now have some photos to show you. Please identify anyone you know."

At this point, she displayed a photo lineup of people including some random government employees.

After a pretense of examining each photo carefully, Jones pointed to Ernie Pedersen. "That's the man," he said smugly. "Talk to him, and he'll let you know who was behind the murder. My identification should help you nail him."

"Yes, I do believe we have that man. Unfortunately, we are unable to ask him questions from his current whereabouts in the morgue. What we need to know is, can you help us identify someone who was working with Mr. Pedersen."

Jones looked stunned. Sudhan realized that her earlier warning about being safer in jail had just hit home. Now he was visibly worried. He began to sweat profusely.

"Man, I had no idea. I met that guy in Fisherman's Folly. There are all kinds of people there. He must have gotten my name through Q-Anon."

"Well, let's show you a few more photos and you tell me if you recognize someone else."

This time Sudhan mixed various people into the photo lineup, including people who worked at or frequented Fisherman's Folly, as well as Roy Williams and Billy Stanton. She included Stanton on the chance that he had played some part in the case. She wanted to corroborate Torres's information.

Jones studied the photos. He recognized some of the regulars from the bar and the waitstaff but quickly zeroed in on one photo.

"I remember now. I've seen this guy a few times at Fisherman's Folly. I don't know much else about him." He tried to collect himself and regain his earlier swagger. "So, it looks like I've really helped you after all."

"Oh yes. You've been *very* helpful. But it seems not

absolutely truthful. We have evidence that Dr. Drake was on your boat."

"But…"

Sudhan raised a hand to stop his interruption. "And also, that your DNA was under her fingernails. It seems you were more involved than you admitted."

With the quick turnaround now available for DNA matches, Sudhan knew she had Jones. As she left the interview room, Jones was scratching himself again, slumped deep in his chair.

Chapter Twenty-six

October 8, 2018

Galveston, Texas

In the morning, Marnie got up with Chris and saw him off to work. This whole new relationship thing felt very strange. Seeing a man off to work again, and that man not be Adam, made her feel off-center. After Chris asked her about her plans for the day, she tried to gather her thoughts.

First on the list was a call to Ellie Jean and bring her up to speed. Marnie had to plan out how much she was going to say about Chris. *Might need to know how I feel before I try to explain it.*

Part of her was saying, *Just chill. This is a weird place to be—in the middle of a murder investigation. This fling is just that—for him as well as me. Who knows? At the end of this intense time, we might share a little kiss and part ways as close friends.* Part of her was saying that wasn't her style. She had no idea what she wanted now. She didn't know what Chris's modus operandi was.

What do I need to do today? Walk the dogs. Call Ellie Jean. Call Louise. Figure out what she's doing and ask if I can tag along.

The phone rang. Glancing at the phone, Marnie was relieved to see Louise was calling her.

"Hi Marnie, I'm going nuts. Can you join me for a walk before the kids get up? We're letting them sleep in and Didier said he would get them ready for school without me."

"Be there in fifteen," Marnie said.

Well, that was one and three on the list. She had until noon her time to place a call to Ellie Jean.

Marnie and the dogs hopped out of the car at the seawall. Louise was already there, staring at the Gulf. The air was still and carried a fishy smell.

Louise turned to Marnie. "I find myself thinking about how time passes and how people and places change. Didier likes to tell his groups about the indigenous people who were here before the Spanish arrived. Did you know that the Karankawas helped their invaders survive? Some historical documents describe them as ferocious thieves while others point out they cried at the drop of a hat and loved dogs."

"I must be channeling their spirits then, minus the ferocity," Marnie laughed. "So, what are your plans for the day?"

"I'm doing mommy/living chores today to keep my mind off things—grocery store, hardware store. I can't even think about shopping online. I need to keep moving. I'll pick up the kids and spend some time with them before they go to their grandparents."

Marnie matched Louise's pace as they headed east atop the seawall. "Are they okay?"

"Yeah, they were pretty shaken up last night, but will probably be better today. We talked to them about safety precautions so they're prepared, if, God forbid, there's ever a next time. Do you and Chris want to come over for dinner? We can order take-out. Since it's Friday, the kids are spending the night with my parents. Maybe we can compare notes and see what Chris learns today."

"Sure, sounds like a plan. Mind if I tag along on your errands? I could use a few things as well. Then, I think I'll go for a long run and settle the pups in for the night."

"Of course. Warning, it's going to be a dull outing."

"I could use some Louise time. Dull sounds good today," Marnie said, putting her arm around her friend's shoulder. "I'll call Chris when I get home and we'll bring over food. Somewhere in there, I have to give Ellie Jean a call. I'm a little afraid of that conversation."

"You'll be fine. Kids are resilient. What's the story with Chris?"

"Don't I wish I knew. This whole week has been nuts and then I fall in love again? It makes no sense but that's how I feel. Part of me thinks it's just a reaction to the stress of everything. Louise, I haven't felt this way since I met Adam. Chris's probably thinking it's all a fun adventure. I don't even know him."

With this confession, Louise burst out laughing and soon Marnie joined her.

After they caught their breath, Marnie said, "What a couple of goofs we are! Love and death intertwined. We could be in a romance novel."

"Or more like a mystery novel." Louise paused. "I just can't wrap my head around what's going on. First Gen turns up dead. Then, we find out she was being pressured to alter her findings. Next, Mom and the kids get attacked."

Marnie thought about it. "The information that Chris's investigator dug up was damaging to several people. I've wondered if someone looked into any of our lives how suspicious we might seem."

Marnie's phone rang. "Hello," she said.

"Marnie, this is Kathy Walsh. I'm getting a bad feeling. Things aren't right here. Roy Williams for one thing…"

"Slow down, Kathy." Marnie placed her phone on speaker so that Louise could hear.

"Roy? What about him?" Marnie asked, shooting Louise a meaningful glance.

"I'm not sure. He gave me the third degree about your tour. I've worked for him for a long time. He's always been a demanding boss, but now he scares me. He's agitated. And it's not just Roy. I tried to talk to his superior at work, but Dr. Thatcher brushed me off—basically told me to mind my own business. He said something about our mission at the lab being sensitive and sabotage could be dangerous. After our chat the other day, you were the only one I could think of to call."

Kathy continued, "With Gen's murder and then her missing research, well, I had to do something. I left an anonymous message on an EPA hotline."

"I think that was a good idea," Marnie said. "We've been gathering information about the lab ourselves. It seems like some powerful people don't want Gen's research to proceed. At this point, we're working with the police. I'll pass this information along to Detective Sudhan."

"Okay, I just wanted to warn you in case something happens…"

A little late for that. Marnie said, "Take care, Kathy. I'll be in touch."

"What do you think?" Louise asked.

"I think Roy Williams always gave us the creeps. Gen was definitely not a fan of his," Marnie said. "I also feel like we're getting close to knowing what happened."

"Let's tackle these errands. Then, you can talk to Ellie Jean and Chris. We'll meet up tonight as planned."

***

Chris had left Marnie's early. He needed to get to the office and tackle the two days of work he had ignored. It had definitely been an interesting two days. He already knew that the story of Gennifer Drake's murder was making news beyond Galveston. Dallas and Houston were reprinting his stories. The risks to public health coupled with a mysterious murder, the added twists of transsexuality and a possible cover up by the government, were all ingredients for a great story with his byline.

All of this rocked his world. But nothing seemed to have shaken his world as much as getting to know Marnie. He hadn't been this smitten since his first love back in middle school. He couldn't understand it. She was smart and funny, caring and passionate, and something of a stunner. But he'd had other relationships with women who had many of these qualities that didn't pan out. Where she thought this was going after her twenty years of marriage, he had no idea.

The newsroom was humming along when he got there. His administrative assistant, Ms. Willa Owens, wouldn't arrive before 8:30 a.m. She had been keeping the newspaper running for thirty years. She never came in before 8:30 and never left after 4:30. She said that, after her first ten years of working in the newspaper, she knew that the world kept turning without her overtime. A person had to take the long view. The eight hours she spent at the newspaper during the day was enough time to report the news properly. Which was important since printing the truth could change history. Her real job was to make sure that the nuts and bolts of the place worked for others. Chris couldn't fathom what he would do when the inevitable happened and she retired.

He had ninety minutes to go through his voice mails and emails before she arrived. After quickly checking the first twenty calls, he took a minute to write down information from a call from the EPA. Marnie had told him she was in contact with someone there.

Tom Assan, the assistant editor, poked his head into Chris's office. "Hey Chris, did you get the voicemail from a Bert Springer yet? He called three times yesterday saying that he had concerns about, let me see," he looked at a notepad, "'suppression of research at the Gulf National Laboratory'. I told him to leave you a voicemail."

"Thanks. Let me check on it," Chris replied. *This must be the surveyor Marnie told me about.* He clicked through a few more of his voicemails to Bert's message.

"Hello, my name is Dr. Bertram Springer. I have some serious concerns about activity at the Gulf National Laboratory. Please call me ASAP." He left his contact info.

Chris immediately called Springer, who answered on the first ring. "Hi, this is Chris Hill from the Bay City Daily returning your call."

Bert thanked him for calling back and launched into his concerns.

"I've never called a newspaper before, so I'm not sure how this works. But here goes. I'm a microbiologist, recently assigned to perform a survey for the U.S. Biosafety Association at the Gulf National Laboratory's Insectary Division. For some reason, my partner never finished his part of our report and now I can't get in touch with him. It's as if he dropped off the face of the earth. I would normally just relax about these delays, but my gut tells me that there is something wrong there. My partner's unfinished report was supposed to cover ongoing research into dengue by Dr. Gennifer Drake. I've recently learned that she was murdered."

Chris was speechless for a minute. Bert was definitely one of the missing pieces of the puzzle. "Yes," Chris said. "We're investigating the events surrounding her murder."

"Her death validates my concerns. I was impressed by Dr. Drake when I met her. I've seen online that there have been cases of serious dengue fever in the Galveston area recently as well as other areas of South Texas. You should know I called the EPA Hotline to register my concern about what's happening at the Gulf National Lab."

"We're also in contact with them. Is there anything else you want to share?"

"The director of the insectary division is acting strange. I've been doing these surveys for over five years and our clients want our reports submitted so their labs can be certified. His lack of concern is way off base. Am I making sense, or do I sound like a crackpot?"

"Not at all. What you're telling me could be very helpful. Let me get back to you after I run down a few new leads. Thanks, Dr. Springer." Chris hung up and turned to his computer.

By late afternoon, he was making notes when Willa came in to review some business details.

"I really can't deal with this stuff right now. Can it wait a day or two? I have some important leads on Dr. Drake's murder."

Willa gave Chris a solemn stare. "Of course, it can wait. Gennifer Drake was a friend of mine. She was incredibly helpful at the cat sanctuary and was in the process of adopting a second cat. You find her killer!"

As soon as she left, he opened the folder Savannah had given him when their meeting had ended so abruptly the day before. He quickly flipped through the pages they had covered together until he came to the last entry, a profile on Director Roy Williams.

"Holy shit!" he whispered aloud as he read Savannah's notes.

Roy Williams, MA microbiology U.T.M.B.

Salary $140K

Paid time off 21 days

Travel July 2017-June 2018 included three overseas trips to Europe and South America. Stayed in five-star hotels. Always with a companion.

Acquisitions—Collects antique toys. Mostly purchased at auctions attended by collectors with similar "tastes" i.e. toys that belonged to children of notorious strongmen.

Bottom line: Expenses exceed income by $100K.

Savannah added an emoji with three eyes, tongue sticking out entitled "Weirdo!"

"Holy, holy, holy shit!" Chris murmured. He checked his watch and realized it was time to join the others.

Chapter Twenty-seven

October 8, 2018

Galveston, Texas

Roy opened the door to his apartment at the Galveston Arms, an eight story, high-end condominium complex. His unit was at the end of the top floor with panoramic views of the Gulf and Galveston Bay, with floor to ceiling windows on three walls, and Danish modern furniture. No tacky seashore décor in his sanctuary. He felt a sense of relief when he closed the door behind him.

He poured himself a glass of Merlot and sank into his leather shiatsu massage chair and activated it. The alcohol and the vibrations helped calm his nerves.

After twenty minutes and a second glass of wine, he pulled himself up and went into his master bathroom to examine the wounds on his face and leg. *Damn mongrel!* The black fixtures were set off against a textured red wall while another wall was composed of full-length mirrors. This was his favorite room. Recently, however, he found himself looking away from his reflected image.

While Roy had previously indulged in long sessions of self-admiration, he now rushed from the shower to grab a bath towel to cover his torso. He especially hated to look at his profile with its early-stage spare tire. *Had Lindsey from Virology actually said he had such a "sweet droopy ass" the last time they hooked up?*

Having been blessed with a physique worthy of a Greco-Roman sculpture for his first thirty-nine years, he never bothered to exercise. Hadn't he been able to toss that sniveling surveyor's body into the Dumpster? He took a closer look at the side of his head where the oxygen tank nozzle had given him a nasty bruise. Another battle scar. He wondered if Kathy had noticed the makeup he used to cover the abrasion. Her gaze had lingered when he greeted her the next morning. Then again, he thought she'd been looking at him differently lately.

He rubbed his hand over the stubble coming in on the sides of his otherwise smooth scalp. On closer examination, he saw the majority of tiny hairs were coming in gray. *Damn! I'm about 24 hours from looking like an aging derelict.* He padded out of the bathroom, keeping his eyes averted from the mirrors.

His career at the lab had finally reached a six-figure salary. But it was in the 100,000's and not the 500,000's he needed. He kept his eyes open for extracurricular opportunities to make money and found them, as evidenced by the recent six figure deposit into one of his accounts.

Roy should be celebrating his bonus, but he could only do so alone. How do you explain to friends that you made a windfall by suppressing scientific research which revealed an imminent public health catastrophe caused by global warming? Who would be impressed that you were able to bring down a computer system and delete vital health information from a research study? *Okay, I'm impressed that I could do that.*

Taking a deep breath, he wandered into his collection room. *Looking at my treasures should calm me down.*

The temperature in the room was kept at a constant 65 degrees. The track lighting artfully illuminated his toys. His interest in antique toys had started when he first noticed Nazi memorabilia in a dusty antique store on a trip to Buenos Aires. He was admiring a set of toy stormtroopers when the shop's owner appeared at his side.

Sensing Roy's interest, he explained that the set had belonged to Adolf Eichman's little boy, Dieter, and came to Argentina with the child after the war. The dark history fascinated Roy. He bought the set and kept his eye out for more of the same.

Eventually, he was able to insert himself into the small circle of collectors with similar tastes. Attending "by invitation only" auctions and estate sales gave his international travels a context. He straightened Lucia Pinochet's Barbie Dream House on its special shelf. As a collector, what he relished was the rush he got from beating out a competitor at auction. He smiled as he saw the sledgehammer and wire cutters. Someone would be bidding on these tools someday. With a quick check on the lock of his gun cabinet, he switched off the light and headed to his bedroom.

Thinking about his last meeting with Thatcher, it had not been as positive as he wished. *I might have promised more than I can deliver.* His trips to the hospital hadn't brought the results he desired. The families of the dengue patients had no interest in heading out of town. They willingly answered questions from the county epidemiologist. This led to even more cases being diagnosed and counted. Gennifer Drake's research was gone but her pesky friends were still investigating. He wasn't sure if threatening the children had been enough to scare them off. They would definitely involve the police now.

His ruminations continued. *So what? They don't know who I am. I'm not afraid of taking decisive action. I have a plan.*

He remembered how amped he felt after dealing those satisfying, bone crunching blows to the surveyor. *God that felt good.* It had released some of his rage for the useless piece of shit. He could sense his heart rate rising as he reran the sequence in his mind from that night. His plan had worked. His mutilation of the body had slowed identification.

Reflecting on the excitement of that night on the beach, he felt the stirrings of an erection. Roy gave himself the relief he needed and then returned to his bar and poured another glass of wine.

He moved to the windows overlooking the Gulf and watched the darkening waves breaking on the shore. He would solve the problem of Gen's nosy friends. He looked forward to putting his collection of guns to good use. The chance to use his prize AK-47 was incredibly exciting. It was one of the first batch of rifles built in 1945 to fend off the Nazi invasion of Russia. Seventy years later it still worked like a charm. Its indestructibility and ease of use was the reason it was still the most common rifle in the world and responsible for a quarter million deaths a year. Thinking about that was almost too thrilling.

Roy calmed himself by focusing on his escape plan. He would be leaving town in twenty-four hours with a new identity and a stockpile of money.

Chapter Twenty-eight

October 8, 2018

Galveston, Texas

Dressed in her usual all-black, Marnie looked across Louise's deck at Chris. Hard to believe that twenty-four hours ago they had sat down to speak with Savannah. Since then, the kids had been attacked and they had met with Detective Sudhan about their investigation into Gen's death. A fog was beginning to build across the sunset.

This day has been its own rollercoaster of a ride. After her walk with Louise, she managed to get Ellie Jean on the phone. The year abroad was going well. After a few pleasantries, Marnie told Ellie Jean about the situation in Galveston.

Ellie Jean had been furious with her. She couldn't believe that her mom was risking her life playing detective. Marnie thought that Ellie Jean was being dramatic but had to admit the whole week sounded crazy as she told her the story.

Towards the end of their conversation, Ellie Jean had said, "Let me make this clear, Mother. If you get yourself hurt or killed, I will never ever forgive you. You may have survived being orphaned at twenty, but your parents hadn't courted danger. You get your priorities straight and let the police take it from here."

She'd inwardly laughed at Ellie Jean's firm tone. *That's a reversal in roles.* At the end of the call, they had been able to say they loved each other. Neither of them wanted their last words to be angry.

The bright side of the conversation was that Ellie Jean had been so focused on the events of the week that Marnie didn't need to tell her much about Chris. Which was just as well, since she didn't know how she felt about him or what to say.

With kids and Chico safely ensconced with Nancy for the evening, Marnie and Chris were waiting for Didier and Louise to change clothes and join them for drinks and dinner. They had picked up Thai food and were planning to sit down and share what they knew. Maybe try to figure out what they didn't know.

As Louise walked gracefully onto the veranda, Marnie again admired her for her ability to command an ER like a general. Personally, Marnie had been more comfortable with a calm office practice and was glad she had rarely been called on to start a resuscitation. The last one had been on an infant who was brought in for paleness and turned out to be in cardiac shock from undiagnosed hemolytic anemia. She was glad her training had kicked in enough to do the basics of CPR and that the ambulance had arrived in five minutes. That was enough emergency medicine to last her for the next ten years.

Didier came out soon after Louise. After taking a group of bird watchers on a tour, the only difference in his clothes from this morning, cargo pants and a long-sleeved tee shirt, were that these were clean.

They sat on the veranda to watch the sunset and have their cocktails of choice. Beer for Marnie, bourbon for Chris, and wine for Louise and Didier. The day's last light was casting a red glow over the bayous that coursed through the wetlands.

Louise spoke first. "Marnie, I followed up on your phone call with Anne. She said she was putting her team together to look at irregularities in the lab's

221

finances and see if there's a questionable money trail. We need to get all our ducks in a row."

"My day at the newspaper was very interesting," Chris said. "I spoke to Dr. Springer, one of the surveyors on site at the lab. He reiterated that he thought there were some irregularities going on there. His partner in the survey has disappeared, along with his report. Mr. Williams was inappropriate about the situation when Springer spoke to him."

Marnie added, "I spoke to Iliana today. She confirmed that her John Doe was the missing surveyor."

"And here's the biggest lead. Savannah uncovered information about Roy Williams's finances—they don't add up. He also has some creepy and expensive hobbies. He has good reason to be on the take," Chris said. "I think we can assume that Williams is up to his ass in alligators."

Louise added to the conversation. "Sudhan told me that she might have a lead on the jailbird as the murderer. But that alone doesn't explain who put him up to it. Maybe this information sheds light on the why. Sudhan said she'd keep us posted on the investigation."

Didier said, "I'm very concerned about the safety of us all. If it is Williams who threatened the children, he may be getting desperate."

Marnie continued to stare at the spot where the sky met the sea, thinking about her call with Ellie Jean and her own thoughts of mass murderers. They were rarely pegged by their neighbors or their families as "people who would do such things." On the other hand, Williams gave her the creeps. He was someone who would think about committing a crime only if he had an escape plan. Did that make him more or less likely to be a killer?

Just then she heard a click. Without thinking, she shouted, "On the floor!"

Everyone looked at her in astonishment.

Reflexively, she grabbed Louise's arm and pulled her down.

Chris and Didier followed suit just as an array of bullets splattered the veranda at waist height.

Didier started to combat crawl into the house, yelling at people to follow him. As they got inside, staying low, they each pulled out their cell phones and started dialing 9-1-1.

Another spray of bullets blasted through the windows.

They slithered in a tight group towards a small interior hallway bathroom, leaving four phones dialing 9-1-1. With the house on stilts, there was no basement. They felt silly huddled in a bathroom waiting for what felt like inevitable slaughter. Ellie Jean's words echoed in Marnie's head.

Didier said, "I think we need to spread out and see if we can get the drop on this guy or at least not let him take us out in one fell swoop."

"I'm so glad the kids aren't here," whispered Louise. Everyone was shaking and terrified.

"I'm going to leave the bathroom and go right," Didier said.

Chris replied, "I'll go left towards the living room."

Knowing that the current advice in an active shooter situation was to take a role in their own defense, Marnie gave a tight smile at Louise and said, "Let's follow our men."

At the count of three, they ran out of the bathroom in crouched positions in two different directions. Marnie stopped to listen and decided that the bullets were coming from the rear of the house. She pointed to the front of the house, indicating that they should head out that way.

There was an open front yard for about twenty yards and then the cover of some scrub and dunes. Louise and Didier had headed out the east side of the house, away from the setting sun. It seemed strangely quiet after the rain of bullets.

Had the shooter fled?

As they reached the front door a blast sent them

back into the house. Chris flipped over a large chair and Marnie and he huddled behind it.

Now what?

They waited again.

Chris grabbed a large lamp that had fallen by the chair. He stood up and heaved it far from them. A blast of bullets hit the area where the lamp had fallen. Marnie and he looked at each other.

"Let's make noise and maybe Louise and Didier will get away," Marnie whispered.

They started grabbing anything within reach and heaving it as far as they could away from them. After a blast, they would quietly move to a new spot and start launching stuff again.

Chris whispered, "I think the gun fire is getting closer."

"I agree," Marnie said. "Stay together or separate?"

"More targets are better."

Chris bent over and gave Marnie a passionate kiss, which seemed both out of place and life affirming. Then, he bolted to the dining room.

His path was lit up by a spray of bullets.

Marnie sat, paralyzed with fear. *How long has this been going on?* It seemed like an eternity but had been only fifteen minutes by her watch. How much longer before their calls and the sound of gun fire would bring the police to their aid?

Motioning her to move to the west exit, Chris indicated that he wanted to throw stuff at her current location.

Well, that is motivating.

After Chris threw something toward the kitchen, Marnie made a break for the veranda and a possible exit.

She left the house and ran low to a pier underneath it. Feeling safer with a large strong beam to lean up against, she started looking at the layout. Chris was still pinned in the house, but she hoped Louise and Didier had made it to cover. She couldn't spot them.

Inching her way towards the front of the house, she saw a flash of gunfire coming from the western edge of that area. Whoever was shooting at them was silhouetted against the last glow of the sunset but was shrouded off and on in fog.

She could barely hear the whir of approaching sirens. The shooter moved closer to the house. Different areas of the house would light up after a crash of some sort. The shooter was definitely advancing and pinning Chris in the kitchen. There was no way to stop the shooter without becoming a target herself.

Then, she spotted a dark shape emerge from the fog behind the shooter. At the last second, she saw the shooter whirl in that direction.

Marnie sprinted towards the back of the shooter and tackled him from his blind side as he got a round off. She heard Didier scream.

The shooter was down, but Marnie only had his legs. He started clubbing her with the rifle and then, as he wielded the barrel at her, she heard, "Police, drop the rifle."

The shooter raised his AK-47 towards someone behind Marnie. A shot rang out. The shooter lay still.

Marnie rolled over and stared at Detective Sudhan who was in a three-point stance with her Glock 22 trained on the shooter.

"Are you okay?" Sudhan asked.

Marnie took stock of herself and realized that she was bruised where the rifle had hit her shoulders but no other place. "I'm okay." She looked up to see Louise bent over Didier.

"Help me!" Louise screamed.

Marnie ran to her side. "What do you need me to do?"

"Give me your shirt and put pressure here." Louise pointed to Didier's left side above his spleen where she had placed her jacket to soak up blood.

Glad she still had her sports bra, Marnie removed her shirt, handed it to Louise, and did as she was told.

Louise quickly took Marnie's shirt, rolled it into a bandana and wrapped it around Didier's thigh above his femoral artery. Creating a tourniquet, she slowed the blood shooting from an open wound in Didier's leg.

Chris appeared with his own shirt wrapped around his arm. "How can I help?" he asked.

***

Louise reached up, expertly tied the shirt into a bandage, then pointed to an area on Didier's pelvis and said to Chris, "Take your good hand and put pressure here."

She moved to Didier's head and took his carotid pulse. It was fast but steady. *How long do we have?*

"I love you," she whispered, and Didier fluttered his eyes open. He seemed to blink a response and faded out again.

The front yard suddenly lit up with emergency vehicles.

"Search the area!" Sudhan yelled. Her officers fanned out.

Paramedic Brian leaped out of the vehicle and said, "We're here now, Dr. Finnerty."

They transferred Didier onto a gurney and lifted him into the ambulance with Marnie and Chris still keeping pressure on the wounds. A second EMT took over Louise's tourniquet roll.

Brian started one IV in Didier's left arm, then another on the right.

His colleague reported Didier's vital signs, "BP 75 systolic, pulse 130."

Brian squeezed one of the IV bags to speed up the infusion. Louise remained at Didier's side holding pressure on his wounds. Turning their roles over to the paramedics, Marnie and Chris backed out of the ambulance.

Louise heard the EMT calling a report into the ER. In her mind, Louise pictured the staff preparing for a trauma resuscitation. They disappeared into the night, lights and sirens blazing.

***

The second ambulance attendants came up to Chris. "Let's get you to the hospital also."

"No, I'm fine. It's just a deep scratch from some flying debris."

An EMT handed Marnie a blanket.

Covered in Didier's blood, Chris and Marnie turned to Sudhan.

"How did you get here so fast?" they asked in unison.

"I was on my way to bring you up to speed on the investigation when I heard the gunshots. I radioed for back up. I crept up the driveway, parking out of the way of the next wave of help. I got to the edge of the yard just as Didier jumped the shooter."

Looking at Marnie, she continued. "You were stupid and brave to tackle him like that. I was right behind you and had no choice but to fire. Hard to believe that twenty years on the force and that was the first time I had to shoot. Are the children hiding here? The dogs?"

"No," said Marnie. "Thankfully, the children and Chico are at Nancy's for a sleepover and my dogs are safe at home."

"You two need to go in the ambulance and get checked out—no argument. You can check on Didier and be there for Louise."

Sudhan directed her gaze to the two EMTs hunched over the lifeless body in the yard. They were not performing CPR.

"The shooter is Roy Williams, and it appears he's beyond emergency treatment. I'll follow you to the hospital as soon as possible and let you know why his identity is no surprise."

Chapter Twenty-nine

October 8-9, 2018

Galveston, Texas

Marnie and Chris rode in silence to the hospital. As her adrenaline ebbed, Marnie started to get the shakes. She wrapped the blanket tighter. She knew that the gravity of Didier's injuries would make survival touch and go.

"It's a good sign that Didier didn't arrest out in the field. Cardiac arrest outside a hospital has less than a 10% survival rate," Marnie told Chris. "I'm so scared. If Didier doesn't make it, I will never forgive myself."

Chris seemed unsure of what to say. "Then it really is good that his heart kept working." He paused. "Whatever happens, it's not your fault. You didn't drag anyone into this with their eyes closed."

"Yes, but if I hadn't gone searching for Gen's thumb drive, if I hadn't insisted Louise get involved, I don't think any of this would have happened."

Chris reached over and took her hand. "Who knows what would have happened. We involved the police, and still, Williams came after us. Now we need to be there for Louise and Didier."

The ambulance pulled up to the emergency bay. With the help of the attendants, Marnie and Chris stepped out of the van and through the ER doors. The noise and lights were disorienting. As the staff asked her questions, Marnie could barely hear or see them. *Feels very different from this side of the desk.* She knew her injuries were minor, but because she was associated with the tragedy that had struck Dr. Finnerty, she was given VIP treatment.

After being whisked into an ER triage bay, she was asked to disrobe and undergo an examination. As an eager tech was looking for a place for an IV line, she broke through her daze and grabbed her hand. "I'm fine, really. I don't need an IV."

She looked up at the nurse in charge and said, "I have some bruises on my back and shoulders. Nothing more. What I need to know is Didier's condition and where Louise is."

The nurse turned to her and she read his name tag, Bob Janssen.

"Didier made it to surgery. Stable but critical. Louise is cleaning up and will be in the surgery waiting room."

Finally, the name registered with Marnie. "Your wife saved my life. She saved all our lives."

A look of pride flashed over Bob's face. "Thank you. Let me get you some scrubs and a wash basin, and then you can join Louise. She needs you. It looks like Chris will need some stitches. He's in Room 8."

After cleaning up, Marnie went to Chris's room. "How are you feeling?"

"Sore, relieved to be here. What's the word?"

"Didier is alive and in surgery," Marnie said.

Chris reached for Marnie's hand. "Of all the crazy things I've been thinking about, I wondered how you recognized the sound of a gun click."

Marnie gave a sad smile. "Something I've rarely told anyone is that I hunted pheasants with my grandfather when I would visit during medical school. He grew up during the depression and dust bowl in southeast Colorado. Supplementing the family coffers with game was a survival skill. One day, a friend of his wanted to take us to a shooting range and show us his automatic weapon. My grandfather shrugged his shoulders and said okay. The click of the magazine going into the gun before its rapid-fire pops has stayed with me. My grandfather was not impressed. He said it was a good weapon for killing humans and not for hunting. He hoped it would never need to be used inside the U.S. borders."

Marnie gave Chris's hand a squeeze. "I'm going to find Louise."

In a corner of the surgery waiting room, Marnie spotted Louise with the hospital chaplain. She joined them.

Louise reached for Marnie's hand and held it. "He was in bad shape, but luckily never lost his blood pressure or had a cardiac arrest. One of our best surgeons was on duty. God, I feel so useless. Waiting is so hard."

"I am so sorry, Louise. I feel like this is my fault."

"Don't be ridiculous. If you hadn't warned us, we would be dead. It took all of us to survive this madman. Didier's going to make it. He has to…"

They sat like that for three hours. Talking some. Sitting in silence.

Chris joined them and then left again to get them coffee and food. They nibbled and waited.

At one point, Marnie called her pet sitter to take care of her dogs for a few days. Louise called Nancy. After she had made sure that the children were asleep, Nancy left Claude in charge and joined them.

About every hour, a nurse would come out and give them progress reports. Several of the bullets had passed through Didier's abdominal cavity. They had removed his ruptured spleen and repaired his lacerated femoral artery. They completed a thorough survey to rule out any other injuries. He was maintaining his blood pressure with the help of transfusions and IV fluids.

Three and a half hours passed before the surgeon came out. They searched his face for clues as he was pulling off his mask. The nurse near him was smiling and the relief in the room became palpable.

"He's stable and we're moving him to the ICU," he began, maintaining eye contact with Louise. "We may have to go back in, but for right now we feel the best thing to do is to give him a break. There is no active bleeding at this time."

The surgeon shook his head and continued glumly. "Getting sprayed by an AK-47 is not good for the human body."

Louise collapsed back into the chair.

Marnie had goosebumps. *Please, please Lord, spare us one.*

In unison, the group said, "Thank you."

Then, they gathered up their paraphernalia and headed to the ICU.

Marnie looked at Chris. "I think you should go and get some rest. You'll probably have a full day at the paper tomorrow. I can call when we know something. You can call when you need to know what the status is."

Chris gave a sigh. "I'll go after Sudhan gets here and lets us know the story. I won't be able to sleep. Cleaning up and getting to the paper are top priorities."

In short order, Sudhan arrived at the ICU waiting room. They had the room to themselves.

"Bob gave me an update," Detective Sudhan said. "We're all so glad that he's made it this far. The whole hospital is pulling for Didier. I know you have a lot of questions and I'll give you the story as I know it. I think you may have facts to add.

"So, my part in this story starts with Gen's death. From her autopsy, we know that she had been in the Gulf and was killed after making it to the beach," Sudhan explained.

"Louise's tip that there was a jailbird with some information gave us an angle. Today—or yesterday I guess—we were able to zero in on a Travis Jones. He proved an easy nut to crack since he had talked a lot during his opioid withdrawal. Apparently, his job was to load her full of drugs and dump her at sea. He hadn't counted on how strong she was nor did he calculate a lethal dose correctly. She awakened early. They struggled and she went into the water. Travis tried to say his part of the story ended there but from his phone record, we know that he made a call soon after the fight."

Sudhan paused at this point.

Marnie sat pale and quiet, imagining the last moments of Gen's life. The grief was almost too much. Then she got angry.

"Who did he call?" Marnie asked.

Sudhan replied, "Pedersen, the missing surveyor, now identified, but formerly a John Doe who was found in a Dumpster about a day after Gen was found. Ironically, that Dumpster is only emptied once a month during the off season. Just happened to be at the right time for us. Pedersen's face had been smashed and his fingertips removed. His wife ID'd the body a few days ago and DNA confirmation came yesterday."

Marnie said, "At dinner the other night you thought he was the surveyor. It definitely fits with what Dr. Springer said to me about his partner going missing. Has anyone talked to him?"

"Not yet," Sudan said. "On the list for today."

Louise asked, "What did Pedersen do after the phone call?"

Sudhan took a deep breath. "The plot thickens. Our other break came when a long shot match of a DNA sample from our John Doe matched DNA from fibers from a shirt found over Gen's face. Pedersen's shirt. So now we have Ernie Pedersen connected to Gen's death. Based on the trauma to Gen's face where Pedersen's DNA was found, the medical examiner says she was suffocated."

"Where does Roy Williams fit into this?" Marnie asked.

"I'll get to him. Pedersen's wife told us her husband

had some financial problems. When we told Travis Jones that we knew about his phone call to Pedersen, he emphasized the point that Gen was alive when she made it to shore. After Jones's phone call, we believe Ernie scoured the beach, found and killed Gen. We suggested to Jones that he had stalked Pedersen and killed him in a gruesome way to clean up his involvement in the case. He claimed no way would he do something like that. Then, he told us about his phone contact with a person unknown. He was supposed to destroy his burner phone but thought he might need it if things went south. He told us where to find it in his house.

"Through phone records, we were able to track the receiving phone to the areas frequented by Roy Williams. Jones identified him in a photo line-up as someone he had seen around. We were closing in on Williams and proceeded to get a court order to search his place today. As I headed out to update you, I received a call that the search had turned up some odd artifacts, including a cache of weapons."

Chris said, "Here's where I have information to add. Looks like we were narrowing the suspects down to Williams at the same time you were. A deep dive into his finances revealed some incriminating information. I was beginning to tell the group about my investigator's findings when a spray of bullets interrupted us."

A nurse came into the room. "Mr. LaSalle is waking up from anesthesia. He's not very alert but I thought Dr. Finnerty might want to come in."

Louise jumped up. "I can't think that I have much to add at this point, but Marnie, will you let me know what you find out?"

"Sure," Marnie answered.

Nancy and Louise left the room.

Marnie turned back to Sudhan. "The question is, who was paying Williams?"

Sudhan exhaled, clearly exhausted by recent events.

"I think those answers may be coming from other sources. My own role in the investigation will be circumscribed by my local jurisdiction. I, of course, will assist federal law enforcement as much as I can."

Detective Sudhan stood up. "I will be taking my leave from you for now. I need to get to the station. Please call me if I can be of any help. Bob will let me know how Didier is progressing."

Looking over her shoulder, she gave Chris a stern look. "I'll need to look at your notes later today."

He nodded.

After Sudhan's departure, Chris and Marnie sat silent for a minute.

Chris said, "I'm going to go home, clean up, and go to the newspaper. It's 4:00 a.m. and the day's going to be busy."

As usual, Marnie's mind had been planning what needed to happen outside of the hospital.

"I was wondering if you could ask Rosa to take her workmen and a cleaning crew over to Louise's house as soon as the police allow entry. Louise will need to go and get stuff for herself and her family and it must be a disaster. I'll pay whatever it takes."

Chris laughed. "Thai food is splayed all over that house! Excellent suggestion. Rosa will be thrilled to have such a constructive way to help her favorite ER doctor."

After Chris's exit, Marnie went into the ICU to bring Louise up to speed. She was relieved to see Didier off the ventilator. There were still tubes everywhere—a chest tube, a nasogastric tube, a central venous line, two more IVs, and suction drains. Louise had tears streaming down her face as she held his hand.

"They were able to extubate him a little while ago. He actually followed a few simple commands. The bleeding has stopped. Mom left to help with the kids."

Marnie said her silent prayers of thanks to whatever powers had intervened. She took her place beside her "sister" and sat there through the rest of the early morning.

Chapter Thirty

October 10, 2018

Washington, D.C.

Anne welcomed the group to the split level she shared with her husband, Ed, a professor of economics at American University. Ed was in the kitchen preparing a tray of baked goods for the group as Anne took drink orders. They were all energized by the mission that Anne had proposed.

Dave Yardly appeared on the screen as they gathered at the kitchen table. The dark hair and full mustache that Anne remembered had gone grey. He had the same intense eyes that softened when he smiled.

"Man, it's good to see your faces again! I feel as if I've been thrown to the lions out here," Dave began. "None of you look a day over twenty-nine."

The group laughed at the corny joke.

"When Anne called me, I thought it might be a set up. I kid you not. I guess I don't need to tell you what it's been like," Dave said.

"No shit! I spend my days writing press releases that make me cry," said Joann Damian, an assistant director in Communications.

Anne was very happy to have found Joann on the employee roster. They would need someone who could negotiate with the media.

"Y'all better get another drink before I tell you what I've been able to learn about our friends at the Gulf National Lab," said Dave.

The use of the second person plural by the Massachusetts native gave the group another laugh. What Dave went on to describe killed the levity immediately.

"It turns out that the director at Gulf National Laboratory was promoted to the post right after our current director was tapped to lead the EPA. The lab is a research facility that operates under the umbrella of the University of Texas. But this is important, funding is provided for operations by the National Institute of Allergy and Infectious Diseases. Stay with me. The NIAID is one of the institutes making up the National Institutes of Health. Naturally, Big Pharma and the hydrocarbon folks have been interested in pushing research dollars in directions that benefit them. Even before the climate deniers took office in 2017, industry had been, let's call it "incentivizing" scientists to join the administrative ranks of various research facilities, including NIH. The more things went the way the industry wanted, the larger the incentives."

Phil Tran, a scientist from the Office of Research and Development interjected, "How do you know this stuff, Dave? I mean, we're going to need to be sure what we're up against."

Sarah Corelli, from the General Counsel office, nodded in agreement.

"Because I was offered incentives," Dave explained. "Simple as that. After the offer, which I declined, of course, I decided to keep my eyes open. I don't have enough to take anyone down, but I sure have my suspicions. As you know, Region 6 is right in the heart of the oil patch. Our director, Bella Smithers, a Republican fembot if there ever was one, is too clueless to catch on. That's one of the reasons she got appointed."

"So, what's our next step, Dave?" asked Anne.

"We expose Dr. Thatcher, the director at the Gulf National Lab. He's been shepherded through the ranks by the fossil fuel industry, right along with our esteemed director. We take this mess from Galveston—suppressed research and murder—as far as it can go. We'll do it the old-fashioned way. We expose them in the public forum. I'm planning to talk to the editor at the Galveston paper tomorrow."

Anne took control. "Joann, we'll need your help on how to make these disclosures without sounding like the disgruntled employees that we are. We'll need someone with appropriate access to follow the money trail. And Sarah needs to be in the loop to keep us out of legal jeopardy. We don't want anyone labeling this as fake news. And you all know of whom I speak."

More questions were posed. Assignments were made. The group was energized.

Chapter Thirty-one

October 11, 2018

Galveston and Dallas, Texas

At the Bay City Daily, Chris had spent the previous day getting caught up. Tom and Willa had been taking care of business during Chris's physical and emotional absence, but responsibilities were piling up. Chris, Tom, Willa, the paper's lawyer, Marnie and Sudhan were now in a conference room awaiting a call from Deputy Regional Director Dave Yardly. When Chris told Sudhan what he had learned from the EPA, she had asked to be present in case new information about Dr. Drake's murder was revealed. Marnie insisted on being present as well.

As Chris waited impatiently for the phone call, Willa replaced the uneaten kolache at his place with an apple.

At the appointed hour, Dave Yardly called. He briefly discussed his credentials and welcomed Chris to verify them.

"I'd like to propose an exposé. An exposé by your paper of my organization," Yardly said.

Chris sat up straight and dropped the apple he had unconsciously started eating. "You have my attention."

Once the video and audio connections had been fine-tuned, introductions were made. There were two separate video link ups going on, one from Dallas and one from Alexandria. Out of sight of the camera, Tom was busy verifying the EPA players' identities with the help of facial recognition software. The newspaper had to be careful that they were not getting suckered. He gave Chris a thumbs up, and they were off and running.

Dave Yardly began, "We received two calls on our Environmental Community Access Hotline related to events in Galveston. Specifically, regarding the Gulf National Laboratory. One caller identified himself as a surveyor who had been tasked with inspecting a division at the lab. He was concerned that there could be irregularities related to the suppression of research on a sensitive, climate change topic. The second call came in minutes later and was anonymous. The female caller voiced a similar concern and went on further to claim that the matter was related to the murder of a researcher at the lab. I'm aware that the murder has been covered by your paper."

Chris exhaled. All he could say was, "Please continue."

"A group of us have assembled to do what we can to set things right. As I explained yesterday, this group is extracurricular and acting on our collective conscience to do what we can to stop the current assault on science and reason at the EPA. An assault that has been years in the making by those in industry and the political toadies on their payroll." Dave's cheeks were flushed. He hadn't taken a breath since he started speaking.

Joann Damian from Communications in Alexandria jumped in. "We have solid information that efforts have been made from the top down to curb, stifle, and suffocate scientific interventions to mitigate the effects of climate change on the environment. Operatives within the agency have been charged to silence opposition and to suppress research in the area. At enormous cost to human health and safety."

"How have these "operatives" been recruited?

Why would they agree to interfere this way?" Chris asked, somewhat incredulous.

"In the time-honored fashion," Dave continued. "Money and professional advancement."

"We want to build an airtight case when we present our conclusions to the leadership of the agency," explained Sarah Corelli from the Office of Regional Counsel. "We believe that the knowledge that the Bay City Daily is going to print an exposé will produce the results we want."

"What results are you hoping for?" Chris asked, aware that these people were putting their careers on the line.

"The resignation of the EPA director and a thorough house cleaning at the regional levels," Dave replied firmly.

"Whew," said Chris. The people at the table looked at each other in amazement.

Detective Sudhan was next to speak. "You implied that you could connect all this to the murder of Dr. Gennifer Drake. How is that?"

"Thanks to some incredible sleuthing by our colleagues in finance," Dave explained, "we've been able to track unauthorized 'incentives' from the level of the Director of the EPA to the head of the lab, a man named Dr. Thomas Thatcher. He has been granted the discretion on how to allocate funds to achieve the desired ends that we just laid out. So, essentially, here is where we stand. Our group can connect the dots from the top down to Thatcher. We hope the Bay City Daily and the Gulf County Police can connect the dots from the bottom up. Thatcher was paying someone off at the Gulf National Lab. Once we know who that was, we have an unbroken chain of deceit."

Chris and Sudhan exchanged looks.

Chris took the floor. "We have the information you need. The only wrinkle is that the person linking all of this together is a dead man as of two weeks ago. But the money trail is well documented. So, yes, we can put this together and would be happy to publish as soon as you give us the green light. We also have Dr. Drake's thumb drive with her research on it. We sent a copy of it to Anne Hallam a few days ago."

Chris explained the details of the murders of Dr. Drake and the second surveyor. They concluded the meeting by describing the bizarre and violent deterioration of the late Roy Williams, the missing link.

After the phone call, Marnie said, "I think we will get justice for Gen and, more importantly, stop these abuses from continuing. That's what Gen was asking me to do in her last letter."

Chris nodded. He thought this exposé would bring some solace to Louise and Marnie.

Chapter Thirty-two

October 14, 2018

Dallas, Texas

It was a crisp fall day in Dallas when Chris and Marnie stepped out of the elevator and onto the floor which housed the offices of the EPA Region 6. On their early flight from Houston Hobby Airport, the plane made a broad circle to the east over the Port of Houston. The ship channel was lined with refineries and teamed with tankers, barges, and tugboats. Chris wondered what his ancestors would have thought. *How on earth had sleepy, backwater Houston surpassed Galveston as the commercial hub of the Gulf Coast?*

Dave Yardly greeted them as soon as they entered the office suite. The two men shook hands. This was their first face-to-face meeting. They had been in close phone and email contact for days, working out their game plan.

"Good flight? Coffee? Anything to eat?" Dave rushed through the amenities, clearly anxious to get to work.

Chris was smiling at Dave's energy. "Good flight. I'm fed and caffeinated."

"I'll take some coffee," Marnie said.

Anne stepped forward. "Hi, I'm Anne Hallam. So glad to meet you."

Marnie and Chris each warmly shook her hand. "Same here," Marnie said. "We would never have gotten to the bottom of this mess without you. Nancy's so excited to see you after this meeting. She was happy to have a reason to come with us to Dallas."

"We decided to spend the night so we would have plenty of time to catch up," Anne said. "It looks like a beautiful day to be outside. We're thinking about a visit to the sculpture garden."

Dave indicated it was time to get started and the group took their seats. He reviewed the agenda.

"Let me go over the guest list," Dave began. "The most important attendee is William Oakes, Acting Deputy Director of the EPA." He then rattled off the names of five more participants, all from the uppermost echelon of leadership at the EPA.

"Why so many with "Acting" in their titles?" Marnie asked.

"The agency has been running on a skeleton staff since the election. The new administration cleaned house to make sure the EPA would be amenable to a 'business friendly' relationship. But the work of the agency didn't stop. There were reports to sign, invoices to approve. Those who remained were mostly pigeon-holed as acting until the new director could find loyal replacements." Dave escorted them to the conference room reserved for the meeting. Dave's assistant, Jarred, helped Chris load his presentation. The title blandly announced "2018 Initiative for Biosafety in the U.S. Energy Industry: Loosening Regulations."

The intern was excused from the room and instructed to meet the attendees in the reception area and direct them to the meeting.

"This is a closed-door session, Jarred. No one else comes or goes without my okay. I'll ask you to wait outside," Dave said.

With Jarred out of earshot, Dave chuckled. "Nice title, Chris."

Promptly at 10:00 a.m., the participants began

arriving one by one. Dave introduced them to Chris Hill. Marnie assumed the role of assistant and took a seat next to Chris.

Acting Deputy Director William Oakes took his place at the head of the table. He gave Dave and Chris appraising looks and nodded in what seemed to be a supportive fashion. He cleared his throat and brought the meeting to order. "I want Dave to use the next few minutes to bring the group up to speed on several issues of grave importance. What you are about to hear is going to make waves, big waves, at the agency. The information was too sensitive to share electronically, so you will be hearing this for the first time."

Dave explained that he was prepared, with the help of Mr. Chris Hill, the editor of the Bay City Daily, to present a proposed exposé with the potential of changing the current course of the EPA.

"Chris will be taking you through the materials," Dave said.

Chris hoped he looked more confident than he felt. He advanced the slide show from the "2018 Initiative, etc." to a mockup of the front page of his newspaper with the headline:

GULF NATIONAL LAB IMPLICATED IN
SUPPRESSION OF CLIMATE CHANGE
RESEARCH. DIRECTOR RESIGNS.

Murmurs of surprise arose from the group in attendance. When they turned their attention back to him, Chris began speaking.

"Thank you, Dave. And many thanks to all of you for taking the time to assemble here today. What you see on the screen is the headline of what we have been calling Version One of our exposé. Let me summarize what happened in Galveston between September 23 and October 9 of this year."

With that, he led them through the gruesome confluence of events that resulted in the attempted suppression of climate change research and the murder of its author, the murder of the unscrupulous surveyor, and a police shootout that took the life of corrupt Gulf National Lab Insectary Division Chief, Roy Williams.

Chris continued with the next slide which read:

"The investigation uncovered evidence that Mr. Williams was being paid by the director of the lab to destroy research with implications for climate change. A member of his division was on the verge of publishing startling research on the spread of a deadly tropical disease in the southern U.S. as a result of global warming."

There was a knock on the door. Dave opened it a few inches and spoke to Jarred who escorted a late arrival to the meeting room.

Chris replaced his slide with the "2018 Initiative…"

Dave motioned the late arrival to take the remaining seat at the round conference table.

"Sorry I'm late. My secretary had this meeting starting at 10:30." He stated somewhat gruffly.

The group turned their attention to the well-dressed sixtyish gentleman with an impressive head of silver hair. He was clearly put off by the perceived miscommunication.

"Don't worry, I'll catch up. Relaxing biosafety regulations, right?" said the late arrival.

"Let me introduce Dr. Thomas Thatcher, Director of the Gulf National Laboratory," Dave said. "Why don't you get back to where we were, Chris?"

The "2018 Initiative…" was replaced by the front-page mockup. It took Thatcher a few seconds to realize that the slide had advanced. As he was reading it, those in attendance turned from the screen to Thatcher. The slide directly implicated him.

"What is this? I'm not going to listen to this crap," Thatcher barked. He stood up ready to go.

All eyes were on him.

"I think you better stay right where you are until we're done here." Dave motioned to the two security guards, who, as instructed, were monitoring the door after the arrival of Thatcher.

Chris proceeded. "As I said, there is a Version Two." He advanced to a second headline:

EPA LEADERSHIP DIRECTLY RESPONSIBLE FOR SUPPRESSION OF CLIMATE CHANGE RESEARCH. MONEY TRAIL AND PAYOFFS LEAD FROM GNL SCANDAL TO DIRECTOR OF THE AGENCY.

Dave took over the meeting at that point. He explained how two hotline calls had set a series of events in motion. With the urging of concerned EPA employees and some inventive financial audits, he was ready to go on the record with the assertion that the director of the EPA had a network in place from the top down charged with suppressing climate change research.

Dave continued, "Then, from the bottom up, the Bay City Daily and local law enforcement have connected the dots in Galveston to implicate Dr. Thatcher in the payoffs to former division chief, Roy Williams."

All eyes returned to Thatcher.

Chris watched the man.

He was unrecognizable from the cocky, self-assured man who blamed his secretary for his tardiness. The tan he had acquired from his daily beach walks had been replaced by a grey pallor. He was visibly sweating.

Director Oakes poured Thatcher a glass of water. The rest of the meeting played out like a Greek tragedy in front of the audience of career EPA professionals in attendance.

Thatcher sang like a canary. He readily accepted and signed an agreement for an offer of early retirement with no indictment in exchange for names, dates, and account information regarding the payoffs. He swore he had no personal knowledge of the murders.

Chris explained to the group that the police investigation could not implicate Thatcher in the murders. It appeared that Williams and his henchmen had gone rogue. After another twenty minutes, Thatcher was allowed to slink off, followed by angry and mystified stares.

As had been previously worked out between Chris, Dave Yardly, and Director Oakes, the paper would only publish Version One of the exposé if the Director of the EPA and those on his unofficial payroll were forced to resign. The EPA would have an opportunity to clear the rot from its ranks and get back to its original mission. Eliminating the corruption at the top of the hierarchy would minimize the damage done to the integrity of the Gulf National Lab. As far as the public was concerned, that would be the extent of it.

The group approved a strategy and timeline to bring this to fruition. Initially shocked by the degree of transgressions, they were elated about the leverage they now had to turn the EPA in a different direction.

Chris and Marnie gathered their few things together and said their good-byes to Anne. They were taking an earlier flight back to Houston. Chris needed to get to the newspaper. He knew he and Dave would be in close contact over the next several days.

Chapter Thirty-three

October 24, 2018

Dallas, Texas

At 7 p.m., Dave Yardly was gazing out his office window. This time he was watching the sunset, eyes trained west over the urban sprawl as commuters drove home on the North Dallas Expressway. *All those cars. Emissions continued to rise when fuel efficiency regulations were relaxed.*

Nonetheless, he smiled as he contemplated the evening's planned conference call to Anne and the gang in D.C. It had been a good day. The staff was buoyed by the unexpected and rapid-fire changes. Morale was on the upswing. He turned down an invitation to join his staff at happy hour to celebrate. He had another meeting to attend.

Dave glanced at his notes. He wanted to present the group a blow-by-blow of the meeting and events that had resulted from their efforts. The Director's resignation had been made public that same afternoon.

In our unlikely, uncompensated and unsung way, we made history. The Director of the EPA's resignation made headlines on all the news outlets. It came as no surprise as he had been under intense scrutiny and criticism for his lavish expenditures.

Most people following the story of his downfall

didn't know that he was joined by an exodus of like-minded scoundrels. They were the lackeys he had appointed to carry out his Make American Energy Great Again agenda. Only Anne's group, the editor of the Bay City Daily, and those in attendance at the Region 6 meeting would know the full story.

Dave logged into the meeting already in progress in Anne's dining room. When his face appeared on the screen, it was met with applause and lifted glasses of champagne. He uncorked the bottle of Dom Perignon that he had saved for the occasion. The pop was met by even more applause. Dave had to endure an off-key rendition of "For He's a Jolly Good Fellow." Then, he told the rowdy group the details of the meeting that had restored the integrity of the organization—the organization to which they had dedicated their professional lives.

Toasts were offered all around. The loudest applause was saved for the toast to Anne Hallam. Their success would have been impossible without her courage and determination.

***

Galveston, Texas

Didier's recovery was slow but steady. He had required only one surgery after the initial admission to the hospital. After a week, he was moved out of the ICU. The children had been able to see him and, as their anxiety had lessened, they had been able to return to school. On the day of discharge, Louise was as eager to get him home as he was to go there. With Nancy's backup, Louise had been working extra shifts so that she could be off for two weeks after his return. She had been able to check on Didier during work time thanks to her supportive partners. She joked that she was a much better doctor than nurse but was up for some on-the-job training. Life was getting back to normal, even if it was a new normal.

After the violence that had threatened her husband, children and mother, Louise was slowly regaining her equilibrium. She had to steady her nerves once back in the ER to deal with the violent tragedies that struck her patients. She knew it would take time. She counted her blessings.

As autumn progressed, the number of dengue cases dropped off. Louise was gratified to learn that her patient, Diego Jimenez, had survived his illness and was on the long road to recovery. Others had not been so fortunate.

***

Marnie was alternating between being at the hospital, assisting Chris with the fallout from the investigation, and helping with the Finnerty/LaSalle house restoration. Rosa's crew had made some changes to the layout to help Didier when he went home.

Her calls to Ellie Jean had been somber but not filled with tension. As the EPA stories came out, Ellie Jean was gratified and impressed that her mother had helped uncover such a horrendous abuse of power.

On her walks with the pups, Marnie had been able to think about a future with Chris. Many obstacles were in their paths—mostly that they had firm anchors in different cities. But there seemed no reason to rush to a decision either way. She stopped in her tracks, gazing at the still Gulf, when she realized she was thinking about the *future*. A concept that had eluded her since she'd lost Adam. Missing Adam was like a physical ache, but its intensity was lessening with time.

Chris had been working around the clock to get the story straight and deal with the news that had spun off as a result of the exposé. She had flown to New York with him when he was invited to appear on some of the national morning talk shows. Upon their return, Chris had decided to take his job on the road and drive back to Colorado with Marnie. She needed to head home to put her garden to bed and get her house ready for winter. Gen's death had made her think that life is short and needed to be lived fully. Another gift from her wise friend? Gen had always been helpful in sorting through emotions and commitments. Marnie found herself thinking WWGD—*what would Gen do*—about Chris and her. There still seemed to be answers coming from that source.

***

Louise parked in front of Marnie's house. She was pleased to see her friend ready and sitting on the porch. One dog on her lap and the other at her feet.

"I thought you'd still be packing," Louise said as she navigated the uneven stone steps leading to the porch.

"Nope. I woke up early and got to work. It was hard to fit it all in the car since I needed to make room for Chris. I plan to ship some of the mementos I'd gathered. Garrett insisted that I take anything I wanted from Gen's closet." Marnie herded the dogs inside and grabbed her purse and the package wrapped in brown paper.

"It's been a wild ride, hasn't it?" Louise asked, pulling the car into traffic.

Marnie nodded. Her eyes welled up again. "We did our best by Gen."

"I'm glad Billy Stanton was finally cleared. He was in a tough spot with his home situation and working under Roy," Louise said.

She parked in the lab's visitor's lot. As they

approached the security check, Louise put a smile on her face.

"This place will forever give me the creeps," Marnie said. "I hope to never come back here after today."

Kathy met them at the door. Hugs all around. "Let's go to my office. Billy's waiting for us there. I can't tell you how life in the Insectary Division has improved since Roy, er, left. We have a new interim chief, and we hope to keep her." Kathy shot a look at Louise and Marnie.

Billy hopped up when they entered Kathy's office. Louise thought he still looked tired, but the anxious demeanor she'd witnessed at Gen's memorial had disappeared. He met them with a broad smile. "Thanks for coming."

"Billy's been working with Gen's research, getting it ready for publication," Kathy began. "Our new chief was able to shake some money loose to fund him for a full-time position. We will be able to keep Gen's research going."

Billy continued to beam and turned his attention to the bulky package in Marnie's arms. "Is that it?"

"Yes, I hope you like it. You and the whole lab, really." Marnie and Louise tore the paper off to reveal a framed portrait of Dr. Gennifer Drake. Her direct gaze was softened by a faint smile.

"It's going to hang outside her office, well, my office, where she can keep an eye on all of us. Let's head up there."

Billy took off, chattering about his work. The three women followed.

Louise turned to Marnie and said, "I'm glad that Gen's work will get the recognition it deserves. I think she will forgive us if we aren't frequent visitors."

Epilogue

October 30, 2018

Galveston, Texas

Marnie and Chris woke up early on the day of their departure. They were planning a leisurely drive north but had one more meeting to attend on The Island. Marnie's car was packed to the gills. So, with the dogs in tow, they took Chris's car and headed west along the sleepy seawall, past the empty Pleasure Pier and numerous pastel motels. As the landscape opened up, the early morning light glimmered on the Gulf of Mexico to their left and cast a warm glow on the salt marshes to the right.

Chris turned toward the entrance to the Galveston State Park and followed the instructions given to them by Louise. They parked at a turnout for the Clapper Rail nature trail. Then, getting out of the car, they took the exuberant pups down a short path through the tall reeds. A fifteen-foot observation deck came into view. It was accessed by a ramp that circled the structure and provided a generous platform with a three-hundred-and-sixty-degree view of the wetlands.

Marnie saw that Didier was topside in a camp chair, his cane nearby. He was pointing east, toward Oak Bayou as Cora and Noah trained their binoculars in that direction and squealed with delight as a flock of roseate spoonbills took flight. Louise and Nancy were pouring coffee while Claude was passing out breakfast tacos. Garrett was serving his signature Mimosas.

Chris and Marnie hesitated part way down the path. They stopped to enjoy the scene of family and friends. They heard more guests crunching behind them and looked back to see Iliana Sudhan and her husband, Bob, approach. Kathy Walsh and her husband were close behind. It was Iliana who looked at them with her characteristically direct expression and asked, "What are you two waiting for?"

With a wide smile, Marnie said, "Just savoring this moment in time."

Acknowledgements

I wrote most of *Break Bone Fever* with my mother's eight murder mysteries looking over my shoulder. Catherine Rae published her New York City murder mysteries after age sixty-five. When I causally mentioned to Wanda that I had always thought Galveston was the perfect site for a thriller, she immediately replied, "Let's do it."

The staffs at Galveston's Bryan Museum of Texas History, the Ocean Star Offshore Drilling Rig and Museum, and the Galvez Hotel patiently answered my many questions. Thanks to my sister-in-law, Kathleen Wright Rae, for her early reading and encouragement, my colleague Vanessa Tilney, M.D., a graduate of U.T. Medical Branch, for her ear and suggestions, and my friend and published author, Patty Dann, for her sage advice. I was happy that my husband, Cody Arnold, was not surprised that I threw myself into this project and remained confident that the finished product would find and entertain readers.

—Dr. Mary Rae

While this book is dedicated to our mothers, I do not want to undervalue the contribution of my father. Refusing to let me say that something was too hard, he taught me the value of persistence and grit. It was just my mom who kept saying I should write a book.

I would also like to thank my older sister who taught me to love reading and my younger sister for her faithful confidence in my ability. Some of this book draws on the experience of my brothers who, despite their struggles, had *joie de vivre* that was infectious. My nephew, Brent Adkins was incredibly helpful with checking the authenticity of life on an oil rig.

Many friends read and encouraged us with helpful edits. The Maikoviches gave generously of their time and energy. My children also edited and encouraged. And, of course, I have to thank my spouse and partner of forty-four years who always had faith that I would someday finish a book. Lastly, we would like to thank our publisher/executive editor Brittiany Koren, who has built a business which encourages and supports new authors. It was fun to inhabit the world of Marnie and Louise and Galveston.

—Dr. Wanda Venters

About the Authors

Dr. Mary Rae grew up in New York and graduated from Colgate University before attending the University of Oklahoma College of Medicine. She trained in Emergency Medicine, which she practiced in Texas for twenty years before transitioning to Primary Care. During her ten years in Houston, she enjoyed exploring the Gulf Coast. Shortly after retiring from medicine in 2020, she and her husband moved to California. She plans to use her time to continue writing, improve her Spanish and French, and learn how to garden on the West Coast.

A native of Oklahoma City, **Dr. Wanda Venters** attended Yale for her undergraduate studies. She returned to Oklahoma City for her medical degree and completed her pediatric residency in San Antonio with the U.S. Army. Retiring from her pediatric practice after three decades, she began her second career as a writer in 2019. She lives in Colorado with her husband, two labradoodles and a Siamese cat. She has three grown children and three grandchildren. She is an avid gardener, golfs with more enthusiasm than skill, and enjoys a craft beer. You can follow her and the Unicorn family on Facebook at https://www.facebook.com/dr.wandaventers/ or at her blog www.parentingunicorns.com.